LOVE
at the end of
DAYS

Tera Shanley

OMNIFIC PUBLISHING
LOS ANGELES

Omnific Publishing
1901 Avenue of the Stars, 2nd floor
Los Angeles, CA 90067
www.omnificpublishing.com

First Omnific eBook edition, October 2014
First Omnific trade paperback edition, October 2014

Library of Congress Cataloguing-in-Publication Data

Shanley, Tera.
   Love at the End of Days / Tera Shanley – 1st ed.
   ISBN: 978-1-623421-55-7
   1. Contemporary Romance — Fiction. 2. Zombies — Fiction.
   3. Apocalypse — Fiction. 4. Urban Fantasy — Fiction. I. Title

10 9 8 7 6 5 4 3 2 1

Cover Design by Micha Stone and Amy Brokaw
Interior Book Design by Coreen Montagna

Printed in the United States of America

For zombie slaying warrior woman, Midian.

Chapter One

No one, in the history of all of mankind, had ever been as big an idiot as Sean Daniels.

He tapped the yellow number two pencil in quick rhythm against the stack of weekly guard assignments and stilled his drumming foot. He had to settle down. She was taken. He had missed his chance and missed it big.

Laney Landry was perfect, and he hadn't seen it until it was too late. Until she'd given her heart to another man because Sean hadn't nurtured it enough. Hell, he hadn't nurtured it at all.

He let out an explosive sigh and leaned back into the creaking office chair. Dead Run River hadn't changed all that much in the year since she'd left with Derek Mitchell. But him? She'd started a change in him the likes of which he'd never undergone his entire twenty-eight years.

It had started slowly, like a small ember throwing a lazy spark onto dry tinder. The night she'd admitted she was leaving with Mitchell, something had gone cold in his gut, a clawing at him that said he'd made a terrible mistake, and it was much too late to right the wrong. She'd chosen, and it hadn't been him. It's not like he could blame her. She'd put herself out there time and time again only for him to swat her down like some jungle cat teaching its young to stop playing with mice and hunt them instead.

But there had been Aria. Aria-the-Dead, the wife he'd coveted even after her heart stopped beating. Even after she had come looking for him with her empty eyes and bloodstained summer dress. He hadn't been worthy of Laney when she'd been ready. He'd only just laid Aria to rest, and if he was honest with himself, Laney scared the shit out of him.

She was impulsive, deadly, brave, smart-mouthed, and wouldn't take an order from him if her life depended on it. She was perfect. He had just been too messed up with the second death of his wife to see it.

"Sean!" Mel snapped from the open doorway. "I've called you three times. You alive in here?"

He jumped up like he'd been caught rifling through someone else's underwear drawer. "What?"

She took a long, slow breath, and her moss green eyes focused on him. "She's here."

His face was a careful mask of ambivalence, but inside, tiny explosions were pinging against his organs. Laney.

His hand shook so badly as he set the number two on the stack of papers, he accidentally knocked a jar of paperclips to the ground with a clatter.

Well, hiding his emotions from Mel to spare her feelings was going swimmingly.

Her eyes held the slightest hint of sadness in their seafoam depths before she washed her face clean of the vulnerability. "Leave them. And Sean?"

He hesitated just a moment before bringing his apologetic gaze to hers. He really was sorry they hadn't managed to be more than friends. She deserved more. "Yeah?"

A slow grin crooked her lips. "It's okay. I know what she meant to you." She turned, and he followed her out of the small log cabin that served as guard headquarters and his office.

Maybe if he could explain. "I just thought I'd never have to see her and Mitchell again and I would eventually be able to move on. And now she's back and it's making me—"

"Crazy?" she offered.

He huffed a surprised laugh. "Yeah. Crazy works."

"Have you made any headway with moving on over the past year?" she asked.

He couldn't bring himself to admit such a weakness out loud, so he shook his head instead.

"Then maybe seeing her will be your answer. She's moved on. It's time you do too."

The Dead Run River colony leader set a quick pace, and Sean jogged to keep up. The winding trail that led to the front gates was littered with dry plants curling into themselves in preparation for the long, frigid Rocky Mountain winter, and pines that stretched to the clouds towered over them in a protective canopy.

Finn, his second-in-command, was talking to Sean's four-year-old daughter, Adrianna, just inside the towering wooden front gates of the colony. The gates that kept humans in and Deads out.

"Hey, Ade," he said as the little dark-headed girl waved. She looked so much like her mother, it sometimes struck him like a blow. "You been good for Mr. Finn today?"

"Yeah, and he taught me how to aim his gun."

Sean arched an eyebrow at the muscle-bound behemoth. "Unloaded?"

Finn cocked a toothy grin. "For now."

A clearing stood between the treeline and the large felled timbers constructed in an impenetrable wall to keep Deads out. And in that clearing was the red truck they'd come into Dead Run River in after the fall of his own colony near Denver the year before. The paint was chipped in a few places, and the Chevy sported a few new dings here and there, but it was mostly as he remembered it. Guist, who had asked for gate duty that day, was clapping Mitchell on the back and grinning from ear to ear. Sean's heart picked up in a thumping cadence to match the pounding of peppered gunfire.

There she was.

From where he stood, he had a perfect view of her face. She smiled at Eloise who had already made her way to them. Laney's dark hair was pulled back from her face, and her cheeks glowed with a rosy hue to match her full and smiling lips.

He closed his eyes to steady himself, and Mel leaned her head against his shoulder. "It's hard having something you want so badly just out of your reach, isn't it?"

He draped his arm around her shoulder in understanding. Nothing had worked out the way it was supposed to. Not for him and not for Mel.

Laney unzipped her jacket and exposed a sweater-clad belly swelling with child.

A knife. It was a knife in his gut.

"Steady there, Captain," Mel murmured. "You'll give yourself away with that face."

"Did you know?"

"No. Doesn't even look like they told Guist."

Indeed, it didn't. Guist's expression had gone completely blank, and a big dumb smile slowly spread across his face, wide enough to crack it open completely.

"Appear weak when you are strong, and strong when you are weak," Mel murmured.

"Quoting *The Art of War* to me right now isn't really helping. That's the book I gave her last year."

Mel looked steadily at the happy reunion in front of them. "I know."

Vanessa chatted with her brother Nelson as they strolled along the barbed wire path that led from the garden gates to the colony entrance.

"Well if I show you favoritism, it'll cause dissension among the ranks," she said.

"Yeah, but it's garden duty. It's not guard duty. Everyone knows I'm your brother, and nobody cares if I get a longer lunch than them. Plus, Laney is going to teach me to shoot, and there isn't enough time if I don't have a longer lunch."

Vanessa pulled a face. Laney. There she was again, all pretty and irresistible and irritating. Even Nelson couldn't hide his gigantic crush on the canker sore. What was it about her?

"Eloise!" a ragged scream sounded.

Vanessa jerked her head up. Speak of the devil and she shall appear.

"What the hell is Laney screeching about," she mumbled.

It was then that she saw the unbridled fear in her nemesis's face. And she wasn't looking at Vanessa or Nelson. She was looking off into the woods.

Fear crashed against her insides, filling her until it was difficult to breathe and even harder to move. "Nelson," she whispered, shoving her brother behind her.

The monster crashing through the woods was huge. How had a creature so foul looking once been human? Even hunched over in full sprint, he had to be six-five. His face was the color of a gray-sky morning and tatters of flesh hung from his sagging cheeks. His filmy, empty eyes were trained on her as he picked up speed and bellowed. The fence between them wouldn't hold him—not at his size. Not with his determination.

A shot zinged through the woods, echoing as the bullet found nothing to lodge itself in. Laney had missed, and he was bearing down on them. Too late to run. They'd never make it to the gate in front of or behind them. She was so frozen, the cry for help that bubbled forth sat lodged in her closing throat.

The Dead lifted his hands and lunged the last few yards between them, and she screamed as the final shot rang out.

Vanessa sat up, gasping for breath that wouldn't come easily. Her lungs burned to be fed oxygen, but her tensed body wouldn't give it. Sweat trickled between her breasts, at odds with the cold autumn air that seeped in through the sealant between the logs of her small room to prickle her skin.

That dream. No, that *nightmare*. She hadn't had that nightmare since she'd started the guard training program three months earlier. Why her dream decided to edit out her friend, Eloise, was a mystery. She was always missing, though her real memories of that day included the strawberry blonde down to the most minute details. She could see the way Eloise crumpled to the ground in a faint. She could see Laney cradling her friend's limp body and yelling for help. The monster's body, jerking and stilling across the electrified fence just feet from them, and Mitchell. Mitchell had come running at Laney's cry and had eyes only for her. Vanessa should've known right then. He hadn't even spared her a glance as he passed. How had she ever thought she stood a chance with him after that moment?

Stupid. It was the apocalypse for chrissakes. It was the dumbest move to get attached to a zombie snack. Everyone left or died.

Dim morning light filtered through the simple window by the door into her small cabin room. Her table sat cluttered with notes on guns and ammunition, knife positions, and saber strokes. Drawings of night-vision glasses and lists of bug-out bag essentials littered the ground beneath. She'd be more prepared for the monsters next time. Training kept the fear at bay.

A cold and unlit lantern sat over the pages, waiting to illuminate the darkness. A crudely made table sat under a weathered mirror and served as home to an old fashioned washbasin filled with clean water. She'd collected the splinters from the floor boards in her tender feet the first few months she'd lived here, and now they were worn and smooth. Her bed was on the wall beside an old wood-burning stove, her savior on cold Colorado nights. Pictures Nelson had sketched for her dotted the wall above the writing table, and a small chest of drawers filled the corner, holding everything she owned. It wasn't much, but it was hers.

The water from the washbasin was as cold as a mountain spring, but it washed away the last shaking rivulets of that awful dream. With her teeth newly brushed, she gave the mirror a quick glance before turning around and leaning against the table. She used to love the routine of primping and preening in the mornings. Of brushing every hair into place and slathering on the perfect shade of lip gloss. Even after the Dead outbreak, she'd kept up appearances. Now, she looked like a ghost of her former self. What fun was it to look in the mirror every day and see the haunted planes of her face that were so unlike her old self? Besides, guard training didn't require perfectly rosed cheeks and mascara. It required a competent trigger finger and more care for the person next to you than for yourself. And for some reason, over the past year, one had become more important than the other.

She dressed quickly in standard-issue gray cargo pants and a tight-fitting, black, thermal sweater. The leather of her holster let off a familiar fragrance as she latched it around her waist, and she checked her Glock 17 before sliding it into place. A simple, plum-colored hairband held her long, blond tresses away from her face, and a pair of sturdy hiking boots covered her woolen-socked feet. With one last look at the room, she strapped an M16A2 across her back and shut the door behind her. The definition of "accessorizing" sure had changed since the outbreak.

Frozen breath puffed in front of her as she jogged up the winding dirt path that led to the mess hall. The trail snaked around clusters of giant pines and huge ferns and foliage growing dormant with the cold weather. The end of the world had been great for plant life. The jungle was retaking the earth without droves of humans to pollute it and cut it down. Go weeds.

If she was early enough to the mess hall, she'd be able to snag a seat for both her and Nelson, and maybe a few of her teammates who were straggling in for a quick breakfast before PT.

Just as she threw open the door, a mountain of a man, not paying attention in the least bit, crashed into her like a Mac truck.

"Whoa!" he yelled as he caught her arms, preventing her from falling backward. His fingers seriously almost fit all the way around her puny bicep.

"What the hell?" she groused, upright again. His hands were annoying, touching her like they were. She judo-chopped one, and he let go.

Staring at her stiffened palm like it had grown a brain of its own, she lifted her gaze to the most intense pair of blue eyes she'd ever seen. Oh, she knew who he was. Anyone with the ability to ovulate had every angle of Sean-freaking-sexy-man-Daniels' face memorized.

"You just karate-chopped me." He sounded almost hurt as he rubbed the inside of his thumb slowly. The smirk on his face said she hadn't hurt him at all.

"I don't know why I just did that. I don't even know karate."

"Hey, I know you. You're…"

Seconds ticked by, and she snorted. "Nicely done. You can't even remember my name? It's not like there're millions of us here."

His eyes narrowed, and she blew past him. He made her heart do flip-flops in an uncomfortable way when he was standing so close to her, and escape seemed like the best option to be able to breathe again. Damn his beautiful face.

She hunched against the humor in his voice when he called, "It was nice to meet you."

She wouldn't look back at him — no way. Her neck itched where he was no doubt staring at her as she left, and she didn't want to see whatever expression was on his face. Nice to meet her? He'd been her commanding officer for months! Granted he wasn't in charge of training new recruits, but it wasn't as if there were a ton of girls signing up to brain Deads. And Dead Run River numbered in the hundreds, not thousands. And thirdly, she wasn't exactly an eyesore.

Nelson waved from a table in the back. She should've known he'd be there even earlier than her. He rose with the dawn even more readily than she did. The breakfast line was long, and by the time she finally sidled up next to her brother on the bench seat, she only had a few minutes to eat. Her teammates were nowhere to be found, so she ate with the tenacity of a starving wolfhound gnawing on a bone.

Nelson stared. "What's wrong with you?"

A bite of egg flopped out of her mouth, and she frowned at its gumption. "Nothing. Had a bad dream is all. And I'm going to be late to PT if I don't hurry."

"Oh, that reminds me. Steven said—" Nelson searched the rafters for inspiration "—Finn is out. Brewster is in."

She choked on a half-chewed biscuit. "Bruiser's in?"

"No, Brewster," he clarified.

"Same thing." She gulped her warm milk and bolted for the trashcan. "See you at dinner."

Brewster was the worst. He was mean, tyrannical, and had a particular taste for picking on five-foot-two blond girls with meagerly controlled bitchy retorts. Where the hell was Finn this morning? What could be so important that he'd bail on early morning PT and leave the new recruits in the hands of that pretentious pride-squisher?

She ran. Finn was good with *on time*, but old Bruiser's mantra was that *ten minutes early meant you were late*.

With a silent curse on Finn flung out into the universe, she rounded a trio of fat-trunked pines that hid guard headquarters. Freaking seriously? All seven of the other new recruits were lined up doing jumping jacks, and from the sweat pouring down Boris Finch's face, they'd likely been at it for a while. Fantastic. Maybe Brewster wouldn't notice if she just slid on into the back row and looked sweaty.

"Summers!" he barked as she jumped into her first jack. "Up front and center!"

"What crappy timing," she muttered as she made her way to the front.

"What's that, recruit?"

She smiled cheerily. "What happy timing, sir."

"Shut up and give me sixty."

"Hmm? Sixty what?"

"Push-ups, Summers! And I swear to all that is wrong with this mucked up earth, if you smart-mouth me today, I'm going to make your life miserable."

She dropped to her hands and knees and started pumping them out.

"Get off your knees," Brewster said blandly. "You wanted to be a guard with the big boys. Do you see them doing girly push-ups?"

"No, sir." But in her defense, they were still doing jumping jacks and not push-ups at all. Brewster probably wouldn't want to hear the shortcomings of his argument, though.

"Then you won't be doing those girly push-ups either! Sixty. Start over."

Her arms turned to Jell-O-textured fettuccini noodles about half way through, but somehow she managed. She couldn't hold her Glock in her numb fingers now even if she wanted to, but she'd done it, and the success counted.

"Now, I want you to make tracks around the fence line of Dead Run River. Rifles above your heads. And knees to the chest, worms. I don't have all day."

Vanessa followed Boris down the trail that would lead to the fence line, and Brewster happily screamed in her ear about her many inadequacies for the first two miles. After that, he paid more attention to Boris, who had lagged behind and allowed her to pass. It wasn't until the final straightaway, miles later, when Brewster commanded, "Halt!"

She peeked around Steven Carpenter's broad and heaving shoulders. The other recruits moved off the trail to let the oncoming group pass, but she found herself locked into place. She was hallucinating.

Mitchell led the group through the woods like he belonged there. Like he'd never left.

"Mitchell?" Vanessa squeaked.

He snapped whiskey-colored eyes to her and stopped. She bolted for him but within two steps skidded to a stop. She wasn't hallucinating. Laney was beside him, and her proudly displayed stomach told of a child to come. His child.

Something dark and terrible churned within her and fury blasted through her veins. Not at them. At herself. She should never have let him affect her like this. Not after all this time. It was just a stupid crush! Her gaze drifted to Sean. How could it not? His blue eyes were practically glowing like a freaking bug light.

She recognized his look of utter despair. It likely mirrored her own in that horrible moment.

Chapter Two

The trail glided along the fence line and cut in toward the mess hall. It was late for breakfast and too early for lunch, but Eloise and Laney had enlightened their companions that if the two of them didn't eat, they'd adopt sourer dispositions than even the grumpiest Dead. Food it was.

Sean pitied the new recruits. Finn had been given the morning off to hang out with Adrianna and meet up with Laney, and Ned Brewster was the one leading PT. The old badger was relentless, and from the recruits' flushed and grim faces, he'd been in an especially unsavory mood.

"Halt," Brewster called out. The sound of the command echoed off the trees, and the eight trainees stopped in their tracks. They moved to the side to let the group pass. All but one.

A tiny woman with rosy cheeks and hazel eyes stood frozen with her gaze locked on Mitchell.

A tremor of uncertainty tainted the edges of her question. "Mitchell?"

A mixture of hope and desolation churned in her eyes. The ghost of a smile faded from her full lips as swiftly as it had arrived. She charged at a motionless Mitchell for two steps that spoke of her relief, but her abrupt halt said she'd seen Laney. Maybe Sean's heart wasn't the only one that had been broken that day a year ago. Was that what he looked like?

"Hi, Vanessa," Laney said, breaking the resounding silence that seemed to fill every space between the ancient evergreens. "It's good to see you again."

The small statement, void of emotion, seemed to snap the woman out of herself. She snorted. "Not likely. As I recall we weren't the best of friends. You back to annoy the shit out of me some more? It *has* become a tad boring around here."

"Ha."

Everyone turned and looked at Sean with the oddest expressions on their faces. Had he laughed out loud? He cleared his throat and gave an apologetic shrug. She had a mouth on her for such a tiny little thing. "I know you."

"You should. You ran me over this morning and forced me to use my karate moves on you."

He'd had a hard time taking his gaze off her this morning. Maybe it had to do with her rush to escape him or the angry blush that had crept into her cheeks when she figured out he didn't remember her name. More likely it was because he was unsettled with why he hadn't noticed a face as pretty as hers before now. Even winded, she was attractive. This pining for Laney had clearly gone on too long.

Mel cleared her throat, and Mitchell led them past the recruits. Sean stopped in front of the woman, and she dragged her eyes away from Mitchell's back long enough to grace Sean with their blue-green color.

"What's your name?" he asked.

"Who wants to know?"

He gave her a charming grin. Games were a delicious distraction from the chronic ache that had taken over his chest cavity. "You know who. Don't make me call you 'recruit' like the rest of these yahoos. Just give me your name."

"Vanessa Summers. Sir."

He narrowed his eyes at the last word. It was meant to distance herself from him.

"Hmm." He nodded respectfully to Brewster. "Carry on."

"Line 'em up, maggots!" the drill sergeant bellowed.

Vanessa lifted her M16A2 over her head with one final mind-bullet glare for Sean and whirled around to join her team. He watched her go until they disappeared into the trees. What was a girl like that doing in guard training? She hadn't a stitch of makeup on, save maybe a dab of lip balm to protect those perfectly pink lips from the bitter morning wind. Still, her pale skin was flawless, and two perfectly arched eyebrows only a shade or two darker than her hair gave away every emotion she had. The hazel in her eyes was surrounded by dark lashes, and her petite nose turned up at the end in an appealing way. What was she doing hanging around with a bunch of fighters? The occupation didn't tend to attract the best mannered men, and the female guards were usually all gristle. A far cry from the tough-talking woman with the vulnerable eyes.

He turned and trailed the group at a slow walk. Plucking a long blade of dry grass, he rolled it distractedly between his fingers and glanced once more to the place he'd last seen her. Last year there'd been a girl who sat with Laney and her friends from time to time during dinner, but he'd only seen her once or twice, and he hadn't paid her any attention. It had to be her.

And she'd had a thing for Mitchell—that much was written all over her face before she'd rearranged it into a defensive sneer. She looked like a pissed off kitten.

"Daddy, c'mon!" Adrianna yelled from up ahead.

His boots made soft thudding sounds against the dirt path as he jogged to catch up. "Listen, I'm going to take Ade and get some work done. Finn, you go relieve old Bruiser before he kills our recruits."

"Aww," Laney said. "We just got back. Surely work can wait."

Mel frowned at him and spoke up. "Actually, Sean heads up all of the guards now. Fridays are his busiest days because he works out the guard schedules for the entire upcoming week. We can stop by later and visit if you'd like, but I'm afraid he's right."

God bless that intuitive woman.

Laney squeezed Adrianna's hand. "I'll come by later and spring you, okay? We'll go fishing or something."

Adrianna beamed. "Can I, Daddy?"

She looked up with those dark eyes so like her mother's, and he was helpless to deny her. "Of course. You girls have lots of catching up to do." *Thanks*, he mouthed to Laney, who smiled and nodded her head.

Adrianna slipped her tiny hand into his as they headed back to guard headquarters. "You know, you won't be able to come to work with me anymore once you start school next year," he told her. "You'll have work of your own."

"Is Laney going to have a baby?" Adrianna asked.

He swallowed the loss down. "Yes. How do you know about those kinds of things?"

"'Cause Eloise is having a baby. I told her I always wanted a baby brother or sister, and she told me her baby could be like that to me." She beamed up at him. "Now I will have two."

Her hand was so fragile and small in his as he squeezed it. "Well, that's very kind of her to share her baby with you. And between Eloise's and Laney's babies, you will be swimming in little playmates, huh?"

He'd always wished to give her a sibling someday, with the right person, but it just hadn't been meant to be. His chance was now having a child with another man. He cleared his throat as if it would settle the churning emotion in his stomach.

Adrianna kicked a pinecone off the trail. "Mr. Finn said Mommy couldn't have a baby sister for me because she got ate up."

He frowned at the top of the little girl's dark hair. "You've been talking about this a lot lately, haven't you?"

"Yes. You were gonna marry Mel, but we don't go to her house anymore, and Mr. Finn said you and Mel have growing up problems."

"That's grown-up problems. Mr. Finn is right, but, honey—" he squatted down and held her arms so she'd hear the truth of his words "—you can talk to me about this stuff whenever you want to. You know that, right?"

Her lip quivered. "I know, but every time I do, you look really sad. And I want you to be happy, not sad."

He pulled her to him so she wouldn't see the effect her sweet words had on him. He hadn't been doing a very good job of hiding his turmoil, and that had to change. "From here on, I'll be happy, okay? And it'll make me happy if you talk to me about this stuff. Even if it's things I can't give you, like a baby sister or brother, talking about it will make us both feel better."

She nodded against his cheek.

A few hundred more yards of hiking later and he opened his office door for Adrianna. She flopped onto the floor with a drawing book and a pack of colored pencils, and he tackled the stack of paperwork taunting him from the oversized desk. Days like these, he missed working at the sawmill. Paperwork was the worst distraction from things he'd rather not think about. What he wouldn't give for a day of sawing, counting, stacking, sweeping, anything physical that got him out from behind the desk. Most days he was out in the field, and thank goodness for that. If he was trapped in this office more than one day a week, he'd feed himself to a Dead just to escape the tedium. This must've been what it was like for Laney to go from a nomadic Dead-fighting lifestyle to a boring job in the gardens. He regretted stuffing her there, even if his intentions had been to keep her safe. He'd stifled her, and as long as he lived, he'd never do that to another. That promise extended even to Adrianna.

A soft knock on the door had him signing the last page in a hurry. "Come in." With the freshly inked page on the top of the stack, he glanced up to find Laney peeking her head in.

"Can I talk to you?"

He leaned back in his chair and grinned. "That sounds foreboding."

"What I have to say will likely piss you off."

He groaned and leaned on the desk with his knuckles over his smile. "Here an hour and already asking favors?"

"I need a job."

Cocking his head, he said, "Are you sure it's safe for the baby?"

"Well, I'm not signing up for guard duty."

"Oh. What assignment are you asking for then?"

"Cattle? I know I pissed and moaned about how much I hated it, but it offers a chance for more action, and Mitchell has already been assigned guard duty, and he'll be on cattle too so he can make sure I'm okay and—"

"Laney, Laney, okay. You don't have to explain to me. I'm not your keeper. Cattle will be fine, and you can start on Monday if you'd like. I'll go back and add Mitchell to the guard schedule and make sure he's on cattle with you if that's what you want. He has enough field experience that he won't need any training. He'll get back into the swing of things around here soon enough."

She pursed her lips. "It's kind of strange being back here."

"How so?"

"Like this." She waved at the space between them. "I don't know how to be us again, you know? Like after we decided we were better as friends and things were easy. I feel like I have to watch what I say so I don't hurt you or make you mad."

"I'm not the same man I was back then. The reason you're feeling all of that is my fault. I toyed with you and didn't take care with you, and I saw how bad it hurt you." Lying would be best if they ever had a shot at being normal around each other again. "We've both moved on, Laney. I'm happy to see you so happy. I'm glad you're back. Adrianna over there missed you terribly."

"Mel told me you guys aren't together." Her face said she hadn't meant to blurt that little gem out, but there it was, hanging between them.

"We work better as friends." With a sad smile, he said, "Seems I'm better friend than boyfriend material."

"But you said you'd moved on."

He bit back a growl. "Damn it, Laney, you've been back for thirty seconds. I'm not sharing the details of my love life with you."

She narrowed her eyes and stood. "Right. Adrianna, you ready to blow this popsicle stand?"

"What's a popsicle?" his daughter asked.

Shaking her head in mock sadness, Laney said, "That's just a tragedy right there. As soon as it gets cold enough out, we're going to figure out how to make popsicles. Come on. I think I need the grand tour of this place again, and Mel says you're the best one for the job." She turned at the door. "What time should I have her back to your cabin, and where am I allowed to take her?"

"Uh, how about we meet at the mess hall at six, and I'll grab her then. You got the old Mini-14 with you?"

She pointed to the strap that held the assault rifle securely across her back. "Never leave home without it."

"Then I don't care where you take her. I trust you to protect her. You always have."

Laney's eyebrows nearly touched her hairline. "Are you serious right now? I really can't tell if you're joking."

He laughed at the unbridled look of shock that had washed over her face. "I told you — things are different now. Have fun you two."

She gave an absent little wave before Adrianna pulled her the rest of the way through the cabin door.

Maybe things would've been different if he'd gotten his crap together sooner. If he'd treated her differently and hadn't been so careless with her attention. But any man with eyes could see how crazy she was about Mitchell and how head over heels he was about her. When they looked at each other, everything in him sang that things had worked out just like they were supposed to. Why it hurt so dang much, he hadn't a clue, but he had to get hold of the tidal waves of emotion that had come back with Laney's reappearance in Dead Run River.

She and Mitchell were right where they were meant to be. It was him and Vanessa who'd lost out. Vanessa. He wouldn't wish this feeling on anyone and especially not someone so intriguing. The shocked sorrow in her expression played across his mind time and again. Finn would know more about her.

He snatched his jacket and bolted for the door. Vanessa, that delicate and fierce wounded bird, made an irresistible distraction.

When Vanessa was younger, before the end of the world, she had seen a *Seventeen* magazine article with a picture of a girl all curled up on her bed, mooning about a breakup with her boyfriend. Oh, for the love of peanuts, she was now that girl. When had the transformation occurred? The one where she went from strong, unfeeling Vanessa to emo, tear-stained, sensitive-about-other's-feelings Vanessa. New Vanessa was a total drag. She wiped her eyes and sat up in her bed. Even the happy purple comforter didn't bring her joy. Apparently, she couldn't just live on the simple things anymore. Apparently, her stupid heart thought she needed love and friends and a family. Ugh! What a mouse she'd become.

She flung her hunting knife into the wall over her writing desk, and as it vibrated against the wooden board it had lodged in, someone in the next room yelled, "Knock it off!"

"Sorry," she called. She wasn't sorry.

And who could she talk to about all of this? Eloise had come to be her closest friend in the past year, but at the moment she was probably trading secret ingredients for stretchmark cream and baby-growing tips with Laney, and no way in hell was she going to go traipsing in on that conversation to talk about her messed-up, leftover feelings for Laney's boinking buddy. In fact, she likely wouldn't be able to confide in Eloise ever again without being suspicious that what she said would somehow make its way back to Laney.

And she couldn't talk to Nelson about it either. He was the best brother she could have asked for, but the kid had his own crush on Laney back in the day. The whole freaking colony was full of Landry worshipers.

The knock on the door was so loud it was borderline rude. "What?" she yelled, not bothering to get up.

Steven Carpenter, another one of the new recruits, shoved open the door and muscled his way into her tiny room. His face was flushed, and he breathed like he'd run through a swamp in soggy boots to get to her. "Mel just posted a supply run call. She said there's room for two new recruits to get some field experience."

Yes, there it was. The solution to all of her problems. Her escape. "Even though we haven't graduated yet?"

The feather mattress sank as he folded himself beside her. "She said if we do well in the field, we'll go through the graduation ceremony when we get back."

She wiped all traces of the traitorous tears from her face with the sleeve of her sweater and lurched for her weapons and jacket. "Where do we sign up?"

"Thata girl. I knew you'd be up for an adventure. Boris, that wanker, was like, *no, there's Deads out there and*—"

"Steven! Where are sign-ups?"

"I'll show you."

She was damn near skipping by the time they tracked down the sign-up sheet. Two senior guards had already scratched their names on it, but she and Steven were the first new recruits.

"Is it first come first serve?"

"Nah, Mel picks. She'll probably talk to Finn about it, and they'll decide who goes based on who would work best together."

Her heart slipped from her throat back into her chest cavity. Chances were she wouldn't be picked. Still, there was hope, and she

TERA SHANLEY

wasn't above begging Finn and Mel to give her an out from her own personal hell. She was running from a possible awkward meeting with some dude she'd barely dated by charging headfirst into a horde of Deads. Questionable logic, yes, but she'd get field experience, speed up graduation, escape Brewster's soul singeing PTs, and she'd finally, finally get a freaking crack at one of the monsters that had scared the old Vanessa right out of her.

Vanessa Summers, she scrawled across the yellowed paper with a grin.

18

Chapter Three

Where was Finn? It wasn't as if the man was an easy miss. He was arguably a giant and roughly the width of the broadside of a barn. Superior genetics had been gifted to the man. He'd been created to be an apocalypse survivor.

Sean checked his watch. He'd spent way too much time looking for his second-in-command, and dinner was creeping up on him. "Tate," he hailed, as one of the guards on duty walked past him in the bustling colony center. "Give me your walkie."

"Yes, sir."

He handed it over, and Sean jammed the speaker. "Anyone seen Finn lately?"

Static.

"He was headed for the showers last I saw him, but that was over an hour ago," came a reply.

"I think he picked up a shift at the garden gates after he finished with the new recruits," came a second.

"Appreciate it." He handed the radio back to Tate and jogged for the trail that led to the back gate of colony.

The garden gates were usually protected by two senior guards, and today was no exception. They saluted as Sean opened the gates and scanned the woods outside the barbed-wire fence. Now that the main fence was finally completed, the next task would be to erect a fortress around the pathway that led to the separate gardens outside colony. As it stood, the ground was too cold and hard to dig proper post holes, so that chore would have to hold until spring. For now, all that stood between Deads combing the woods for a meal and Sean's flesh was a three-foot-tall fence, embellished with bells and electrified for good measure. It wouldn't stop the monsters hunting them, but it would slow them down. Sometimes that extra few seconds was the difference between life and death.

He'd touched an electric fence once on a dare, back before the outbreak, when he'd had endless summers to spend with his friends back in Montana. Felt like getting kicked in the back by a horse with hellfire-shod, dagger hooves. The memory had him clenching his arms a little closer to his sides as he jogged for the next set of looming gates. Towering pines had been used to erect them, and he called out when he reached the other side.

Finn tugged it open and grinned. "Hey, boss."

"I've been looking everywhere for you."

"Not everywhere."

The heavy doors closed behind him with a thud. "Everywhere but here. You got a minute?"

Finn's dark eyebrows lowered, and he nodded his head at the other guard. "You got this for a minute?"

The guard saluted Sean and took his position while Sean and Finn wandered toward a trio of hay bales the garden workers used as bench seats when they took their lunches.

Sean didn't much feel like sitting, but Finn plopped down on the biggest one like he hadn't a care in the world. "Look, I wanted to know about one of your new recruits."

"Boris will come along once he loses the weight. He'll need a little more time than the rest, but he'll be good in a pinch."

"No, not Boris. A woman on your team. Vanessa."

Finn's face went comically blank. Not a muscle twitched, and Sean waved a hand in front of his unblinking eyes. When a flicker of life returned, he said, "Sean, Vanessa couldn't be less your type if she tried."

"And how do you know what my type is?"

"I knew Aria, remember? She was the sweetest woman on the planet. You had your thing with Laney last year, and I thought you'd rip each other's throats out, you were that mismatched. Vanessa is a ball-buster. You won't have a shot in hell at compromising with that woman." He leaned forward and rubbed his face. "I don't know what's been going on with you, and you don't seem inclined to share, so I don't ask out of respect for our longstanding working relationship. But I know you. I've guarded you and your family for years, and I know when something is up. You and Aria—that was right, you two were a good match. Vanessa couldn't be further from her, do you get what I'm saying?"

Sean slumped into the hay bale beside Finn's. "Aria was my perfect match. Before the outbreak. I don't know if you noticed, but I'm not the same person I was four years ago. I liked my boring desk job and my benefits. I liked Aria seeming happy with me taking care of her. But I screwed up. Instead of giving her weapons to fight what was happening, I coddled her, sheltered her. It was her inability to defend herself that got her killed, and that falls on me. I just couldn't see that until Laney came along and set me straight. I need a partner who will fight beside me. One I don't have to obsess over whether they're tucked away safe somewhere when things get gritty."

Finn shook his head slowly. "I get where you're coming from, man. I do. But you're looking in the wrong place on this one. Vanessa ain't it. She's not good for anyone but the fighter next to her right now, and you have Adrianna to worry about."

Sean opened his mouth to argue, but the pulling of the gate stopped him. Vanessa ran through with the frantic pace of the hunted and didn't stop until she came to a clearing some distance off from them. "Shut it, shut it, shut it," she chanted as the guard pushed the gates back together again.

Heaving breath, she made a scared noise in the back of her throat and looked around with wide, panicked eyes. Over and over she wiped the palms of her hands on her cargo pants. What could've frightened the woman that much?

"Are there Deads out there?" Finn asked as he reached for his rifle.

"N-No," she stammered, her throat moving as she swallowed.

"Then why the hell did you blast through those gates like the engine of a crazy-train?"

"Sorry," she squeaked as her frightened gaze collided with Sean's.

"You okay?" he asked.

"Of course I'm okay," she snapped.

He held his hands up in surrender as she marched toward them.

Angry little fists blasted onto her hips as she glared at near eye-level with Finn. "I need to talk to you. Alone, if you don't mind."

"If it's about your feminine problems, I told you before, I don't want to hear about it. Anything else you can say in front of your commanding officer." Finn gestured languidly to Sean.

Even from there he could see her hands shaking as she fought to keep them on her hips. Something had spooked her and bad, though the glare she was bestowing upon him made it really hard to give in to his protective instincts. She might actually give him a fist to the face if he tried to help. Curiosity piqued, he cocked his head and stayed right at the safe distance he was.

"Fine," she grumbled ungraciously. "Mel posted sign-ups for a supply run."

"And?"

Her hands flopped to her sides, and in a much more reasonable tone, she said, "And I want in."

Two beats of thick silence passed before Finn asked, "Why?"

"I want the field experience. And it'll help me to graduate."

"Okay," he drawled. "Now, care to share the real reason?"

"What are you talking about?"

"You running in here like a bat out of hell kind of screams desperation, Summers. Now, every one of those recruits, except maybe Boris, will be signing up for that supply run for the same reasons you just listed, but you came flying in here like a cannon and asked me a favor. I'm not telling you yes or no until you tell me what I'm getting myself into."

For several tense moments she stared, a myriad of emotions playing across her face. Seething anger, resignation, fear, and anger again. Finally, she said, "Forget it," and spun for the gate. Without a glance back she barked for the guard to open up and left.

Before she was out of the gate though, she pulled her Glock and held it ready. The woman was a mystery. If she was so scared of Deads, why was she in guard training? And why on this tainted earth would she ever want to sign up for a supply run?

"What do you think?" he asked Finn.

"Hell no."

"But it's not because she's a girl, right?"

"What? No! Gender has nothing to do with this. Laney put all those misconceptions to rest long ago. And Vanessa's fierce. But she's green, and she's definitely hiding something. I can't risk putting a team with her when her reasons for being there are some super-secret mystery, which will no doubt reveal itself at the worst possible time when we're out in the field and surrounded by Deads."

"What's she like in training?"

"Intense, which is great, but it's the *I need to graduate or else my life is over* kind of intensity, you know? She's mouthy but good. Scary good, and her knife-throwing skills put the rest of the new recruits to shame, but she's a liability until she wrestles whatever demon she's fighting right now. This supply run is too soon for her. I'll see what Mel thinks, but it's a no for me."

Sean rubbed the two-day scruff on his face and frowned at the gate where Vanessa had disappeared. "I think with the right team, the supply run might be exactly what she needs to get over whatever is ailing her. If she fails, she fails, no graduation, and she can move on."

"No, it's not if she fails, she fails. If she fails, she dies, or worse, takes her own team down with her and has to live with that kind of poison. It's not like starting her out on patrol, Sean. We'd be okay-ing her to spend a week outside the gates with Deads who haven't found a meal in a while."

"You'll take the Terminator. That truck is made to protect. You'll be careful where you make camp and teach her how to keep a wary eye until it comes natural. This could be her test. The one that makes or breaks her. She knows what's at stake. If she thinks she's ready, maybe she is."

"You think she's ready after her mini panic attack just walking to the gardens? You know she used to run the gardens, right? She walked it every day, and now she breaks out in hives over it."

"I don't think that determines how she'll do in the field. That could work itself out with one Dead encounter. One Dead kill. You just don't know until you give her a shot."

"Seaaan," Finn groaned, rubbing his hands through his cropped hair.

"I'm not trying to piss you off, man. It's up to you and Mel. I'm just offering advice." He clapped him on the back and stood. "Now, get back to work, you lazy sod. The gardens aren't going to protect themselves, you know."

Sean, that dick, staring at her with that dumb smirk on his face while Finn ran her down. Now she was going to be stuck in make-out town where the featured stars were Laney and Mitchell. Gag her with a jump rope.

"Vanessa!" Eloise called from a table to the right.

She veered toward her with a dinner tray in hand before realizing Laney was sitting with her. Quick as a whip, she did an about-face for an empty table in the corner. Nope. She wasn't ready to play nice quite yet.

"Why are you sitting alone?" Nelson asked, sliding into the bench seat beside her.

"I don't feel like playing Chatty Cathy over dinner tonight, that's all."

His golden brown hair shone in the evening light of the illuminated mess hall as he searched the room. "Ooooooh, Laney's back, huh? I'm sure Eloise has enough room in her heart for both of you."

"Shut up."

She slid a glance to the mess line. Sean stood there talking with his daughter as he stacked a double portion of food onto his tray. What was it about men who were good with children that made them so attractive? He wore a tight fitting gray shirt over forest green cargo pants. Even from where she sat in the corner, the outlines of his flexed triceps as he moved were obvious. He was tall, six-foot maybe, with a body that said he was disciplined with PT and patrols. His short, summer-kissed chestnut hair only enhanced the impossible blue of his eyes.

As he started to turn, she went back to eating and avoided direct eye contact. He'd been at Dead Run River an entire year, and he hadn't crossed her path much in that time. Their schedules and duties were different, and she'd rarely seen him eat in the mess hall. And admittedly, on his part, he'd barely noticed her at all. So why was he everywhere her eyes landed today? She bit back a growl and spooned another heap of beef stew into her maw. The entire day had been one disappointing experiment in annoying.

"Hey," Mitchell said from above her. She tried to keep the panic from her face. "Can I sit down?" he asked.

"I'd rather you not."

The bench screeched across the wooden floorboards as he pulled it out and sat anyway.

"Your wifey is going to be pissed when she sees you talking to me."

"Laney's not like that. I just wanted to apologize for everything that happened when I left. You came to tell me your feelings, and I was short with you. I just didn't want to lead you on, and I had no plans on coming back."

"Nyaah, stop talking. I really don't want to have this discussion. Whatever you need from me, you have it. I forgive you. I absolve you from any further guilt. Just please, please don't talk about it anymore. It doesn't make anything better. It's just embarrassing."

His dark eyes swirled with worry or guilt, or maybe both. "No hard feelings?"

"Nope."

"Liar."

She shrugged. What was the point in arguing? "Now move along, Mitchell. You're harshing my dinner, and I have important things to discuss with Nelson that don't involve you."

"What things?" Nelson whispered as Mitchell made his way back to Laney's table.

"I signed up for a supply run, but I won't get it. Finn already said no. Just wanted to give you a heads up."

"Why would you do that? Do you have a death wish? Look, I was okay when you said you needed to do guard training, but that was because I thought you'd be on patrol inside the colony gates, not gallivanting out in the forest playing pew-pew-bang-bang with a horde of hungry Deads." He leaned back and crossed his arms, a sure sign of stubbornness if she'd ever seen one. "I'm glad you didn't get it."

"Don't say that. I really wanted to go."

"I want you to live. You're being selfish with this. You're all I have left, and you're flinging yourself into danger like you couldn't care less whether you live or die. Cut it out."

A guard stood on one of the tables in the front of the room. "Jackson, Keeter, Carpenter, and Summers—if you're in here, Mel needs to see you at guard headquarters right away."

Vanessa frowned. What had she done now? If that old boot Brewster had turned her in again for her creative way with words, she swore she'd spit in his coffee first chance she got.

"You want the rest of my stew?"

Nelson answered by sliding her bowl in front of himself and going to work on the half-eaten meal.

"See you tomorrow," she muttered and stepped over the bench.

Steven and the other two guards were nowhere to be seen, so she took the trail illuminated by solar lights that would lead her to headquarters alone. Such a feeling of doom filled her. Maybe she was being cut from the program already. Maybe she should've put more effort into respecting her commanding officers.

Dawdling, putting off the inevitable, she meandered through the quiet woods until she came to the lantern-lit cabin that served as the meeting place for PT in the mornings. Steven paced the porch and fixed her with a relieved smile when she stumbled around a giant evergreen. "Mel wanted me to wait for you. Come on. Jackson and Keeter already have their orders."

"Orders?" She followed Steven into the dimly lit room and sat in a chair in front of the sprawling desk where Mel sat.

Mel was a good leader for Dead Run River. She was patient but firm, and the colony had flourished under her. She also had an excellent poker face. There was no acknowledgment of them for a full three minutes as Mel's pen scratched across a piece of paper. Vanessa's palms began to sweat, and more than once, she tugged at the collar of her shirt that seemed to be growing tighter by the moment.

"Almost all of our new recruits signed up for the supply run," the striking woman began. "But we only have two spots open for them because of the risk. Any more, and there isn't enough experience among the team. Are you both sure you want to do this as your first mission?"

"Yes!" Steven all but yelped.

"Wait, you're saying I'm one of the picks for the supply run?" Vanessa asked.

"Does that surprise you?"

"Yes and no. No, because I know I'm ready. Yes, because Finn didn't agree when I talked to him earlier today."

Mel nodded and leaned forward over the desk. "He had some valid arguments, but you've got a champion in your corner. Someone who agrees with you that you are up for the challenge. I've listened to both sides of the argument and am willing to give you a try if this is what you really want. There will be contingencies though. If you prove you aren't up to snuff during this mission, you will be let go from the program with no chance of graduation. You will start work immediately in the gardens in your previous position. That's if you survive. However, if you prove yourself an asset, you'll graduate as soon as you get back. It'll be up to your commanding officers to decide, so my suggestion is that you play nice with them. Become part of the team. Be of use to your colony."

A slow hope had been building, and by the end of Mel's speech, Vanessa was on the edge of her seat, gripping the arms of the chair. "Yes. My answer is yes."

"Great. You both will participate in PT in the morning, and then the rest of the day is yours. You'll meet at the front gates and leave at first light on Sunday."

"Oh Mylanta, thank you, Mel. You don't know how much this means. Thank you!" She didn't even wait for Steven before she bolted out the door at a giddy, slightly psychotic run.

She'd been picked out of all of them. Yeah, so there was a lot at stake. Her life, for instance, but still. This was what she'd been training for. What she'd sacrificed her comfort for. She had to celebrate with someone!

Nelson was out. He was going to be pissed when he found out and would slurp the wind right out of her sails. She'd deal with that tidal wave tomorrow. Right now, she needed a friend who would actually be happy for her.

She'd just have to wrestle Eloise away from Laney for the night.

Chapter Four

Eloise didn't know she was being hunted yet.

Vanessa eyed her and Laney's deep conversation with narrowed eyes. They talked with conspiratorial smiles, and their foreheads tipped forward in a triangle of secrecy. Did she look that dumb when she talked to Eloise?

"Hey, El, sorry to break up the gab-fest," Vanessa said as she approached the picnic table they were tucked into.

Laney gave a short laugh. "The smile on your face says you're not sorry."

"Yeah, I'm not sorry. Can I talk to you a minute?" she asked Eloise.

"You know you could give Laney a chance, and then you guys wouldn't have to split custody."

"Nah, I'm not into three-ways."

"It's fine, El," Laney said with a patient look. "I'm going to grab a shower. Been looking forward to hot water again."

"What's up?" Eloise asked as Laney plodded off.

"Guess what?"

Eloise opened her mouth, but Vanessa held up her hand. "You'll never guess, so I'm just going to tell you. I was picked for the supply run on Sunday!"

After trying to lean forward, Eloise seemed to give up, apparently realizing she was still growing the moon in her stomach. "And you wanted that?"

"Yes! And before you pooh-pooh this, know that I came to you first out of everyone because I knew you'd be happy for me. It's something I want. It's a big deal for me to get to go."

A beatific grin spread across her lightly freckled face. "Well if you're happy, I'm happy. Let's go get a drink at Ricky's to celebrate."

"El, I love you for offering, but in case you've forgotten, you're about thirty-seven months pregnant, and bathtub booze isn't recommended for fetuses."

With an eye roll, Eloise heaved herself up and waddled toward the trail that would lead to the moonshine shack at the back of Dead Run River. "I'll drink water," she called over her shoulder.

"I believe the menu specifically says they only have rot gut or bathtub wine."

"Are you going to come up with problems all day or solutions?" Eloise called over her shoulder.

"Okay then," Vanessa murmured and followed her friend. She could use a Ricky's schnockering. After all, this could very well be one of her last days on earth.

It wasn't a spinning room or splitting headache that kept Vanessa awake that night. Sure, she drank too much as a sober Eloise laughed and looked on. And she'd danced on the rickety bar top and sung terrible karaoke minus the karaoke machine. But she'd been lucky or unlucky enough to become violently ill in the woods on the way home, and now the only remnant of her wild night was pain behind her eyes. As she lay there in the comfort of her bed with the crackling wood-burning stove sending waves of heat behind her, it wasn't a hangover that kept her eyes from closing.

Imagination could be a terrible thing. Before the end of the world, creativity was cultured and nurtured, fleshed out until a talent was revealed. In current times, imagination was a tiny, pin-less grenade lurking deep within the brain tissues in the darkest hours of night. So morbid were her imaginings, she couldn't close her eyes against the world if she tried. Scenes of Deads clawing at her legs, or of hiding in a small, dark place as moaners scuffled just outside, or of the team being taken and leaving her all alone played across the backs of her eyelids any time she blinked. No way was she inviting the kinds of nightmares that danced just beyond the edges of sleep.

The knock on the door in the middle of the night would've pissed her off a lot more if she'd been anywhere near hibernation.

Thick, flannel pajamas shielded her from the offending bite of the wind as she opened the door. Finn stood there, a stark and giant silhouette against the star-cluttered night sky.

"No thanks," she said blandly. "I'm trying to cut back on my booty calls." She tried to close the door, but Finn shoved his foot in front of it.

"Vanessa," he growled in a hoarse and sleep-filled voice.

"Fiiine," she groaned. "But no kissing. I can't have you falling in love with me."

She couldn't be positive in the dim moonlight, but she was pretty sure his eye twitched.

"Grab your weapons," he said, pushing his way into the room.

"Ooh wee, you like it rough. You're dangerous and I approve."

"Vanessa! Stop trying to be a pain in my ass and get ready. I have something to show you."

"All right, all right, don't get your panties in a twist." She cracked an uncontrolled grin. "Do you want me to undress fast or slow?"

"I'll meet you outside," Finn muttered through her cackles.

"That was the last one, I swear!" Vanessa called as he slammed the door.

Five minutes, one pair of cargo pants, a thermal sweater, a jacket, a pistol, a rifle, and a pocket full of ammo later, and Vanessa was filling her lungs with frigid front porch air. Finn looked like he was asleep in one of the rocking chairs, so she thoughtfully kicked his boot until he lurched awake.

"Let's do this. I have PT in three hours."

After a stretch and an under-the-breath oath, Finn led the way down one of the winding paths. The further they got away from the cabin, the more the sense of wrongness sent little, tinkling warning bells off inside of her.

The woods of Dead Run River were magic at night. Small solar lights dotted the edges of the trails and could be seen through the trees like fairies sleeping on flowers. The closer they got to the front gate, however, the fewer lights there were to guide them.

"Finn, where are you taking me?"

"You'll see. It's show and tell. First I'll show you. Then I'll tell you."

She threw a baleful glance at the quiet woods behind her. This was a bad idea, following Finn, the mysterious Yeti, into the forest at night. If she weren't still battling the remnants of a moonshine headache, she would've remembered to ask for an explanation before she'd left her cabin.

It wasn't until Finn led her all the way to the front gates of Dead Run River and ripped the engine of a small four-wheeler that she balked completely.

"Aw, heck no am I getting on that thing and zipping around Dead infested woods with no protection. Heck. Freaking. No."

He held his hand out and commanded, "Get on."

Crossing her arms, she refused. "This is the part where you're pissed Mel went over you on the supply run decision, and you're going to drop me in the woods in some effed up game to see if I can make my way back to the colony. Screw you, Finn. I'm not playing."

"For the billionth time, Summers, you can't talk to your commanding officers like that, or it affects your graduation score. I swear I won't leave you in the woods. Now get on, or there won't be a supply run. This little test was approved by Mel, and we both have final say." His hand hung in the air between them, inviting her to hop on. Quiet steel laced his voice as he said, "Now, Summers."

She denied his offered palm, her fists clenched in anger, and slid onto the back, holding onto his taut waist. "I swear if you leave me in those woods, I'll kill you."

"I won't. Besides, it's not me who needs killin' tonight."

How could words chill her blood to ice in such a way?

Two guards opened the gates and closed them again as Finn pulled the ATV down the road. She hadn't been outside of the colony gates, besides the short walk to the gardens, since she'd come to Dead Run River eighteen months after the outbreak. Now she felt completely stripped naked against the elements and unprepared for the fear that bathed her like arctic rain water.

On and on they drove through shallow springs and frozen marsh, through overgrown thickets and piney woods. Limbs whipped at her face as if they were begging her to turn around, but on Finn drove as Vanessa scanned the uneven terrain fearfully for Deads. It was dark, and sight distance was severely limited. Time and time again, she imagined a movement just beyond the beyond.

Finn hit the brake and cut the engine. "Now listen up, because I'm not explaining this twice. For some reason, Sean has taken it upon himself to vouch for your abilities out in the field."

"Sean? What's he have to do with dragging me out into the woods?"

"Listen! Your success affects him in two ways. One—his word is very important in Dead Run River and with the troops. He doesn't need you proving him wrong and dying on the supply run."

"Thanks for the vote of confidence."

"Two—he's now volunteered to go on the supply run, probably to save you from yourself, and I can't have you getting him hurt, do you understand? I've been a personal guard for Sean and Adrianna for a long time. They're like family to me, and I'll be damned if you're going to get your first shot at a Dead in a situation where it really matters. Where Sean's life is dependent on you not freezing up and jerking the trigger wide. So, tonight you get practice to ease my mind. Tonight you'll kill your first Dead." He pulled a gleaming buck knife from a leather sheath on his belt and grabbed her arm.

"What are you doing?" she screeched, heart pounding into her throat. Snatching her arm away she scrambled off of the four-wheeler and rounded on him. "You were going to cut me!"

"It's cold now, and there aren't as many Deads in the mountains this time of year. They can't move very well in this climate. We need something to draw them in. Your hollering will work fine, but we'd do better with blood."

"Oh, my blood is what you want? All right, Mr. Sensitivity. Have you ever had someone drag you from your bed in the middle of the night, drive you out in the woods, and pull a freaking saber on you? Hmm?"

A long sigh escaped Finn in a cloud of cold smoke. He clicked a tiny flashlight on and rolled up his sleep to reveal a long, silver slivered scar across his forearm. "Yes."

"Well…touché, but you're still a megadick, Finneas."

His eyes narrowed to slits in the dim illumination of the flashlight. "Don't call me that."

She shoved her arm toward him. "Do it fast," she breathed over the hammering of her heartbeat.

And he did.

One swift motion was all it took. The touch of cold metal cut through layers of skin and she gasped as warmth trickled out of her arm. She held it to her chest like it would ease the pain, but it didn't help.

"Don't waste it, love. Go be a good little hunter and spread the bait around."

"This isn't the bait," she growled. "I'm the bait."

"Good girl. This is a rite of passage, you know."

"Oh goody, so the other rookies have their turn next?"

"No. They've all killed a Dead before and know how it is."

She dribbled crimson droplets over a giant fern and leveled him a look. "Boris hasn't."

"He's not making it past training, and you know it."

"Or you're using this as an excuse to try and scare me off the mission. Am I getting warmer?"

Finn sighed and scrubbed his hand down his face. "No, actually. I want you to succeed, but I can't take you out there on a mission untested. I just can't. You have to show me you can fight Deads. The cut helps prove you can fight one while distracted and hurt. That shit will happen daily out the supply run, and you need to be prepared. Whatever you imagine it's like out there, it's not. Tonight we'll be lucky to attract one, maybe two Deads in this kind of weather. It's a controlled test, and I'm right here with you. You aren't the first one to go through this kind of trial, Summers. Quit belly-aching and just get it done."

Finn was awfully chatty tonight, which was a new and unwelcome trait. Usually he was level-headed and a man of few words. Tonight he was just seven shades of annoying. A controlled test? Sure there weren't many moaners walking around the woods right now, and sure Finn was sitting behind her with a small arsenal to assist her. And yes, she hadn't ever killed a Dead and probably should tackle that little fear before she went out on a mission. But they were out in the woods in the middle of the night to fight a real, wild Dead. Why couldn't he just cage one up and feed it for a while, tame it a little, and let her shank it through the bars of its little zombie prison? That sounded way less scary than bleeding her and drawing one to her.

Unless he was trying to toughen her up.

The Deads they would face in the ravaged fallen cities wouldn't be caged. They'd be running at her team in droves. If the packs were small in the mountains because of cold, or altitude, or whatever pattern Finn had noticed in his years of hunting them, they would be milling around in hordes in the warmer cities nestled in the valleys.

She understood it. Killing a caged Dead wouldn't prove her battle-readiness or boost her confidence in her abilities. Hunting, waiting, and adapting to the terrifying situation she was in right now would. Maybe Finn was right. Maybe she needed this.

Her breath shook, and she clamped her jaw and gritted out, "Is this the part where you leave me?"

"I told you I wasn't going to do that. Teammates don't leave their men behind. Now stand a little further into that clearing so you don't have trees right at your back."

Her traitorous voice shook to match her hands. "Are you going to help me?"

"Yes, but not with weapons. You'll shoot the Deads that come your way or we'll both die. My survival depends on you, Vanessa. Protect us both. Clear your mind, and ready your Glock. If you run your clip down, switch to knives, and then to your rifle. The guns will be loud and draw more in, so use knives when they're close enough. Don't panic. I'm right here, so listen to my instructions, okay? They aren't quiet or stealthy, and the grass is dry. Listen. Use your senses. Mother Nature will warn you when something doesn't belong in her forest."

The tremor in her body had reached her lips, and she clenched her jaw to keep her teeth from clacking together. Fantastic. Zombie Miyagi back there was telling her to find her inner chi, and all she really wanted to do was hop on the back of that little ATV and zip on back to safety.

Grass crackled behind her, and she spun, pulling her Glock out of its holster. The light of Finn's flashlight followed where she aimed, but nothing was there. Nothing but the laughing wind. Another movement sounded from behind, and she spun with a pitiful whimper. It was so hard to breath and getting more difficult by the moment. She was going to suffocate long before she ever saw a Dead in the dark.

"Settle down, and take a deep breath. You can do this," Finn said from the comfort of the ATV seat.

She heard the moaning long before she heard the running. At least two Deads were hunting her, but in her panic she couldn't decipher the direction they were coming from. The groaning became louder, and Finn pulled his flashlight to the left. All she could see was deep, black darkness, and then, on the blue edges of the pitiful light, two Deads appeared. Their faces were sunken in, and one of them didn't have lips to cover his gnashing teeth. Filmy gray eyes focused on her, and their emaciated arms and clawed fingers lifted and reached for her.

"Vanessa, what are you waiting for? Shoot now."

She stood frozen in place, reliving that horrid moment a year ago when the Dead had crashed through the woods toward her, Eloise and Nelson. Her finger sat useless on the trigger as they ran for her. Thirty yards. Twenty yards. Ten.

"Shoot now!"

Finn's command scared her into pulling the trigger, and the first Dead dropped. With no time to aim, the other was on her, and she fell backward. She hit the ground hard as the clammy skin of the creature's hands clawed at her back, and she pushed his chest just enough to keep his mouth from the tender flesh over her jugular.

"Finn!" she screamed.

"Knives!"

With her bleeding forearm pinned against the monster's chest, she reached for the knife she kept stashed in her boot. She was losing strength in the arm, and her own blood splattered against her neck. Grunting with the effort, she pulled the knife and screamed as she sank it into the Dead's temple. The cold body went limp as he died his final death, and she pushed him off her and scrambled away.

"Jerk!" she screeched, rounding on Finn with the fury of an erupting volcano. "You were going to let me die and not lift a finger to help."

Finn shook his head slowly back and forth. "You're wrong." He pointed the flashlight at three felled Deads near the ATV. "I was helping." He jerked his head to the side, listening. "Vanessa, what is the first rule you learned about Deads from your training?"

"Uhh…" *Think, think, think.* "They travel in groups?"

"Yep. Where's your pistol?"

"Crap." She searched the ground near the knifed Dead. "I must've dropped it in the scuffle." Adrenaline surged through her body, making it difficult to focus on anything other than fleeing.

"Better find it quick. We've got more company."

It was then that she heard it. The groaning of countless Deads coming in fast. Stiff, dried grass whispered under their clumsy footfalls as she scoured the ground for her handgun. Her panicked fingers fell over rocks and stumps, sticks, and brush but still couldn't find the weapon. There. Lurching for it, she pulled it up in one swift motion toward the crashing noise. "I thought you said there weren't as many of them in the cold."

Finn stood stiff and waiting as she took her position at his back. Confusion flashed through his eyes as he scanned the woods. "I was wrong."

"What do we do?"

He tilted his head and looked up at the trees and cursed. "Too old, we can't reach the bottom limbs. Head for the ATV."

He didn't have to tell her twice. She was high-knee scrambling before he even got the entire sentence out.

"There they are," Finn whispered. "Turn it on, and put it in first gear while I pick them off."

Shot after careful shot fired and served as a soundtrack to her internal panic when the engine only gave a whine as she twisted the key. Again, she turned it. "Finn?"

"Keep trying. She takes a tender touch is all. She'll start up."

Over and over she turned it to nothing, and the moaning got louder. Finally, the engine roared to life but there wasn't time to escape what was coming for them, and Finn was in trouble. She pulled up her Glock and steadied her breathing. Shot, aim, shot, aim, shot, aim, until her clip clicked with an echoing, empty sound. Finn had already switched weapons but the running corpses just kept coming. Closer and closer they pushed until the darkness was filled with nightmares.

A scream sat in her throat, readied to be of use in her last moments of life. Finn sprinted for the ATV and grabbed the bars around her waist. "Clear a path!" he yelled.

She pulled her rifle around front and leaned to the side to give him room to see where he was driving them, and she picked them off in the harsh illumination of the headlights. It was a good plan until they came to a cluster of monsters. Finn pulled off into the woods and hit the gas so hard her stomach lurched. Deads ran clumsily after them, and any in front, she took a shot at. Some she missed on account of the jerky terrain, but most fell on the spot. Her arms shook from the adrenaline, and a piece of her that she wouldn't give a voice wanted to sob. Finn checked his position and turned the four-wheeler north. The moaning sounded farther off, but it never disappeared completely, and that feeling of being hunted clung to her like a second, suffocating skin. There were no words here. Just a hope that they'd make it to the Dead Run River gates before the monsters did. Hopefully Finn could find his way in the dark, even after they'd got turned around in the woods. All she could do was trust him.

The ATV bumped and bounced across the uneven ground, but Finn never let off the gas. If she didn't know any better, she'd say he was spooked too. The lights of their ride illuminated the wooden posts of the gate, but they were too far to one side. He rocketed down the fence line until they came to the entrance.

Two guards filed out of the opening, and the leader, a squat man with a ready scowl, said, "Bite check."

Finn pulled off his shirt and hopped off the back before tugging at the fly of his pants.

"Bite check?" She'd had one when she first came through colony gates, but it was done in private and by a female guard.

"Vanessa, take your clothes off."

"What? No, thanks. Hard pass."

"Nobody gets in the gate without us making sure they aren't going to turn Dead on us. Clothes off!" barked the guard.

"All of them?"

Finn leveled her a look of impatience and snarled, "There are a whole lot of Deads headed our way. Can you not hear them? If you don't want to be zombie chow, I'd suggest you take your friggin' clothes off."

Good enough for her. She stripped faster than a lady-of-the-night named Cinnamon. She didn't even care about the smirk from the guard and definitely didn't bother to dress herself before she went sprinting for the opening gates. Finn at least had his pants back on before he pulled the four-wheeler through and the gates thudded closed.

After hobbling into her clothes, she collapsed onto the trail and stared at the twinkling stars as she waited for her breathing to slow.

She was different now. Down to her bones, she was a different person than the one who'd left these gates an hour before. Her arm hurt like hellfire, and she may very well never catch her breath again, but she'd thought she was a goner. A slow smile crooked her lips.

The stout guard stood over her. "Did you kill your first Dead out there, little lady?"

"No," Finn said. "She killed her first thirty."

The guard just stared at him like he was waiting for the punch line as Finn pulled her to her feet. His chuckle matched hers. She was downright giddy under the drunken adrenaline crash that left her woozier than the bathtub wine she'd chugged. He pulled her into a rough hug and slapped her on the back so hard she nearly lost her breath all over again, but she didn't mind. They'd lived.

The clawing at the gate was a stark reminder of what could've been, but tonight, they were alive, and she'd helped keep them that way. Victory.

"I owe you an apology, Summers. That wasn't…" Finn seemed to struggle for words as he eased away from her. "Deads don't usually act like that this time of year." He cast a dark look at the gate that stood between them and the horde. "I really thought you'd only get a shot at one or two." He gripped her shoulder and shook her gently, then smiled. "You did good. I think you've earned a day off of PT. Get some rest, and we'll leave first thing Sunday morning."

Finn's approval suddenly meant a lot more than she'd expected it to. It had sat in her craw when he'd rejected her as a candidate for the supply run, but now he was okay with it.

She gave a little salute. "Yes, sir," she said with a saucy grin and turned for home.

Something about the near-death experience exhausted her. She wouldn't have a problem in the world with falling asleep now in the safety of her little cabin room.

In the morning, she'd probably wonder if she'd dreamed this.

Chapter Five

Vanessa meandered up the trail toward the showers. She'd slept until noon, and anyone without the day off was busy at their job assignment. She'd passed only two people by the time she reached the six wooden stalls in the clearing. Only one pair of legs graced the men's side, and she had her choice of showers on the women's. Hanging her shower bag on the faucet and hitting the tap, she hung her clean clothes across the stall door and waited for the water to warm to steaming. One quick temperature check later, and she was stripping out of her pajamas and carefully unwrapping her hastily bandaged arm.

So tired was she after the Dead hunt, she'd washed the cut as best she could in the washbasin and performed a quick wrap job on it. Without pain meds, she'd woken up several times during her slumber when she'd lain on it wrong, or when the uncomfortable throbbing pulled her from sleep. If it got infected, she was definitely going to shoot Finn in the leg or maybe the arm.

The water turned brown under her as she washed dried blood from the wound, and when the rivers swirling around the drain turned clear again, she leaned her forehead against the shower wall and absorbed every drop of warm water she could. Who knew when the next hot shower would be.

With a towel tightly wrapped around her body, she wrung out the long tresses of her blond hair until water didn't pour from it anymore. No way did the thought of pulling the rough, thermal sweater over the freshly washed and unbandaged cut on her arm sound appealing. Maybe she could get away with escaping to her room in just a towel. It was cold, but a faster pace would warm her enough until she got to the heat of her room.

Peeking around the stall, not a soul was in a sight. With her shower bag and a wad of clothing, both clean and dirty, in hand, she slid her boots onto her moist feet and bolted for the safety of the trees.

"Vanessa?"

She skidded to a stop and hunched into herself. Slowly, she turned.

"I thought that was you," Sean said with an amused grin.

He wore a tight, black cotton shirt over dark cargo pants, and little drops of water clung to the ends of his short hair. His face had been shaven clean, emphasizing every sharp angle of his face. The slant of his eyes was downright cat-like when he was smirking like that.

She cleared her throat. "I heard you vouched for me."

His dancing eyes dropped to her towel, held stubbornly in place by her clenched fist, and then to her untied and floppy boots. His appraisal stopped at her arm, and a deep frown furrowed his brow. "What happened?" he asked, running a towel over his hair.

Dead Run River wasn't an overwhelming size, and rumors ran rampant. Idle gossip spoke of Sean's epically stubborn protectiveness, to the point of fault for the man. And the stubborn pull of his narrowed eyes to the wound said he was only playing at patience. Treading carefully was a solid plan when it came to pacifying a predator.

She smirked. "I fell."

His approach was unwavering and slow, like he was trying not to startle her into fleeing. Smart man. When he stood directly in front of her in that unnerving way of his, he brushed a light finger in a line down the uninjured part of her arm, tracing but not touching the slice on her arm.

"Did Finn do this?" The intensity of the blue in his eyes swirled like the Bering Sea in the middle of a hurricane.

She nodded carefully. This was it. He'd freak out and ream Finn and ruin the experience completely.

A slow smile curved his sensuous lips. "Did you kill a Dead?"

Okay, or maybe his protectiveness was only reserved for people in his inner circle. The relief sent a flutter into her throat, and she huffed a laugh. "I'm a Dead-slaying virgin no longer."

"He wouldn't have taken you hunting if he didn't have faith you could manage it, you know."

"I'm beginning to see that. His methods kind of sucked though."

"Come on. I'll take you down to Doc so he can check that out. We need that taken care of before the supply run tomorrow." He led her down the path without a backward glance. "It wasn't his method."

"What do you mean?"

He graced her with a wry smile over his shoulder. "It was my method."

A tiny gasp escaped her. "You were the one who cut Finn?"

"I trained him, but I needed to know he'd be good under pressure if I was going to take him as a personal guard for Adrianna and myself. Most colony leaders have enemies—people hungry for that power for the wrong reasons, and I was no different. I needed someone I could trust."

"Right, stab your friends to test their loyalty. Got it. Finn said you're coming on the supply run. If it's to keep an eye on me, don't bother. I'll be fine without a babysitter."

"I haven't decided if I'm leading it yet or not. Finn doesn't think I should. I haven't gone on one in six months. He probably thought I had retired, and it would've made his job much easier."

"Retired? You're twenty-eight, not eighty."

His shoulders rose as he inhaled deeply and released it. "Things are different when you have a kid to think about."

"It's settled then. You stay here, and we'll be back with the supplies shortly."

He hopped the medical office stairs by twos and held the door open for her. Clasping the towel even tighter, she took a seat on the table Sean pointed to.

"Hey, Doc, you in here?" Sean called.

Dr. Mackey stuck his head out of a lab room in the back. "What's happened?" he asked with a frown.

"It's not me. It's her." He gestured to Vanessa, and she fidgeted under Dr. Mackey's scrutiny.

"Nasty looking cut you got there. Do I need to worry about where you got a knife wound this big?"

She shrugged noncommittally. Doc didn't have to know about her near-death experience any more than Sean did.

With stitches, fresh bandages, a bitter drink that most definitely dulled the edges of the pain, and strict instructions on keeping the injury clean, she left the office with Sean trailing her. "Well, it's been real, and it's been fun, but it hasn't been real fun. See you on the flip side, Sean."

"All right, I can take the hint. You're trying to shake me."

"Yep. Later."

He stood on the porch of the medical cabin as she scurried up the trail with her shower supplies. Braving a glance back only once, her heart hammered as Sean watched her leave with an unfathomable expression on his face. Thoughtful and serious—maybe even calculating. The look scared her, but for the life of her, she couldn't figure out why. She turned back around and double-timed it up the trail to her cabin.

Sean was a dangerous man. That was for certain. Honorable, a good friend and father, but those devilishly good looks were the perfect disguise. Men like him made broken promises and left women like her to pick up the pieces. It was a lucky break she was leaving him behind in the morning because she'd be damned if she would trust her heart with another man again.

Sean watched her leave with an odd sensation in his gut. The instincts to go with her and to run away in the opposite direction warred with each other and made it hard to stay in place. For a year, he had scarcely noticed her, and now she was everywhere, filling him with something he couldn't explain. Something scary.

With an explosive sigh, he sunk into the rocking chair on the medical office porch. She'd looked good sashaying off in her little towel that simultaneously left too little and too much to the imagination. He'd had to stop himself several times from touching the ends of her damp hair while Doc stitched her up. What was wrong with him? Was his heart so desperate to find relief from Laney that it would latch onto the first good-looking woman who halfway pissed him off? Finn was right. Vanessa was nothing like Aria. And she sure as hell wouldn't be any good for him.

The guilt over his late wife hit him in the gut, like it always did when he thought of another woman. She'd died almost four years ago, but he'd only just mustered the courage to put her down last year. How weak he'd been to let her go all that time as a monster.

"I'm scared," were her last words, and he buried his face in his hands as the pain from that memory washed over him.

Laney had been right to run from him. He wasn't right for anyone. He did two things well: good fathering and good leadership. Caring for a woman in a way she deserved was simply beyond his abilities. He'd spare Vanessa the pain and stay away from her. The supply run would have to make do without him.

Mel needed his answer, so he stood and headed for her cabin at the top of the colony.

After a firm rap at her door, she called, "Come in."

Mel was sitting down to lunch in her formal dining room with a dainty napkin laid in her lap. "I thought you would be coming by." She pushed a shallow stack of paperwork closer toward the edge of the table.

Even months after deciding there was nothing romantic with Mel, it still felt strange stepping into her home. It was impossible to know where he stood with her. If Mel didn't want to be read, she was proficient at keeping her thoughts and opinions deeply guarded. She could hate him for all he knew, but she'd still be a mask of politeness for the rest of their days.

She motioned for him to take a seat beside her, and he cleared his throat. "I'm out on the supply run. I can recommend a replacement though."

She tilted her chin. "Why the change of heart?"

"It wasn't really a change of heart, Mel. I came in here to vouch for Vanessa yesterday. I didn't think you were going to ask me to lead the team."

"I have my reasons for doing so."

"Which are?"

She pursed her lips and dropped her gaze to the paperwork. "Doc needs a med run. It's the focus of this mission, and I need someone I can trust to get the job done right out there."

Sean fingered through the five sheets of paper. "I don't even recognize most of the things he needs. How are we supposed to track all of this down?"

"You'll be taking one of Dr. Mackey's assistants to aid you in finding what you need."

He jerked his gaze to hers. "We can't bring a civilian on a supply run, Mel. You know that. The last time we did that, half the team was eaten by the third day trying to protect the helpless bugger. We're already on a steep learning curve with Vanessa—"

"I thought you said she was ready."

"She is, but she's still green."

"She's not green anymore."

"And what do you mean by that? I heard about Finn's little test last night. Killing one Dead doesn't make her experienced. Surely you know that."

"Killing one Dead, no. Killing thirty or so gives her enough experience to retract her 'novice' label."

Gripping his hands under the table, he leaned forward. "What do you mean thirty?"

"The Deads' movements around here have shifted. It seems they aren't as affected by the cold as they have been in past years. Finn miscalculated how many would be roaming the woods last night, and they had to fight their way out of a horde. Vanessa was a warrior."

Stark pride warred with gut-searing anger that she was ever placed in such an uncontrolled environment for her first kill.

"Sean," Mel said softly. "We need you on this one. Who can you name that will get the civilian back alive with everything we need for vaccine dispersion? Dr. Mackey is so close to having the medicine ready to administer, but we're at a standstill until we get these supplies. Every day, people are dying, and we are on the cusp of preventing some of them. We can't help the ones who are eaten, but a single bite? They won't be a threat anymore. Just a scar and a story for the grandkids."

Sean sighed, long and slow. "I quit doing supply runs because Adrianna is old enough to ask me not to go."

"Laney and I have already worked out a schedule and talked with Adrianna about it. Your daughter has chosen to stay with Laney until you return." She smiled. "Likely because Laney's promised to teach her how to use a crossbow."

Sean snorted. "Figures. Of course she'd bribe her with weaponry."

The corner of Mel's lip twitched. "If she is going to survive this world, she'll need everything Laney can teach her. And she'll need that vaccine."

Sean rubbed his eyes with the heels of his hands like it would ward off the coming headache. Put that way, how could he refuse? The colony needed his expertise. Adrianna needed it. No one had been on more successful supply runs, and at his very core, he was and would always be a soldier. Dead Run River had a need, and he had a need to fill it. "At least send a civilian who has pulled the trigger on a pistol before. I'd like to think we've learned our lesson after the last one."

A slow grin took Mel's face. "I knew you'd come through."

"Don't count your chicks before they hatch. We aren't back alive just yet."

And with every obstacle stacking against them, odds were they weren't coming back human.

Chapter Six

Thank the powers that be that Finn had decided against cutting Vanessa's knife-throwing arm. With the bandaged one limp at her side, she hurled another blade that toppled end over end until it lodged itself in the target-painted tree. *Thunk.*

"Hey," came a soft voice behind her.

Laney stood beside a great evergreen with a backpack slung over one shoulder.

"No, thanks," Vanessa said, turning once again to pitch another knife. "I'm not interested in buying any Girl Scout cookies today." *Thunk.*

"Eloise told me you were accepted for the supply run. She said you hang out here and practice most days. I asked Guist to help me pack a go-bag for you."

Vanessa eyed the offered backpack suspiciously. "I can pack my own bag." *Thunk.*

"I know you can. I just thought maybe I could offer advice from what I learned as a fighter all those years. I messed up a lot in the beginning, and I thought it could be easier for you."

"Why do you care if it's easier for me?" *Thunk.* "I thought you would be skipping all over this place when I left."

"Vanessa, I'm not trying to run you off. Eloise told me how much your friendship means to her. I left her with a good-bye note last year, and you were there for her through most of her pregnancy. I know me coming back has thrown a wrench in things around here, but I don't want to rip Eloise up with our squabbling."

"Well, maybe you'll get lucky, and I'll get tickled by a Dead on the mission. Then you can have her all to yourself. Shit. Why do you do this? How can one person make me feel all guilty just being myself? I just wanted to get over him, you know? Just not think of you two anymore, and now I can't escape your legions of fans. Sucks filling that shadow."

Laney shifted her weight and looked down at the toe of her boot. "I'm sorry," she muttered, and spun to leave.

"Waaait." Damn it, Laney was really going to get her to bury the hatchet, wasn't she? Didn't Laney get that her bitterness was the only thing keeping her from pining for the man who'd rejected her so epically she'd never want another partner again? "Fancy a knife throw?"

"Ha, heck no. I'm terrible at knives. I mean, I'm impressively bad."

That little tidbit drew her up short. "What is this? The invincible Laney Landry sucks at something?"

"Admittedly so. I used to practice all the time, but I just didn't ever get it."

Vanessa flipped a blade in the air and caught it by the hilt over and over. Somehow, Laney's admission to a weakness made her hate her nemesis less. She narrowed her eyes to slits. "Okay, I'm going to say this once, and if it leaves here, I'll deny it for eternity."

Laney's mouth quirked with amusement. "Okay."

"I never thanked you for saving my brother and me that day by the gardens."

Laney arched one perfectly shaped eyebrow. "And you still haven't."

"That's as close as you're getting, Landry. Take it or leave it. It was pretty cool of you to put yourself out there and protect a person you hated. Even if you were only trying to save Eloise, my brother was saved in the process, and he's all I have, you know?"

Laney wiped off a tree stump in a half-hearted attempt and sat down. "I know how that is." Her smile could've belonged on a ghost for as sad as it was. "I had a brother. Jarren. He was all I had too, and he died the day before I came to Dead Run River last year. Losing him was—I don't think I'll ever be the same."

Vanessa's innards churned like she was being burned from the inside out. She hadn't known about Laney's loss. She was naturally and harshly honest with people, but if she'd known Laney was going through hell, she would've cut her some slack at least. Losing Nelson was completely unimaginable, and Laney had gone to work and undergone all of those horrible tests, all while mourning her brother's passing. It made her sick and ashamed. "I didn't know."

"I didn't want you to. I didn't want anyone to. Talking about it was impossible. Mitchell was his best friend. We'd all grown up together, and that loss was a secret hurt we shared together."

Vanessa slumped down against a tree under the weight of the new knowledge. Here she'd been pining at the unfairness of Mitchell picking Laney when they had this deep, rich history together. They'd been through the apocalypse together for crying out loud. She'd known him for only a second compared to Laney. She'd misjudged every single thing, and suddenly, she couldn't trust herself. The conversation had become too deep and promised to drown her if it continued, so she bailed. "What's so fantastic about this go-bag you guys have packed?"

Laney squatted and pulled at the zippers. "It has the essentials but also a few extras that a lady needs. They wouldn't have taught you about that in training because they think every go-bag is the same. It's not. Canteen with iodine tablets is a must. Purify all water. If you get sick out there, you're just a meal waiting to happen. Guist snagged homemade protein bars for meals on the go, and this blue tarp and rope are all you need for a shelter. Tie the rope in between two trees, toss the tarp over it and hold down the edges with rocks. Here's a first-aid kit with a few extras in it because I know your arm is injured. Extra bandages are in there, and they need to be changed daily. Keep the cut clean. Infection in your arm will be a dinner bell for Deads, and you don't need them hunting you any more than they already will be. Fishing line and flies are in the Tic Tac case along with a spark starter. You'll need to pack an extra pair of clothes and two pair of socks. If yours get wet, switch them. You don't want sore feet on the run. Where do you keep your ammo?"

Vanessa pulled open her cargo pockets and pointed to an ammo pouch on her belt.

"Perfect. I heard you're a bad ass with a gun, so you'll be good on weapons. The hardest part is getting used to traveling with men. Don't take any crap from them."

She gave a wicked grin.

"Not that I thought you would," Laney said with a laugh.

"What's that?" Vanessa pointed to a tangle of flat canvas ropes.

"That is really important. It's a tree harness. Deads can't climb, so if you find yourself in a jam, find a tree and get yourself up it. If you're stuck for a while, don't go to sleep up there without the harness on. This one is mine, and it's smaller and made more for a woman. It's yours while you're out on missions."

"And what if I don't come back?"

"You'll come back. You have a good team with you, and Finn said you guys are taking the Terminator. That truck is a Dead crusher. What tree do you want to climb?"

"Pardon?"

"I need to show you how to secure the harness and you need to get a feel for which trees are best for you to climb."

"Oh, right. Uhhh," she said, searching the immediate forest. Her size was going to hinder her on this one because the older trees' branches were all too high for her to reach.

Laney followed her until she pointed to a smaller pine with branches all closer together near the bottom. She hoisted the harness over her shoulder and climbed, ignoring the burning pain jolting up and down her injured arm. The limbs were tightly packed together, and she had to shove her way through smaller ones that bent easily. Sap caked the palms of her hands, and the bark was rough on skin not used to it, but upward she pushed.

"Higher," Laney instructed. "Better to be safe than sorry when you are going to let your body go into an unconscious state of being."

Vanessa obliged until the limbs became too thin to hold her.

"Good, now hook that part over your shoulders and buckle at the waist. And then strap the other end around the tree and tighten it." When that was done, Laney said, "Whew, I'm glad you aren't afraid of heights."

Well, now that Vanessa thought about it, the ground was really far away. A momentary panic seized her when she imagined falling to the ground and hitting every limb on the way down.

"Vanessa," Laney warned. "Look at the trunk in front of you. Put your hand on it. You're safe. Now look at the ladder of limbs going down to the ground. You won't fall. The harness won't let you."

"What if there are Deads below me and I'm out of weapons?"

"Don't let that happen. It's what we call being 'treed.' You'll starve to death long before those Deads give up on you."

"Lovely."

"Okay, now unstrap it, then loop it over your shoulder again, and come on down."

Climbing a tree was much, much harder than it looked. Her fingers were tired where she'd gripped the branches, and the palms of her hands were scuffed up from the rough bark. Her arms shook like autumn leaves by the time she finally reached the ground again, but Laney assured her she'd grow used to climbing, and her body would acclimate to the need to use those muscles with practice. Over and over she wiped the palms of her hands against her pants until the sap was mostly cleaned.

"Okay," Laney said. "I'm going to head back. I have a check-up with Dr. Mackey to see how the baby is doing." She turned to leave.

"Laney?"

"Yeah?"

"Why didn't you pick Sean?"

She opened and closed her mouth as if she were unable to come up with a reasonable explanation. Or maybe she was trying to spare her feelings about Mitchell.

"Honestly," Vanessa encouraged. "Was there a moment when you knew he wasn't the one?"

"He stifled me. I let him for a while, but it wasn't me. I would have been a caged bird under his protection, and I couldn't live that way. Not when Mitchell treated me like I deserved."

Honest words, but they caused such a disappointment within Vanessa. She wouldn't be caged either.

Laney gave a little wave and disappeared into the woods, and Vanessa turned to bury another blade into the bark of the target tree.

The look of disappointment in Nelson's eyes when she'd told him about the supply run the day before hurt like a lash against her heart. Still, in true Nelson fashion, he waited in front of the Terminator with a sack of breakfast food he'd nabbed from the mess hall.

"Here." Jamming the food at her, he hugged her in one fluid motion. "Come back."

It wouldn't do to sob openly in front of her gathering team, so she patted him roughly on the back like she'd seen Dad do before the outbreak and promised she would.

The dim blue light of early dawn illuminated a fog that had settled over the mountain. As she stood there, hugging her brother, a man strode through the mist with a heavy looking bag in one hand and a gait that dripped with confidence. Sean Daniels sauntered toward them with a slight frown on his glorious features and tossed his bag to Jackson, one of the senior guards. Holy guacamole. She'd barely managed to run a brush through the snarls of her hair, and he was approaching the Terminator like a one-man dream team. The freaking fog was actually parting for him. Her heart thumped an erratic rhythm against her sternum.

"Vanessa," Nelson wheezed. "Can't...breathe."

"What are you doing here?" she asked, releasing Nelson from her anaconda grip.

"Nice to see you too, Summers," Sean said, not even bothering to stop on his way to the driver's side of the eighteen-wheeler. "Load up," he commanded.

Nelson said good-bye and scrambled out of the way. The Terminator was a beast. Its grille had been modified into a steel snow plow, and someone much more creative than her had painted murals down both sides. Cartoon zombies bent and folded into endless positions of their final deaths while hellish flames licked the edges of the painting. Across the top, in elegant giant letters, read *No Dead Food Attitude*. Right, no weaklings allowed on this party bus.

Finn, Jackson, a studious looking man named Brandon, and Keeter crawled on the back bench seat with their backpacks shoved under them, leaving the only space for Steven and her up front. Right by Sean.

"I call window," Steven murmured in a sleepy voice.

"But—"

"Sorry, Summers," Finn said with a toothy grin. "He who calls it first, gets it."

After primly throwing him the middle finger, she scooted over beside Sean, who graced her with a hard look. What had she done?

Maybe he was one of those people who was terrible at mornings. Or maybe he was rethinking his decision to vouch for her. Too late now.

The engine roared to life under them, and he threw it in gear. The next few minutes were terrifying, but Sean maneuvered the gigantic vehicle down the switchbacks like he was born to be a trucker. She'd have to make him a T-shirt with that slogan if they survived this.

"So," she started, "if gasoline is only good for about a year, and we're now on year four of the outbreak, how are we still driving around?"

"No."

She scowled at the hard edge in his tone. "No, what?"

"No talking. Everyone is trying to sleep, and you should be too. It's your turn to drive next."

She snorted and waited for the punch line to the joke. When none came she asked, "Are you out of your ever loving mind? I haven't driven since the outbreak, and even before it, I was mostly taking the bus."

"Why's that?" His intensely blue eyes left the road just long enough to paralyze her with his gaze.

"I was trying to be environmentally conscious. I wanted to make my ecological footprint as tiny as it could be to preserve the earth."

The corner of his mouth curved up. "And how'd that work out?"

"Well, Deads ate everyone, and the jungle took over, so I guess the earth didn't need my help after all."

"Should've enjoyed driving while you had the chance. Finn, you're up next."

"Sure, boss," came a rumbled reply from the backseat.

Vanessa's feelings weren't hurt. If she'd been allowed to drive this Moby Dick of a truck, they'd be dead before they made it to Breckenridge. Sean waved to the guards at the front gate as they swung it open wide to allow them to pass. The truck hissed and whistled as he put it into gear and pulled away from the sanctity of Dead Run River.

Her fears and indecision were meaningless now.

Turning back was no longer an option.

Sean was in trouble. Vanessa was so damned cute in the morning, it should've been illegal. One of those verbal types, she'd chattered on, asking questions about every leaf and blade of grass they passed like she'd never been outside the colony in her entire life. He tried to ignore her completely, but she made it very difficult. Mostly because the woman didn't get her feelings hurt. If he told her to shut it, she threw a ready insult at him and went on talking as if he'd never made the effort of being rude.

At the moment, she was sleeping soundly against his shoulder. Long, blond tresses that shone like spun silver in the morning sunlight splayed across his chest like a fan, and for the eight hundredth time, he clenched his teeth against the urge to touch it. A wiser man would've flung her off onto Steven, who was snoring like a freight train against the window and wouldn't notice.

Her hand flopped into his lap, and he tensed against the feel of it. What was he supposed to do now? He wiggled to try to ease it off, but that only made the crotch of his pants become uncomfortably tight with a slow simmering rigidness. Not good. Removing his hand from the wheel, he picked her tiny wrist up between forefinger and thumb and set it back on her own lap.

"You're going to have to be careful with that, boss," Finn murmured.

Glaring through the rearview at Captain Obnoxiously Obvious, he said, "You think?"

"Here," his second-in-command said, "I'll help." Placing his giant paws on either side of her head, he yanked her off Sean and pushed her toward Steven.

"Oow," she howled with an angry grimace.

Sean ducked out of the way as she nailed Finn with the full force of her flinging backpack.

Sean tried not to laugh. Really he did, but the zipper caught Finn in the side of the head, and every time he looked back at the dumbfounded look on Finn's bleeding face, his smile couldn't be contained.

"Vanessa," he chided dutifully when he could keep the laughter from his voice, "blood brings the Deads in, so please, please don't maim your own teammates."

She sat in a cloud of anger with her arms crossed remorselessly over her chest. "I was having a good dream," she said, like that explained away her behavior.

The main drag in Breckenridge appeared over the hill, and she leaned forward with her hands splayed across the dash. Maybe she'd never seen a ghost town before.

Grass didn't grow very well at this altitude, so foliage hadn't exactly taken over, but the dilapidation of the buildings was enough to say no one had cared for this place in years. Paint had chipped, and the wood underneath had rotted in the wet seasons. Roofs sagged under the weight of Mother Nature, and doors to abandoned shops hung open. Rust bathed everything in red hues. The signs that hadn't given up the fight yet clung to weather-eaten chains and nails, and stairs and porches had eroded away to splinters. In a hundred years, there would be no evidence that the ski resort town had ever existed.

A look of desolation clouded Vanessa's face. "We came through here, Nelson and I. It was still beautiful then. Is it like this everywhere?"

He wanted to lie just to save her sadness, but she'd see for herself soon enough. "Yes." Pulling the truck to a stop near the curb, he checked his handguns.

"Where are you going?"

"Not me—we. There's a pharmacy across the street right there. We've hit it a few times, but we left stuff we didn't know about alone. We might get lucky and find some of our supplies in here." Twisting in the seat, he asked, "Brandon, you ready?"

Dr. Mackey's assistant looked terrified. At five-foot-three at best and with a shaky gun hand, his greenish pallor sure wasn't doing him any favors.

Sean handed him the list, and the door creaked loudly as it opened. A lone Dead with splintered legs stumbled slowly across the street, likely attracted to the noise of the Terminator. Her hair was short and stringy, and her eyes were so filmed over they looked white. With her jaw hanging open, her rasping could be heard from here. Mouth breathers. Unsavory.

"Sean?" Vanessa whispered.

"Don't engage her. She's focused on the truck, and gunfire will draw in others." The breeze pushed a metal window frame open on the building behind her, and it creaked loudly, drawing the Dead's flighty attention. He waved to the occupants of the truck. "Go now, while she's turned away from us."

The seven of them sprinted for the pharmacy as quietly as boots on pavement could. The glass doors had been broken long ago, so they just stepped through. Tinkling shards crunched under the thick rubber soles of his shoes, and Sean gestured for Jackson and Keeter to stand guard. The door at the back of the small building was closed, and a quick peek into the window told him some dumb Dead had wandered in there and hit the latch that held the door open. Who knew how long the monster had been stuck in there.

The lurching Dead was clad in only shredded pants, and his gray skin sagged like the Silly Putty Sean had played with as a child. His eyelids had pulled away from his eyes in his emaciated state, and the creature jerked and twitched like a junkie too long off drugs. All Deads were dangerous, but a hungry Dead was riskier still. Vanessa looked borderline panicked when she glanced through the window, but he put an arm out to shush her. He'd do it himself and be quiet about it. *Stay here*, he mouthed.

Finn ambled off to pick through the littered shelves, and Brandon was doing a bang up job of looking nauseous, so Sean took three quick breaths to steel himself and threw the door open. The Dead's reaction was instantaneous. There wasn't a moment of hesitation as he ran toward his chance at a meal. The power of the monster was surprising, and as Sean pressed his forearm against its chest and drove his knife upward, he knew in an instant he'd hit too shallow. A gruesome effect to be sure, but Deads weren't affected by pain. With a guttural moan, it pressed him into a wall and gnashed its rotting teeth around the dagger in its face. All he had to do was get the knife out and— *Pow!*

The Dead went limp and dropped like a stone. Shocked, Sean swung his gaze to the open doorway where Brandon stood with his pistol still aimed in his general direction. Vanessa yanked the gun from him with eyes so big they could've rivaled a wood sprite.

"Why didn't you stop him?" Sean asked.

"Me? This is my fault? I didn't know you gave the idiot a gun."

"Hey," Brandon groused. "I just saved your life. And my IQ is double all of yours combined, so who's the idiot now?"

"Still you," Vanessa deadpanned. "Deads are attracted to sound. Just like Sean explained in the truck."

"Oh," he said with a worried moue.

"We've got company," Jackson called out from up front, and a pepper of gunfire trilled through the building.

If Sean had time to punch Brandon square in the jaw, he'd gladly do it, but right now they had bigger problems than who would win the blame game. Finn stood with an idiotic grin and a box of condoms in his hand. "Stop waggling your eyebrows like that, or I'll shoot you my damned self," Sean growled. "We'll go out the back and circle around to the truck," he called out.

"What about the medical stuff?" Vanessa asked.

"We'll have to try again on our way back. We can't let ourselves get trapped in here. Jackson, Keeter, fall back."

Deads poured by twos into the building like some messed up version of Noah's Ark, and Sean led the others at a sprint out the back door. Another Dead rounded the gigantic garbage bin and almost ran smack into Vanessa.

Sean ordered, "Duck," and popped it the moment she did. At least the woman could obey orders when it mattered.

She and Brandon flanked him, while Finn and the other guards took out any Deads getting too close to their backs.

It was then that they focused on run-and-hide tactics. Deads weren't supernaturally fast or even graceful. As long as no one lagged behind, they could keep ahead of them. In a wide loop, they sprint-ed until they were flush with the Terminator. Heart pounding and adrenaline pumping through every cell in his body, Sean threw open the door, and the others piled in. The Deads knew where they were, and the sound of the shots wouldn't matter. He picked them off until Finn was in and dragging Sean backward.

He slammed the door closed just as the clawing hands of the Deads reached for him.

"Ew," Vanessa said, picking up a severed finger and tossing it out the cracked window before rolling it up again. As if by magic, a tiny bottle of hand sanitizer appeared, and she deftly worked it into her palms.

Something about that struck him as funny. Deads were piling onto their truck, moaning for their death, and Vanessa was focused on the one little nasty occurrence that didn't matter in the big picture.

"What's wrong?" she asked through an offended frown as he turned the key.

The engine roared, and he threw it into first.

"Nothing," he replied. "Nothing at all."

Chapter Seven

Sean was a redwood in a storm. Strong, immovable, steadfast. The durability of his branches offered shelter from the reality of what was happening.

Vanessa had panicked at the first shots Jackson and Keeter fired at the horde, and when that Dead jumped out from behind the Dumpster, she'd frozen. She would've been a goner if not for Sean's cobra-strike thinking. So shaken was she after that, she'd almost lost her lunch. Running for her life left her with a drained and sick feeling deep inside.

But then there had been Sean. There was no hesitation in his command and not a trace of fear in his voice. He'd somehow formed a plan before he even knew there was a need, and because of him, they were all still upright. And able to eat salad. As easily as anything, she could've been one of the masses trotting after them as they sped off in the Terminator. The man wasn't even shaking. One of his hands rested lightly on the wheel, and the other drummed light fingers against the window in rhythm to some song only he knew the cadence to.

No frown let on that he was worried. No tension made his jaw clench. The man had obviously seen more Dead battles than she'd ever comprehend. He'd somehow managed to find a way to turn his fear off. Maybe it was because he naturally put others in front of himself. She could see that. He wouldn't get into the truck until every one of them was safe inside. Or maybe he just didn't have that trigger that released fear endorphins into his system. Such a possibility was frightening. A man without feelings? She scooted a little closer to Steven. Sean was not a person to get too emotionally invested in. He didn't reek of reckless, but his chances of being taken were upped dramatically if he was going to play Captain America and continue putting their safety above his own. Especially trigger-finger-Brandon, who at the moment was heavy-breathing on the back of her neck.

Twisting in her seat, she warned, "I will literally head-butt you if you don't lean back."

"I'm trying to see out the front window," he said.

"Then switch places with me. I'm not traveling all the way to Denver with you air-breathing a hickey on my neck."

Leaning back, he crossed his arms and looked out his own window with a man-pout. She couldn't be sure, but the corner of Sean's mouth twitched into what looked suspiciously like an almost-smile. How many times had he wanted to tell someone off, but couldn't in his position? Thank God she was just a peon foot soldier. She could say whatever she wanted to the other expendables.

"Hey, Brandon? Why don't you explain that little list of yours in case you get yourself killed?" Jackson suggested.

Huh. She liked Jackson even better now. He was average height with light brown hair worn longer. In his mid-forties, he all but dripped with Dead fighting experience and didn't talk very often. When he did, it was apparently to offer legitimately helpful suggestions. Points for him.

"What's to keep you protecting me if I give you all of the information I know?" Brandon asked.

"We'll get you safely back to colony," Sean promised.

There rang such an honest note of conviction in his tone, she almost groaned. The nerd's life would come before all of theirs because of his civilian status.

Brandon swallowed at an annoyingly loud volume. "Dr. Mackey needs to get this vaccine he's extracted from Laney to the masses. And even though there aren't a ton of humans left, there are much more than our small medical cache can handle. To disperse the medicine to other colonies, the main thing we need is a way to get the vaccine from the vial to the vein."

"Dumb it down there for us, Einstein," Vanessa drawled. "We're but a humble crew of uneducated guns for hire."

"Needles," Brandon said flatly. "We need as many needles as we can get our hands on. We also need components for the vaccine itself. We'll need several different types too if we're going to start testing this on people. Here," he said, pointing to the middle of the second page. "These five alone are all variations of a stabilizer. We'll also need antigens, adjuvants, and preservatives before we start poking people."

"Is that the only copy we have of the list?" Keeter asked.

"No," Sean answered. "There is another under the front seat, wrapped in plastic. If the person holding that list is lost, it's up to the rest of the team to complete the mission. This is save-the-world work. If we don't do it, it doesn't get done."

A flutter started in her stomach at his talk about saving the world. She'd never looked at the mission as much more than an escape and a shortcut to guard graduation. This was much bigger than she'd given it credit for. And Sean's deep velvet voice popping it off like that—like it was just another day saving the planet? Well that was just about the sexiest sound that had ever caressed her eardrums.

The brakes hissed as Sean stopped at a dilapidated stop sign and poured over a map he pulled from under the seat. "We'll have to hit up every hospital and medical facility in the Denver area and beyond until we find what Doc needs."

Finn groaned. "I hate hospitals."

"Why?" she asked. "What's wrong with them?"

"They are always infested with Deads who are trapped in the rooms and hallways. And they're the creepiest places you'll ever be in."

Vanessa faced forward and grimaced. Goody. "Say we manage to get past all of the Deads in the hospital, how do we know there will be anything left worth taking?"

"We don't," Sean said. "But there aren't many colonies around here. I sanctioned all of the supply runs for the Denver colony before it fell, and we didn't hit hospitals for any of this stuff. Dead Run River hasn't either. We wouldn't have taken medical supplies that we didn't know the use for, and likely others wouldn't have either."

"Heroin addicts," she said. "Heroin addicts would definitely steal all of the needles."

Sean's dark eyebrow arched, and she couldn't seem to pull her gaze away from the perfection of it. "You know many junkies who survived the outbreak?" He shook his head and dragged his cerulean gaze back to the road before accelerating through the stop sign. "I don't know if you've noticed, but it's survival of the fittest nowadays. The junkies were the first to go. Probably didn't even know what hit 'em."

She dragged a somber gaze to him and let it rest on his. "My parents were junkies."

His mouth opened and closed and such a look of sorrow crossed his features that she couldn't keep the smile from her lips. "Joke."

Glorious blue eyes narrowed in annoyance as masculine chuckles filled the cab of the eighteen-wheeler. In her defense, he'd practically set her up.

"That's a terrible thing to tease about," he grumbled, turning onto an abandoned highway.

Shrugging, she sank into the cushion of the seat. "I'm probably dying today. If I don't have jokes, I don't have anything."

"Don't say that. You aren't dying today." His voice lowered to a barely discernible whisper, and she could almost swear he said, "I won't let you."

He could've also said, "I want to cut you," though, which also made sense. Looking down at her bandaged arm, she sighed. She had that effect on people.

Denver was trashed, and the streets were paved with bones. Fires had consumed large sections of the city until only ash and charred ruins remained, never to be refurbished or cared for again. The destruction sent an ache through her. She sent a silent thank you into the universe for Nelson never showing interest in leaving the colony. His tender heart would be broken the second he stepped beyond the gates.

As much as she'd hated morning PT, it was a lucky thing she was conditioned for this mission. It wasn't like they could back a roaring truck into the hospital loading docks without attracting some serious Dead attention, so Sean had pulled them right beside an ancient Victorian house about two blocks away and led them inside.

In the mildewed basement there was an entrance to a tunnel that led underground. They'd hoofed it twelve feet under the earth through winding tunnels with a carefully followed map. Plenty of rats were down in the shallow streams of water that coated the tunnels, but nary a Dead to be seen. Sean said they were wary of moisture. What with all the rotting limbs, it made sense some buried instinct inside of the monsters would want to preserve what little they had left.

At the end of a sloshy tunnel main, Sean flicked his flashlight to a rusty ladder. "Up we go. The hospital is just across the street from this exit."

Keeter went first, then Jackson and Brandon. She ended up getting stuck between Sean and Finn. Meh. She'd been in much worse positions than serving as the meat in a sexy manwich. Plus Sean's tight backside was her beacon of glorious light leading out of the depths of the smelly tunnels. She'd slosh through that goulash again if given the option. She'd sworn to herself she wouldn't touch, but there wasn't a good enough reason on earth not to look.

As Keeter pushed aside the heavy metal mesh cover from inside a tangle of bramble vines, the storm clouds above only lent to the ominous sinking feeling that had settled into her gut. She pulled her Glock as soon as she was out. The street was bare of Deads, but they'd likely drawn any moaners in the area to the place the truck was now parked. Should be interesting getting back inside their escape vehicle with all of their appendages intact.

Blinking against the gray light that was still leaps and bounds brighter than the black pitch they'd been immersed in for the past twenty minutes, she tilted her head back. Legions of black birds circled the wind currents above the city.

"Crows," Finn said in a hushed voice.

She wasn't one to believe in omens, but gooseflesh rippled across her skin. Maybe she was a little 'stitious, if not *super*stitious.

Following Sean's silent approach to a set of double doors behind a circular drive, she covered their backs as the others pried the once automatic double doors open.

Movement, subtle and small, drew the aim of her handgun. A Dead lay between two overgrown shrubs. Like a moth to blue flame, she was drawn to the emaciated creature.

Clack. Clack. Clack.

His eyes were closed, but the soft snapping of his teeth sounded from the landscaping. His fingertips twitched in rhythm to the noise. Sean brushed her elbow and jerked his head toward the opened doors.

"What's wrong with him?" she whispered.

"He's dying. Starving."

"Oh." The Dead looked pitiful. "Do we put him out of his misery?"

"No. He'll die on his own in a few months."

A few months in this state? Sean started to move off, but she snatched a knife from her belt before she could change her mind. With a grunt, she thrust the blade down at the Dead's temple, and just before it pierced him, his filmy eyes opened. Stifling a shriek, she stayed her course, and when his body was limp, the blade was wiped across a tuft of grass and returned to its sheath.

Sean stood watching with his eyebrows furrowed. "You can't spare pity for Deads, Vanessa. It's a waste. They won't appreciate the sentiment, and they won't hesitate even a second before eating you."

"I didn't do it for the Dead. I did it for the person he used to be."

His expression softened, and she followed the others through the hospital doors. Inside, Brandon discussed the most likely places for the items on the list, and Steven, Jackson, and Keeter made sure the area was secure. Silently, they moved through the dark hallways. Dim light streamed through open windows and created stripes across the dingy tile floors. Each room had to be checked for wandering Deads, and Vanessa stopped when she came to a slowly jiggling door handle protecting a closed door. Sean put his finger over his lips and twitched his head to keep going.

The not knowing was terror inducing. How many Deads were in there? How had they managed to lock themselves in? Would they make an ill-timed escape and come up from behind the team to catch them unaware?

The hallways were littered with debris and broken glass. A layer of dust coated everything except well-worn trails down the middle of the floors. The air was saturated with moist rot, and a steady *drip, drip, drip* echoed off the walls.

Finn had been right. Hospitals were downright creepy.

Vanessa clicked her flashlight on and held it next to the barrel of her gun as they turned down a hallway that led away from the windowed rooms and into darkness. Steadying her breathing, she silently chanted the things she'd learned in guard training to calm her nerves. At this rate, she'd pull a Brandon and yank the weapon with her shaking hands.

Finger beside the trigger, not on it until she was ready.

Calm her breathing.

Deep breath.

Senses open.

If she was aware enough, she'd probably hear them before she saw them.

Walk carefully.

Protect the guard beside her. And Brandon.

Don't get bit.

She could do this.

The only sound that came from the team was that of metal weaponry being checked and the muted scuffle of boots against the filthy floor. She thought she heard scampering footsteps behind her, but when she turned the flashlight down that hall, nothing was there. Her imagination was proving to be much scarier than the actual situation she'd found herself in. When she turned around, she met Sean's questioning gaze and shook her head.

The first medical supply room was empty of Deads, and they filed in before Finn shut the door behind them. Maybe they could get away with a little more noise with the extra layer of protection.

Boxes of supplies were scattered on the tiled floor, and rows of haphazardly strewn bottles, vials, and canisters littered a wall of shelves. Brandon shimmied the empty black duffle from his back and started checking labels against the list he held clutched in his shaking hand. Sean rushed over to help while she and the others ambled around to the other cupboards and sifted through them for anything of use.

Antibiotics had been picked clean in the first year of the outbreak, along with pain killers and vaccines against common illnesses.

She held up a canister of single wrapped sanitary bandages in silent victory. Steven pointed to the duffle that was being filled and kept searching.

Two miniature refrigerators sat quietly in the corner, and she gagged when she opened the first one. Someone had left their lunch in there years before, and the mold inside practically had a face. The next one yielded more success. Vials were lined in carefully labeled rows. She couldn't even guess at the pronunciation, so she waved Brandon over. The smile on his face said they'd found something good. He took everything but two rows and shoved the tiny glass vessels into foam cushioned containers before shoving them into the bag. It wasn't until she swung the flashlight at the slim window on the door that she saw the face. One blink and it was gone.

Sean followed her gaze and whispered, "What's wrong?"

"I thought I saw someone at the door."

"A Dead?"

"I don't know." It had happened so fast. Or maybe it hadn't happened at all.

It was at that moment she heard the moaning, and the window shattered inward. Tiny shards of glass cut her cheeks, and she squeezed her eyes closed against the unexpected pain. Sean grabbed the back of her neck and shoved her behind him, but he couldn't hide what was coming for them.

"How many?" she breathed as the first Dead shoved his arm through the broken window.

"More than our numbers, that's for damned sure," Keeter said, pulling a machete from a sheath behind his back.

Overhead, the sound of running footsteps trilled against the floor of the second story. Sean ducked at the sound and glared at the ceiling. His hand still rested lightly on the back of her neck. She would've told him to shove off if the small gesture didn't comfort her so much.

"Finn?" he asked.

"I heard it too," his second-in-command said. "Whatever it is, it ain't a Dead. We're being set up."

Sean hissed an oath as the door splintered. "Brandon, shoulder that duffle bag now." He searched the room and pulled the miniature refrigerators away from the wall. "Vanessa, find me a vent we can get through, a hole in the wall, anything. Finn!"

Finn tossed him a semi-automatic, and in one smooth motion he pulled it up like it had been born a part of him. "The noise won't matter now. Deads are making enough racket to attract all of Denver," he called over the murmur.

She turned and ripped viciously at the boxes stacked against the wall, desperate for any escape from the room. The walls sunk inward until she couldn't breathe, and she panted as she threw her panic into clearing the wall. One small vent that would fit a child was behind a bookshelf, and she swallowed a sob as another splintering crack sounded from the door. The rhythmic *pop, pop* of calculated gunfire cleared the Deads near the window, but masses were pushing against the door, and all hell was about to break loose in here.

Not a single place to hide. Not for any of them.

"Vanessa," Sean called, backing up to her. When she didn't answer, he gripped her thigh with an impossibly strong and soothing grip. "Back Brandon into that corner. Protect him."

"Sean—" What did she want to say? Something hung in the air between them but what was it? Be safe? They were all about to die, and the tragedy of not enough time ached inside her bones.

His eyes held hers for a brilliant moment before the door flung open. An endless stream of Deads poured through the open doorway like some floodgate to hell had been pried open and all of the lost and damned souls were leaking onto earth.

Keeter threw his weight at the door to try to staunch the flow, but it only slowed them, and several of the Deads had a death grip on his shirt through the small window. The darkness lit up in a desperate smattering of gunfire. The illumination would have been deadly beautiful if the reason for such light's existence wasn't a last effort at survival.

Brandon stood frozen on the outskirts of the chaos, and she grabbed his shirt and dragged him to the farthest corner. If this was her last stand, she was going down fighting that ragged fate.

"Stay here!" she yelled.

His eyes were round behind his glasses, and he nodded solemnly. Just as she turned and lifted her weapon, a knotted rope slapped her in the face, and she lurched back. She craned her neck, and the man who appeared through the now missing tile in the ceiling was more terrifying than the Deads. One side of his face was chiseled, worried, beautiful, while the other side was cut and gray, and his eye had the film of death over it.

"I don't kill women," he said. "I didn't know they had a woman with them until I'd already let my watchdogs out. Climb up, and I'll save you."

Hearing human words come from a decaying Dead's mouth was enough to turn her blood to ice.

Her team was failing. Deads still trickled in. Keeter was nowhere to be seen, and they were losing ground.

"I won't leave without my team." It was a desperate move that could get them all killed, but she couldn't live with herself if she just left them here to be turned.

The man scoffed. "No, no, no, no. I don't share and you're mine. No men. All men die."

"Then I'm not coming! I'll die here, and it'll be on your head. You'll have killed a woman!" She was shrieking—but desperate times and measures.

"Fine!" he bellowed. "Climb up, and I'll leave the rope for them."

"That's not how this is going to work. Them first." She shoved Brandon toward the rope. God, that weenie better not have skipped out on rope climbing day in gym. "Climb."

"I'm not going up there with that psycho," he said in a cracked voice.

They were out of time. She pressed her Glock against his temple. "Climb this damned rope, or I'll pull the trigger." She jerked her head toward the team. "You're wasting their time."

Brandon, thank whatever powers that be, could actually climb a rope.

"Jackson, Steven, you next!" she commanded.

With one small, shocked glance for the rope, they started scrambling up as she took her place near Sean and popped gunfire into the undead. Keeter was twitching on the ground in front of the door, and his presence there prevented more than two coming in at once. He was turning. She swallowed the sorrow down. There was nothing that could be done to save him now. The best she could do was honor his sacrifice by living.

"Finn, you're up," she said over the bellowing. Between the bottleneck and the pile of felled Deads at the doorway, the masses were slowing.

Sean jerked a glance at the rope, and his eyes went round. "What're you still doing here?" Stricken panic laced every word.

"He wants me. He'll pull the rope as soon as I'm up, and you'll all die here. I've got to go last."

A surge of force hit the door, and Keeter opened his eyes with a groan. *Click, click.* Her Glock was empty, and there wasn't enough time to reload. A Dead was already on her, and Sean was backed into the corner by two.

Seamlessly, she pulled a knife and screamed a battle cry as she pushed the Dead against the wall and brained him. Sean was in trouble. Keeter was coming for her, but Sean was pinned on the ground by the weight of the two Deads, straining to keep their teeth away from his face, and if she didn't help him, he was a dead man walking. She couldn't stand the thought of him looking at her like Keeter was, so in one last burst of energy before he was upon her, she pulled a blade and launched it.

Over and over it spun in the air until it landed with a sickening sound into the Dead closest to Sean's neck. It fell away limply just as Keeter reached her. She rolled, but he wasn't a clumsy Dead with decayed flesh and muscle deterioration. He was a newly turned monster with the advantages of a warm, trained body and the strength of a fighter. He grabbed her shoulders with a painful grip, like his fingers were digging through to her marrow, and he groaned in triumph as he lifted her from the floor. A foot above the air, her booted feet dangled as she thrashed and kicked to keep his teeth away from her.

The shot came from above as Finn snipered Keeter-the-Dead from the missing ceiling tile. She toppled to the floor on top of his body and scooted away from him as fast as she could. A tremendous crash sounded from the doorway as Sean pulled over a huge medicine case. Sprinting, he sailed through the air and landed on the rope, he wasn't even done swinging before he began an impossibly fast ascent up to the ceiling.

The cabinet rocked dangerously, and Sean yelled, "Vanessa, move!"

He'd bought her time, but not much.

Her cut arm screamed as she strained to climb the knots in the ropes. Panic and fury drove her. Fear from the grasping hands that now sought her ankles and fury for what they'd done to Keeter. As long as she lived, she'd never be able to picture him as anything other than the monster who'd almost succeeded in killing her. It wasn't fair. He'd probably fought against them for years, and now that glory had been ripped away. Grunting, she pulled herself the rest of the way through the opening and balanced hands and knees on two-by-fours that had been placed strategically as a walkway.

She sat up, breathless, and came face to face with Sean. His eyes swirled like a stormy ocean, and his mouth twitched in the beginnings of a question.

They'd survived.

The clack of weaponry was deafening in the small space. "Get away from her," a voice in the darkness echoed. "She's mine."

Chapter Eight

A hand pulled her roughly back from Sean, and she was shoved forward. "That way," the half-Dead man said, pointing his flashlight to an opening in the wall. His touch on her upper arm chilled the skin there even through the long sleeves of her thermal shirt almost as much as the cold whisper of gun metal against the back of her neck.

"I thought you didn't kill women," she said.

"I don't have a problem with shooting them. Kneel down!" he commanded the rest of her team the moment they were through the opening. He gripped her shirt and shoved her roughly onto a couch.

The room was an entirely different world. It wasn't a hospital room at all, but a luxurious bedroom. How had the man brought it all here? A four-poster bed decorated the back wall with soft, gold-colored sheets, and the walls were adorned with a fashionable wall paper. A sitting area waited in the shadow of a towering bookshelf overflowing with literature. The man shut a tiny, intricately carved door over the small opening in the wall and turned a Dead eye to her.

"What's your name?" Sean asked as he knelt down in front of the wall with the others.

Brandon seemed to be the only one panicking as his eyes shifted from the door and back to the man.

"Jericho. This is my Jericho. Jerry. The walls came tumbling down. Sandman. Sandy. Sanderson. Jerry Sanderson."

She threw Sean a wide-eyed look as the man paced the room and scratched his head with the barrel of his pistol. Something was wrong.

"Jerry, good. Nice to meet you. This is my team, Finn, Jackson, Steven, Brandon, and Vanessa."

"Vanessa. Nessa. I like that name. She's mine now. Not your team anymore."

"She's more than my team, Jerry. She's my wife. Now you wouldn't want to hurt another man's wife, would you?"

Jerry turned a half-Dead appraising glare on her, and when he smiled, the open, rotting cut on the side of his face gaped. "No marriage laws no more. She's my wife now."

"You want Vanessa?" Brandon asked.

Sean threw him a warning glance, which he promptly ignored, and Vanessa shook her head from behind Jerry.

"If you let us go, we'll give you Vanessa."

"Brandon!" Sean yelled.

The click of the gun as Jerry aimed it at Sean cracked against the walls of the open space.

"Listen," Brandon said with a calming wave of his palms. "She's yours. She cleans up pretty. You look awfully lonely here, and we can do without her. Just let us leave."

"You ruined everything," Jerry said. "Do you know how long it takes to get my pets in that room? To trap them there until one of you comes along to try to steal my home from me? I've killed all of you, all of you. This is my Jericho."

"What happened to your face, Jerry?" Sean asked.

"Turning, turning, turning, but I won't go quietly. I've been fighting the monster in me."

Sean's eyes swept over an assortment of vials and needles on a tray table before he dragged his gaze back up to the man's marred face. "Were you one of the doctors who worked here? Have you been experimenting on yourself?"

"They're my pets — my guard dogs against people like you."

"Listen, we have a doctor who's working on a vaccine who might be able to help you. Why don't you come with us, and we'll take you to him?" Sean asked in a calm voice.

"No more people. People are monsters. Can't trust people."

Vanessa gripped the cushion as he swung his gun from each one of her teammates to the next.

"Who first? He said I could have her, and I want her. You can't have her." Again, he pulled the hammer back on the old pistol in his hands and aimed it at Sean.

"Wait." Impossible. It wasn't physically possible for her to watch Sean die. She hadn't been able to do it in the room full of Deads, and she couldn't do it now. "I'll stay with you if you let them go."

"You'll stay with me either way," he said with a monstrous frown.

"Yes, yes, but if you let my friends go and I know they are all right in the world somewhere, I'll stay here willingly. I'll do whatever you want."

"Vanessa," Sean warned.

"You, shut up," Jerry spat as he lifted his gun to him again.

He worried the corner of his rotting lip as he studied her. Still under his gaze, she hoped whatever he saw in her earned her this one favor.

"Give me your gun. Now."

Without hesitation, she pulled her unloaded Glock and slid it across the floor to him.

"And your knives."

"I lost it while fighting the Deads down below." She lifted the edges of her shirt to prove it to him. All that remained was an empty sheath.

His eyes turned lucid for the first time since she'd seen him poke his head out of the ceiling. "Leave, before I change my mind."

Brandon, that traitor, bolted for the door and threw it open before the others even stood up.

"Can I say good-bye to my wife?" Sean asked. "Please. I'm never going to see her again. The least you can do is let me say good-bye."

Moments passed with only a hard and steady look from Jerry before he nodded curtly. "Make it quick."

Finn immediately started twenty questions with Jerry as Sean approached. His intense gaze held her like a caress, and he stroked her cheek with the pad of his thumb. Wrapping his arms around her until his hands tangled with the edge of her shirt, he leaned down and smiled just before he kissed her. His lips were sensuous and moved fluidly against hers until her legs felt like they wouldn't bear weight anymore. Finn spoke loudly about the best way out of the hospital as Sean whispered, "Meet at the tunnels," against her lips.

His hands brushed the bare skin of her exposed back and then something cut painfully into her flesh. Warmth trickled and pooled at the waist of her cargo pants, and it wasn't until he pulled away with a meaningful look that she realized just what he'd done. He'd given her knife back—the one she'd hurled at the Dead to save his life. Now, he was returning the favor.

Her hands shook at the realization that if she didn't use it, she'd become the reluctant partner of the half-monster who argued with Finn near the door.

Okay, she mouthed.

He'd kissed her too well. She was drunk with the taste of him, and her lips were warm and throbbing for more—for everything.

He was using that affection to trick Jerry. *Gah*, she had to get it under control and quick. Her life depended on recovering from whatever Sean had done to shock her system. Kissing Mitchell last year had been fun, but it hadn't been like this.

Her heart pounded as Sean walked away, and she bit her lip in hopes that the pain would evoke some of the inner strength that had vanished since she'd climbed that rope.

The door shutting behind her team was the most desolate sound in the world.

Vanessa swallowed a sob as she ran down another hallway only to realize she'd gotten herself turned around yet again. What if the team had already given up on her? It had been hours. What if they decided they couldn't wait for her any longer and left her alone in this city of Deads?

There. A map decorated a wall by a nurse's stand, and she ran a sleeve over the front of it to clear the dust. Coughing as quietly as she could, she tried to figure out where the front exit was. It had been years since she'd read a map, and her brain function seemed to be working at approximately thirteen percent capacity. Too much had happened over the past several hours for her to be able to focus on the here and now.

A shadow shuffled across the wall of a turn at the end of the hallway. Hang the map! She bolted in the opposite direction.

Just as she recognized where she was, it was too late to slow down. Knife and light in hand, she sprinted past the room they'd been trapped in, now filled with Deads still drawn to their lingering scent. The sound of running and moaning echoed down the hall behind her, but she didn't stop to look. Her nightmares would never let her live it down if she did. What if they'd shut the front door again? She'd be trapped, running these halls forever!

Skidding across the dirty floors, she slammed into a wall and took off for the front check-in. Light filtered in through the front glass, and she nearly cried in relief when she was able to run straight through the still-opened doors. Deads would be on her in fifteen seconds if she slipped, so she carefully thrust one foot in front of the other and booked it.

A hundred yards. Surely they hadn't left yet.

Fifty yards. Surely she'd be able to see them from here!

Twenty-five yards. The iron woven gate was open, but all was black inside.

They weren't there.

Not only that, but she was barreling toward a tunnel she didn't know how to navigate. And a little moisture fear wasn't going to keep the hungry monsters running after her from following her straight inside. She was leading them right into the dark where she'd be lost.

Something as solid as a stone wall caught her the moment she stepped into the pitch, and with a thunderous clang, the iron gate slammed behind her. She filled her lungs to scream, but Sean's face flashed in the dim light, and she nearly melted into him.

Her breathing was shaky and labored and seemed to fill every inch of the tunnel space as the Deads reached the gate and stretched their hands through the bars in desperation.

"I thought you'd left," she gasped. "I thought you'd left me here."

Sean cradled the sides of her face and pressed his forehead against hers. "Never. I knew you'd get back to us."

"To be fair, we did almost die waiting here for you," Brandon said matter-of-factly.

The black rage Brandon's treachery filled her with was more than she could handle. How could he even think of whining about the inconvenience she'd caused while trying to escape a psychopath and horde of Deads? One which the little twit had happily thrown her to. With a screech, she launched herself at Brandon's stupid face.

"Ow, you're hurting me!" he said as his back hit the tunnel wall.

"I think that's the point," Finn offered as she got her first good fist across his jaw.

Punching someone sounded awesome in theory, but in actuality, it hurt like hell. The possibility that she'd broken her fist right in half seemed likely, which only added fuel to the fire that was burning her up. "You gave me to that man! Just traded me like I was nothing!" Her voice was becoming shrill, but so what? She hoped she burst his eardrums.

He held his mouth as if it would flop onto the floor if he let it go, and he glared at her with shocked disapproval. "You just hit a guy with glasses."

"Well, looks like we're *both* going to the fiery place after we die, now doesn't it? Maybe we can share a room." With that, she shoved him out of her way with her good hand and stomped through the slush down the tunnel. And damn those boys with their echoing chuckles. She could hear every wisp of their obnoxious amusement, which only enraged her more.

Sean had been slowly gutted as they'd waited for her. He'd sworn to have faith in people more, but battling his protective instincts to go back in there to save her, which would get every one of his team members killed, sat heavy in his stomach.

He'd imagined every morbid thing that could be happening to Vanessa in that hospital, and the ache went from a mild dullness to an acute pain.

"She'll make it back to us," Finn chanted on a loop. "She's tough. She's proven herself today. She can do this."

And then she'd been there, running for her life and doing exactly as he'd asked her. She'd run straight to the tunnel even though she likely couldn't see them in the shadows. From the way she barreled into him, she probably hadn't known they were waiting just at the lip of the entrance.

And then she'd let him hold her. That ferocious woman let him comfort her. Some senseless pride arose in him that he'd somehow touched a jungle cat and been rewarded with a purr instead of death.

Even if it was just for a moment, that touch relieved a discomfort he hadn't known he'd been shouldering. She'd been a warrior in there. Unblinking, no hesitation, had gone above and beyond for the team and sacrificed her own safety not once, but twice for them. She was fierce and brave, and watching her closed fist sock that dillhole Brandon in his deserving jaw was just about the sexiest thing he'd ever seen.

Shoving past Brandon and his perpetual pout, he caught up to Vanessa just as she came to the first fork in the tunnel. "This way," he said. The words echoed off the moisture laden walls and sent a trio of rodents scurrying. He couldn't even name a less romantic destination for their first almost-moment.

He leaned closer, but she pulled into herself and crossed her arms over her chest. Whatever had happened in that room up there still sat, heavy and suffocating, on her. He swallowed the cold lump that threatened to choke off his air. He didn't even want to know. She was safe, and that had to be enough. Any more and he'd go mad hunting down the thing that had hurt her.

Stepping in front of her, he led the team through the tunnels and back to the basement of the house. The Deads had dispersed from the truck with the lack of food, and Finn took the wheel as Sean slid into the backseat next to Vanessa. There was more room to stretch because of the fall of Keeter.

Keeter.

The loss was fire on a soul that had already borne too much. Keeter's death was on him. No matter that he'd barely made it out himself. He led them. Every mistake fell on him.

Leaning his head back against the seat, he closed his eyes against the pain of what was to come. Of telling Keeter's wife she'd never see her husband again. Telling her she'd be raising their young son alone in a world already rich with unfairness.

Vanessa's breathing hitched beside him as Finn turned the engine. She faced away, toward the window, with her forehead against it as if the cool pane was her salvation. For a long time, he watched her struggle to control whatever emotions were overflowing from her body. Tensed muscles, clenched hands, a tightly controlled sniffle. She was a dam in a flood, barely hanging on, and he was adrift on the current of her sadness.

Words wouldn't fix what happened. They would only chip away at her walls until she was lost in front of the team. She couldn't show weakness in front of them. From the way she held it in, she likely knew that already.

Her hands were so soft-looking, clamped together in her lap. Impulsively, he placed his over hers, praying it would give her some of his strength—some of his warmth.

In a move that shocked him into stillness, she turned one petite hand over and brushed her palm against his as she held on. Dragging his gaze away from their intertwined fingers, he searched the side of her jaw, wishing desperately that her hair wasn't hiding her face. If she'd only look at him, he could see the thoughts in her expressive eyes.

She squeezed his hand once and let him go, and just like that, the moment was over and done. His palm still looked the same as it had the minute before, but it had changed somehow. Buzzing with something he couldn't understand, he held it up and clenched it a couple of times to see if the tingling sensation was just in his imagination.

Steven watched him with a thoughtful expression from the seat beside him.

"Finn," he clipped, in charge of himself once again. "Enough hospitals for today. We'll hit the pharmacy and urgent care off the highway and be done for the day. After Keeter—everyone could use some time to process."

"Yep," Finn said, making a right turn at a dangling, unlit streetlight.

If there was even the hint of something amiss, he was calling off these last two stops. They couldn't afford to make any more mistakes, or none of them would make it back to Dead Run River alive. And their ability to gather Dr. Mackey's medical supplies was a mission much more important than any of their lives. The fate of the world hung on their ability to complete the job Mel had asked of them.

The deserted streets were eerily quiet, and Sean leaned forward against the seat in front of him. The further they drove, the more Finn twitched his gaze around to each window and back. Sean wasn't the only one spooked.

"Where are they?"

Finn shook his head and turned down a side road. "Maybe the ones on this side of town were the big herd that migrated into the mountains that Vanessa and I ran into."

"Maybe. Let's go," he said as the truck pulled to a stop in front of a twenty-four-hour pharmacy and general store.

"Vanessa and Finn, you'll be serving as watch-out this time. Radio if there is any activity we need to know about. Jackson, you take the entrance, and Steven and Brandon, you're with me."

Vanessa's vibrant blue eyes held his gaze. Her eyes looked so much brighter with the little bloody cuts that covered her face from the broken window glass. She looked as if she wanted to say something, but instead she slid another magazine into her Glock with a metallic click and followed him out. She needed first aid, but there wasn't time now. The longer they stayed in one area, the bigger the risk.

And he'd be damned if he was putting her at such risk ever again.

Chapter Nine

The last twelve hours had been the longest of Vanessa's entire twenty-four years.

The hospital seemed like days ago, and it had only been this morning. She was dead on her feet by the time evening struck and Finn pulled up to a gated park. Sean hopped out of the front seat and stood in the dull light, entering a lock combination and yanking the chains off to let them pass.

"What is this place?" she asked.

"A sanctuary," Finn offered. "This is where we try to stay on supply runs because it's safer. This place was private land someone had fenced in as a type of game preserve. From what we can tell, he ran controlled hunts for elk and mule deer, and since the property is completely fenced, it's relatively safe from Deads. This will be the only time on this run we're close enough to it to make a night of it."

After Sean pulled the wire gates closed, Finn hit the gas in a slow build. The dirt road had long ago washed out and served as no more than a guideline. A trio of deer with giant antlers bounded in front of the headlights, and the truck jerked as it hit another pothole.

Already, just a couple hundred yards inside the gate, relief filled her veins until she sighed, expelling some of the tension she'd held tightly in check. Existing outside of the safety of Dead Run River gates was more difficult than she ever could've imagined.

A tiny, log hunting cabin came into view, and from the new boards and patched roof, it was obvious someone had been keeping it viable since the outbreak.

Sean hadn't looked at her since he'd held her hand in the truck earlier today. Not really. Other than the occasional glance to make sure she understood a command, the intensity of his knowing gaze had been denied her. He was just like the rest. Guilted into some emotion when a woman gave a little, and then back to a mask of indifference when the moment passed.

Snatching her pack from the floor boards, she hopped from the cab of the Terminator and followed Steven to a fire pit. Finn pulled tinder from his bag, lit it with a fire starter, and fed big dry logs that sat under the sagging porch to the newborn flame.

Vanessa sagged onto a log beside the warmth of the fire. Even the racket of Jackson shooing a couple of raccoons that had taken up residence in the cabin out the front door and right past her couldn't revive her energy. She was exhausted to her very bones. Every tendon and ligament screamed in protest if she moved even a little.

"Give me a minute?" Sean said from behind her.

She thought he was talking to her, but Steven nodded and disappeared into the cabin with the others.

An oversized first-aid kit dangled from Sean's hands as he took a large sitting stone beside her. He didn't ask permission, or if she even needed the attention — he just began picking and choosing supplies for her. Thank goodness, because she hadn't the brain energy to come up with a snarky rejection at the moment.

As he cleaned dried blood and scrapes on her face, he was so close that she could feel the warmth of his strong body seeping through her jacket. Or maybe it was just the heat from the crackling fire and an overactive imagination. One side of his face was in shadow, and the other was illuminated from the flickering glow of the flames. The light bounced off a scar down the side of his face.

Unthinking, she touched it with the tip of her finger, and he froze. "What happened there," she asked, too tired to care about which boundaries she crossed.

His shoulders sank in a sigh. "Supply run a couple years back. We'd gone to this construction site looking for building materials for the cabins in my colony when we were attacked. I was pressed against a wall under this Dead who was a foot taller than me, and to escape his teeth, I had to press my face into a nail sticking out. And when I kicked him off me to save myself, the nail caught me all the way down. No big exciting story—it was just something that happened. It'll happen to you too if you decide to continue a life as a guard. You won't live with an unblemished body anymore." He frowned against the light and gently wiped a stinging cut across the bridge of her nose.

Her pride said she didn't need anyone, least of all a man with fickle attentions, but she swallowed it down. Out there among the Deads, ego could get you killed. "My back could use first aid too. I'd do it myself, but I can't reach it very well, and I don't have a mirror to see what I'm doing."

Worry flitted across the tiny creases in the corners of his eyes for just an instant before it was replaced by a somber mask once again. He finished cleaning a cut at her temple and turned her hips until she faced the cabin. The breeze was chilly as the hem of her shirt was lifted to expose her skin.

"Shit," he murmured. "I didn't know I cut you. I tried not to."

She smiled at their shadows as they danced across the face of the ramshackle cottage. "I keep my knives extra sharp."

"Everything about you is as sharp as your blades, Vanessa," he said in a voice so quiet, she could've imagined it.

Arching against the burning pain as he pressed an alcohol swab over the slice her own knife had taken out of her back, she bit her lip against crying out.

"This is pretty deep. At the very least it needs butterfly bandages and to stay clean. It really needs stitches if you want me to."

With hands clasped against the fear at imagining a needle in her skin, she asked, "What would you do if you were me?"

"Stitches," he said without hesitation. "It'll heal faster and maybe it won't scar as badly. The way it looks wouldn't matter as much to me, but for you it'll be different."

"Why? Because I'm a girl?"

"Maybe. I saw what having scars from Dr. Mackey's tests did to Laney last year, and I don't want the same for you. I don't want you ever wondering if your man will see you differently with scars."

"There's a simple solution for that." She turned and leveled him with a rare seriousness. "I'll never make myself vulnerable enough where a man who didn't appreciate my scars would have the power to hurt me."

The corner of his lip turned up, and he lowered his gaze to the bandages in his hands. "Good girl."

"I still want stitches though. Not because of vanity, but because the faster I heal, the faster I'm at one hundred percent again. I'd like to survive this little road trip."

He led her into the cabin, and when he opened the door said, "Everyone but Finn out. Get started on something to eat while we stitch up Vanessa."

"Why do I have to get out?" Brandon said. "I have more medical experience than both of you combined."

Sean offered the little troll a patient glare. "Vanessa, do you want Brandon to stitch you up instead?"

"Hell no. Get out."

"Whatever," he muttered as he grabbed his pack. "It's your funeral."

"It's stitches, not an appendectomy, and Sean was the one trying *not* to get me eaten by a cannibal today. Plus, he'd feel guiltier if he killed me and plan a much prettier funeral. Also, nice face," she said, pointing her middle finger at his swollen jaw.

He bumped her shoulder on the way out, and Sean excused himself while Finn gathered the lanterns. Whispers of angry words filtered through the window, too low for her to understand, but from the tone in Sean's voice, she'd do best not to piss him off in the future.

The cabin was just as small as the outside suggested. It was made up of one room—a living area and kitchen combined. Couches embroidered with a moose and bear pattern dotted the space, and a leather recliner sat in the corner. Next to the small kitchen, a hand-carved oak dining table waited for dinner to be served, and a deer-antler chandelier hung from the ceiling like some giant spider. Stone edged a wood-burning fireplace where a blaze had been started already.

"Where are you hurt?"

"The answer to that would be everywhere, Finneas."

He gave her an exhausted look. "Stitches?"

She assumed the gauze she'd hastily secured over her knife injury wasn't going to win her any first-aider of the year awards. "On my back."

He lifted the tail of her shirt and undid her shoddy binding, then whistled. "Damn, you have a flap of skin just hanging there. Why didn't you tell us about this earlier?"

"Didn't seem that important at the time." Flashes of the last minutes of Jerry's life danced before her eyes, and she swallowed the bile that filled her throat. Her continued existence depended upon her ability to forget this entire awful day as soon as humanly possible.

"Lay up on the table and pull your shirt up."

He set a needle and sutures beside her, along with a bottle of alcohol and a roll of bandages. The door creaked open, and Sean shut it tenderly behind him like he hadn't just given Brandon the verbal lashing of the dork's life. Finn poured alcohol over Sean's hands once, and then again before he doused the slice in her back with it. She bucked at the unexpected pain and buried her head into her folded arms. Thank God they couldn't see her face. She could only take so much torture in one day, and she was teetering at capacity.

Her shirt crept up higher, and Sean's careful voice asked, "What's this?"

She hadn't actually seen it, but she could imagine what he was asking about. He traced the ache with a light fingertip. Over her ribcage, against the tender flesh of her back, were likely eight perfect finger-shaped bruises with the thumbs against her front.

"Jerry wasn't a gentle monster," she said, biting back the panic of memory.

"Did he—"

"No. It didn't get that far."

Sean, wise man that he was, dropped the subject right there like a flaming coal. And a good thing it was, because she'd rather lick the toilet seat in a men's bathroom than answer any more questions about her time with Jerry.

The stitching wasn't so bad if she concentrated on Sean and Finn's murmured conversation above her. Where they would try to find medical supplies tomorrow. Food rations for the entirety of the trip. How long they guessed the run would last before they'd used up all their stores around the Denver area. Sean's hands stayed steady and warm against her skin as he worked, like he'd stitched up a hundred teammates before her. Maybe he had. Or maybe he was just that confident with everything he did.

"All done," he said with a tiny pat to her unmarred flesh. "Now hop up so we can change the bandages on your arm, and we'll go grab something to eat."

Her stomach threw a little party at those glorious words and let out a rumble of anticipation. She hadn't eaten since that morning.

The stitches pulled tightly against her skin, and she sat up tenderly before removing the bandages from her arm. "If you people would just stop stabbing me, that would be fantastic."

Finn snorted and pressed against the side of the long cut like he was searching for infection. "Maybe if you weren't so mouthy."

"Maybe if you weren't so irritating."

"Maybe if you didn't bring that out in people."

"Okay," Sean said, halting the argument. "Enough. Vanessa, do you want something for the pain?"

"What kind of something?" she asked.

"All herbal. Dr. Mackey sent us with a tea that will dull the edges."

"Or," Finn said with a toothy grin, "we can give you some of the rotgut whiskey Ricky sent with us."

Her stomach churned. "I'll go with the tea. Any more rotgut this week, and I'll likely go blind."

Sean looked at her with frank curiosity, but she shrugged out from under his stare and headed for the door. "Thanks for the stitches—no thanks for causing them," she called over her shoulder.

Jackson had somehow found the time to track down four family-sized cans of beef stew in a hidden cupboard of a pharmacy break room on the way in, and only one of them was rancid. When she approached the fire with her metal plate and spoon, Jackson heaped an extra spoonful on hers and said she'd earned it. She waited a moment longer to see if he would say he was just joking, but when he just stared at her with that serious expression of his, she nodded her thanks. That might've been the nicest thing anyone had ever said to her. Or at least it was the most meaningful compliment. She was part of the team, and it was clear as day Jackson was just fine with it. Huh.

Sean didn't sit by her, or even near her. In fact, everyone seemed to be giving her space. Instead, he sat directly across the fire, which did nothing but illuminate his striking features in the firelight. With a conscious effort, she tried her best to keep her eyes on her plate or anywhere other than him, but time and time again, her gaze was drawn to him like she had no control over her own thoughts or actions anymore.

Maybe it would've been easier to ignore him if she didn't keep catching his eyes on her too. Even the conversation around them didn't seem to hold his attention.

Stupid traitorous heart. She could see what it was doing from a mile away. Latching onto yet another risky man. Well, not this time. She'd learned her lesson with Mitchell and she sure as sugar wasn't going to make such a colossal mistake again.

"I'm going to bed," she said a little too loudly, effectively breaking the spell of Sean's gaze.

She rinsed her dishes off and put them back into her pack before heading inside. No one followed, so she had plenty of time to gently wash her cut up face again and brush her teeth over the sink. With an explosive sigh, she sank into the recliner and curled in on herself. What a day. She could only wish tomorrow would be easier.

Scratch, scratch, scratch.

Vanessa opened her eyes and struggled to adjust to the faint moonlight that penetrated the window. All around her, the deep sleep noises of men filled the room, and she turned her head and searched for the noise that woke her up.

Scratch, scratch.

Heart pounding, she turned to sit up and almost ran head to chest into Sean Daniels. As she opened her mouth to squelch a startled sound, he placed his hand over her lips. Holy crow, he didn't sleep with a shirt on, and the smooth, taut musculature just under his skin's surface beckoned for her touch.

Shhh, he mouthed, before twitching his head toward the window.

A shadow stumbled across the moonlight, and the scratching started again. Okay, the Dead hunting them was creepy, but it was really hard to feel scared with Sean leaning over her like this. There was nowhere for her to go except further into the cushion of the chair as he leaned forward.

Panicked, she pushed her hand against the front seam of his pants.

"What're you doing?" he whispered.

"I'm cock-blocking you."

He banished a smile behind pursed lips, and as soft as a breath, said, "Cock-blocking isn't a literal term, and I'm not here to molest you. Though if you'd like to keep your hand right where it is, I wouldn't mind. It feels nice."

She jerked away and narrowed her eyes.

He leaned into her ear until his lips were so close they tickled the fine hairs on her lobe. "There's a Dead outside. Just one. A fence must be down, and she was attracted to all of the noise we made earlier."

"What do we do?"

"You go back to sleep. I'll take care of her."

Ha! Not likely.

He pushed off her and headed for the fireplace where he pulled out a poker from the hearth set. Without a spare glance for her, and with not a worry in the set of his chiseled jaw, he opened the front door and was back within five tension-filled minutes. Closing the door behind him, he replaced the poker and lay back down beside Finn like he'd simply taken a midnight bathroom break. She looked from the door, to him, and back to the door. Alrighty then. She needed to learn how to turn her fear off like Sean did, and she needed that little talent now.

The sight of Sean's shirtless chest and taut stomach played across her mind until her stomach clenched. She'd known he was fit from the way his simple, dark-colored shirts fit him, but damn, she hadn't expected him to look like that. Every abdominal muscle begged to be caressed by her fingertips, and the light trail of shadow that led from his belly button to the seam of his pants was just about the sexiest temptation she'd ever seen on a man. Even the muscles over his hips had been defined in the dim moonlight, and the triceps of his arms had tensed and flexed as he leaned over her.

She was many things in that moment, but most obviously, she was in trouble.

Chapter Ten

Sean wouldn't have bothered explaining the Dead to Vanessa the night before, but she was awake, and he didn't want her to panic and wake the others. And then she'd put her hand right on his crotch, and he'd just about lost it. The temptation to press himself against the soft palm of her outstretched hand was a slow, inescapable burn. How could a woman be so amusing, and surprising, and sexy in the same instant?

"You all right?" Finn asked, as he pushed the tree off the downed length of fence.

"Yeah, why?"

"You just got this weird look about you. And you haven't ordered anyone around the whole morning. We don't really know what to make of it."

"Just thinking is all, man."

"About her?"

"Who?"

Finn leaned on the shovel he had plucked from up against the fence. "You know who. Laney."

Sean frowned and shook his head. "I actually hadn't thought about her this entire trip until you brought her up. So thanks for that."

"Oh," Finn said. "My bad."

He dug at a new post hole as Sean dragged up the fencing materials they'd found in a shed behind the cabin. The storms must've knocked over the dead tree and the lightning burn down the middle of the trunk likely hadn't helped it stay upright. If they were going to continue to use the sanctuary, they had to make sure they weren't driving into a Dead prison every time they came through the front gates. Fence repairs were a straight line to peace of mind.

"Then are you thinking about Vanessa?" Finn asked, wiping the thin sheen of accumulated sweat from his brow.

"What does it matter what I'm thinking? It's not therapy hour, Finn. Just help me fix the damned fence."

"That's a yes."

"I don't need your advice on the matter. I know where this is going, and why do you care so much?"

Finn jabbed the shovel into the earth. "I just don't want you and Adrianna getting hurt is all."

"Wait, do you like Vanessa?" Sean asked, standing up from the fencing he was untying. "Is that why you get so pissed when I look at her?"

"No! She grates on my last nerve. I mean, don't get me wrong, she's level-eleven hot and she'd be a cat in the sack, but—"

"Enough. Don't talk about her like that. That's an order."

"I knew it. You're falling for Vanessa-the-man-eater-Summers."

Sean jabbed his finger at Finn. "Shut up."

Finn's dark eyebrows arched. "Or what?"

"Or heaven help me, I'm going to lay you out. She's been through hell and back, and your disrespect of her stops right here and now."

Finn leaned against the shovel again. "I have all the respect in the world for Vanessa. Have for a long time. I just wanted to see where you stood with her." He stabbed the soil again. "Now I know."

Sean's fist itched to hit him across his smirking face. Being baited about a woman was infuriating. He didn't know what he was doing and the timing couldn't be worse for him to start seeing Vanessa as anything but a teammate. His churning feelings for her put everyone at risk. It would be his responsibility to make the difficult calls in the days to come, and her presence was clouding that ability. He squatted down and looped his hands behind his head. "I don't know what I'm doing."

"Yes you do," Finn said quietly. "You aren't built to be alone forever. Eventually you were going to move on from Aria. Your heart just landed on Laney first, and now it's rebounded from that hurt and landed on Vanessa. You need a partner—your timing is just terrible."

He licked his lips and said, "I know."

"So turn it off. I've seen you do it a hundred times. Turn that emotion off until you get us back home, and then see where it goes. We all need you to be at your best, but if you're offering protection to one of us over the others, the entire system fails. Your feelings for her will cloud your judgment. It puts us all at risk. Just turn it off."

Finn made it sound like such a simple thing. Sure he'd turned off his fear. He had to be clear-headed to make those hard, in-the-moment decisions for his team. Fear was different from affection though. Turning off his feelings for her would strip his humanity, little by little. His heart would be trained to reject companionship, and after the last four years alone, he didn't want to go back to how he was before. He liked the man he was becoming. But, his team came first. They always had. It's why he had such a high success rate on supply runs. It's why he'd been a respected leader of one of the biggest colonies in the known world for three years before it fell to traitors. If he changed his approach now, people would die. Not just people—friends.

Finn was right. He had to turn it off.

Sean and Finn were gone when she woke up, and the rest of the team sat around white smoke and embers, devouring biscuits and gravy one of them had cooked up in an iron skillet over the fire pit. She took her turn at the food just as Sean came ambling through the woods. His thoughtful eyes were downcast, and when his gaze collided with hers, he looked away so fast it was as if her presence there had burned him.

"We need to be back on the road in ten minutes," he said. "Start loading up."

Sean drove, and she sat behind him, wondering what had changed in the night. He hadn't said a word to her. Not only that, but he was doing a bang-up job of not even gracing her with a glance. Like she didn't exist at all.

A-hole.

She could play that game too. She checked her weapons and put two extra blades in her belt for the day, and when she was thoroughly confident she was ready to take on whatever was coming their way, she leaned her head back and enjoyed the scenic beauty that unfolded just outside the window. No matter that Sean's presence seemed to take up every cubic inch of space in the Terminator, she was over it. So over it. If ever two words described Vanessa Summers, they were 'over' and 'it.' She caught his quick glance in the rearview mirror and crossed her arms over her tripping heartbeat.

Aw, crap.

"Candy bars," Vanessa said, checking her scope again.

"And?" Steven asked.

"And what?"

"You aren't playing the game right! You have to name what you miss and then what you would give up to have that thing again now."

"And I'd give up a fingernail."

"Eh, just rip it off?"

"Yeah, but it has to be the middle finger so I have an excuse to show people my injury and offend them all at once."

Jackson spit over the side of the roof as they moved across the flat gravel grocery store ceiling. "I pick poon."

"Oh, gross on the word choice," she complained as Steven groaned. "And you said *I* was playing the game wrong. Look, Jackson, even after the outbreak, you can still get sex, so you wouldn't really have to give up anything big for it."

"I'd give up my left foot."

"Jackson! Aww, forget it. There." She nodded with her chin at a trio of Deads around the back of the building.

Steven brought the radio to his lips and murmured, "Three Deads on the south side of the building. Nowhere close to an entrance though. They don't seem alerted."

"Copy," came Sean's quiet voice through the static.

"Toilet paper," Jackson said as Vanessa lowered herself to the roof's edge and watched the Deads through her scope.

"That's better. What would you give up?"

"The poison ivy blisters on my ass."

"Jackson! Seriously, you aren't allowed to play this game anymore," she muttered.

Steven's face looked like he'd just sucked a lemon. "Now I won't even be hungry for the crappy lunch I've been looking forward to."

"You and me both."

"What's Sean's beef with you?" he asked after a few moments of kicking pebbles with the toe of his boot.

It had been nearly a week, and Sean had barely said two words to her. He was doing a great job of talking at her, just not *to* her. With everyone else though, he was sweet as blackberry pie. "Heck if I know. I tried to figure out what his deal was the first couple of days, but maybe he just doesn't appreciate my sense of humor or something. What do you want to bet I can hit the one on the right from here?"

"No bet. Sean would explode if we started picking them off and making all that racket without an order."

Getting any kind of reaction from Sean tempted her to put her finger on the trigger, but she couldn't do it. If anything happened to the three men inside because of a stupid mistake on her part, she wouldn't be able to live with it. She pulled her eye back from the crosshairs.

"Your sense of humor is definitely an acquired taste," he said through a slight frown. "Still, it doesn't make sense that he ignores you so obviously. Not as a new recruit."

"At least he's not yelling at me."

Steven gave a wry smile. "Touché." He'd been in trouble the whole week.

She rested her cheek on her arm and glared at the stumbling Deads. "Of course, that may mean that Sean has faith that you are worth the effort of correcting. I get the feeling he's going to fail me and send me packing back to the gardens."

"What? That's stupid."

"He'd be an idiot not to pass you," Jackson agreed.

It was true that she'd contributed to the team. Sure they'd all saved her neck a few times too, but she'd repaid the favor and always jumped right into the workload. "Thanks for the vote of confidence, boys." The trio of Deads had joined up with another small herd and now numbered seven. "Trouble headed our way."

The monsters seemed to wander aimlessly, but they were definitely headed for the front door, which was pried open at the moment. Maybe some instinct pulled them toward their prey.

"Sean?" Steven said into the radio.

"Yeah?"

"You've got incoming. Seven Deads headed toward the front entrance. Can you go out the back?"

"Negative. The back part of the building is collapsed around the door. It's nothing but rubble. We need another ten minutes in here. The pharmacy in this place is big and everything was tossed on the floor."

"How do you want us to handle them?"

Sean's sigh morphed into a growl. "Can you three handle them quietly?"

Steven arched his eyebrow at her. If this was day one of the trip, she would've peed her pants. As it stood, she'd killed more Deads than she could count in hand-to-hand combat and had her rhythm down to a science. She nodded with a toothy grin.

"Yep," Steven said. "I'll radio you when it's done."

"Carpenter?" Sean said over the static.

"Yeah?"

Crackle, crackle, crackle. "Never mind."

Steven took his finger from the button and pointed at her. "That was for you."

She rolled her eyes and stood, wiping the gravel dust from her pants before moving toward the ladder across the roof. Let him try to guess Sean's problem. She was done with that mind game. It got her absolutely nowhere.

She climbed down first, followed by Jackson and Steven. When her hands were warm and comfortable around the hilts of her biggest knives, she loped toward the corner of the building. With one quick glance around the side to make sure the number hadn't grown, she gave a rushed huff of air and sprinted for the loosely strewn herd.

Steven and Jackson ran like the wind beside her, a comfort as it always was to have her team so close by. Whatever was about to happen, they were going to weather it together.

She engaged a scrawny Dead with a tattered button-up shirt and dress pants. Poor sod had probably been getting off work as a banker when he was eaten. So focused were his filmy eyes on her, they followed as she dipped down at the last moment and pummeled him with her shoulder. He flipped over her and hit the ground with a sickening thud, and she brought the blade down on his face. The guttural moan of another was so close, she barely had time to stand with an upward arch of the knife before it was on her. Long, dark hair covered the Dead's face, which made it creepier not to see her features when Vanessa hit her mark with the wet blade.

She kicked the she-monster viciously in the chest, and the Dead crumpled just in time for a pair of cold, clammy hands to clamp around Vanessa's arms. With only an instant to spare, she yanked forward and hurled her opponent over her. The Dead's grip didn't waver, and the bones in his arms made a sickening crack as he flew forward. Two weeks ago, that noise would've brought her food back up. Now, there was a sense of satisfaction that she'd bested a creature evolved to kill her. He had only enough time to stretch his neck toward her before she brought her knife down.

A few seconds and the skirmish was over. Jackson wiped his machete blade on a tuft of grass growing wild out of a huge crack in the parking lot concrete, and Steven was already belting his crowbar.

The smile spreading across his face froze, then fell at something he was looking at behind her. The hair on the back of her neck lifted in the chilly breeze, and she gasped as she turned. "Run," she breathed. "Run!"

There had to be at least twenty of them. She didn't have a guess where they'd been hiding, but there they were, charging the three of them like an angry herd of rhinos.

"Sean, we have to go," Steven huffed into the radio.

"We need another few minutes, can you buy time for us?"

Jackson looked at her in that serious way of his and jabbed a finger at her. "You go in and help them. Steven and I will take the Terminator for a spin and try to lose them. Five minutes is all we can give you."

She nodded and pulled ahead. Blasting through the front doors, she could only hope the Deads followed the others. Not too close, but close enough where the boys could lose them in the Terminator. Where was the pharmacy? Maybe at one time, helpful signs had pointed busy shoppers where to go, but now the store looked like a tornado had hit it. Maybe one had.

Clumsy footsteps squeaked against the tile floors behind her. She couldn't tell how many Deads hadn't been fooled by their bait and switch, but by the sounds of it, probably more than she could handle alone. Dodging upended cans that littered the floor and broom handles that booby trapped the aisles, she bounced toward the back of the store. The sound of her frantic breathing filled her head until it was hard to hear anything else.

She dared a glance over her shoulder to find the Deads weren't being so careful about the debris, and it was to their advantage. One fell, and others used the struggling creature for traction. Shuffling her feet, she skidded to the end of an aisle and lost her balance. With a half shriek, down she went, crashing into a shelf of scattered laundry detergent. Hefting a gallon of winter's eve scented soap, she whacked the closest Dead in the face and scrambled to get up as he fell beside her. When he latched onto her leg with a clawed hand, she brought the detergent down onto his face with as much force as she could muster from her disadvantaged position. Kicking her leg out, she broke the knee cap of the next Dead with a clean snap and pulled her knife upward as it fell onto her. She pushed the body off her just in time for three more Deads to lunge at her.

Hang the no guns rule.

In a smooth motion, she pulled her Glock and pulled the trigger. The intended target fell, and she rolled out of the way as the other two lurched forward over the stiffened bodies of their fallen comrades. She brought the butt of the pistol down on the Dead's face and kicked at the other to give herself time. The Dead sunk her teeth into Vanessa's tough, leather boot, and she screamed as she pulled the trigger. The moaner released the deadly grip of her jaw on Vanessa's shoe and slumped to the side.

An endless trail of Deads streamed down the aisle, and she bolted before she was even upright again. "Sean!"

She was going to die, and she was going to do it alone. Her team wasn't there to back her or protect her weakest side. Slipping again, she twisted to land on her back. No way was she going down crawling away. Can in hand, she chunked it at the closest Dead and rolled to pull a shelf over on top of the other two nearest the fray.

This was it.

Her last stand.

She had been counting, and only two bullets remained in her magazine. One left in the chamber.

She squeezed them off. One. Two. Three. She stood and dropped the Glock before pulling two knives. Hunched inward, ready and enraged by circumstance, she screamed, "Come on!"

And then the aisle lit up like a meteor shower. Deads fell like a domino effect until none remained standing.

She stood there, stunned and ready for a death that wasn't coming, and Sean hooked a hand behind her head and pulled her into his chest.

"I called for you," she said in a voice that sounded very far away.

"I heard you." His voice dripped with emotion as he held her to him like she was part of his skin. She couldn't breathe but couldn't find it in her to care. She'd rather die suffocated by the strength of Sean's arms than the fate that had released its grip on her just moments ago.

"Brandon, shoulder the bag. Finn, you take point. Where are the others?" he asked against her ear.

"Five minutes. They gave us five minutes while they try to lose the bulk of the horde. They're in the Terminator."

"Let's go," he barked and pulled her behind him.

His hands fit perfectly over hers, tanned against her fair skin, like soft leather covering porcelain. She must be in shock. That was the only explanation for the strange crawling sensation from the palm of Sean's hand to hers and up her arm. Like their skin was melding together, and they'd have to stay connected forever or sever their limbs.

It was then she realized how his cold shoulder burned like a wedge of dry ice embedded in her soul.

She dipped to retrieve her gun in a smooth action that didn't dislodge her from his grip. She'd rather face another horde than let go of the comfort that swam in the molecules between their skin.

Chapter Eleven

As long as he lived, Sean wouldn't forget how frightened Vanessa sounded when she'd called his name. To hell with the rest of the medical supplies. He'd burn the entire mission to the ground if it kept her from the gnashing teeth of a Dead.

She fought like some wild thing, cornered and desperate for survival. The Deads closest to her hadn't stood a chance against her fierce, weapon-filled hands. She'd dropped her empty Glock and pulled her blades in one smooth motion. She was fearless.

Chills had rippled up the back of his neck as he raised his rifle to protect her. Enraged, he didn't miss a one. He couldn't. She was ready to die, but he wasn't equipped for the loss.

He'd go back to distancing himself once they got in the truck, but for now, he couldn't pull away from the temptation to touch her. To physically reassure himself she was still breathing—still with him. He clutched her hand like it was a lifeline and he'd been drowning.

He spun just as autumn sunlight warmed his face out front of the store. "You called for me."

Emotion churned in her eyes. "Because I knew you'd come. And if you didn't—" Her delicate neck worked as she swallowed. "If you couldn't, it still felt nice to say your name at the end."

His breath shook as he studied her face. Her perfectly arched eyebrows drew up like she wondered what he was thinking. Her full lips pursed in question, and he fought not to reach out and brush his fingertip across the smooth skin of her cheek.

"That's what I was afraid of," he said, swallowing the urge to take those necessarily horrid words back. He dropped her hand and turned away before he could see the hurt on her face. He wouldn't have the strength not to kiss her if he did.

"We've got company," Finn said.

Sean kneeled beside his second-in-command and steadied the scope of his rifle on the dozen Deads running their way. "Snipe 'em."

By the time the fourth Dead fell, the throaty rumble of the Terminator rattled the asphalt beneath their feet.

"The cavalry is here," Finn said with a grin in his voice.

Sean shouldered his rifle just as the Terminator barreled around the corner and slammed into another cluster of Deads with the metal grille made to maul. Bodies flew through the air, and he yanked open the passenger door. The team was loaded before the second wave even made it to the front of the truck.

Sean pushed Vanessa into the back of the Terminator with Brandon and Finn and slammed the door as he sank into the passenger seat. Deads fisted rotted extremities against the metal sides of the truck like war drums, but she couldn't take her eyes from Sean's turned face. As they pulled away from the horde, he leaned his head against the window and rubbed the stubble on his face like he was irritated. He looked good with scruff, real good, but it hid the scar down the side of his face and that seemed a little tragic. She knew the secret story that went along with the beautiful imperfection, and now the evidence of that was hidden, much like he was doing with his gaze at the moment. What had she done wrong?

"You smell like blood," Brandon said with his nose scrunched up like she was an unsavory offense to his delicate senses.

Finn leaned over Brandon and pulled her forward by the arm until her back was exposed, and then he yanked the hem of her sticky shirt out of the way.

She knew it was bad. Fresh stitches hadn't stood a chance against the strain of fighting for her life, and the warmth of the burn had her gritting her teeth. Really, did guards just have to get used to pain? It had been an annoying constant over the past week. It was becoming quite clear the only dependable occurrence in life after the outbreak was discomfort. And sitting here in a truck full of foul-mouthed men, with Brandon glaring at her like she was a mosquito, with Finn's gargantuan hand wrapped unapologetically around her arm, with Jackson and Steven singing "Dirty Deeds Done Dirt Cheap" at the top of their lungs, and Sean ignoring her once again, it all became a little too irritating to stand.

She opened her mouth to say so, but Finn beat her to it.

"I think we need to be done for the day."

Clacking her mouth shut, she turned a suspicious glare at him. What was his game? Finn-never-cuts-out-early wasn't exactly one for taking an evening off for some rest and relaxation.

"Carpenter!" Finn snapped. "I swear if you don't stop singing the guitar parts to that song, I'm going to put you in a sleeper hold. Hand back the first-aid kit."

Sean jerked his head, and his impossibly blue gaze crashed into hers like a cannon ball. Ignore her all he wanted, and hang his reasons, but worry shaped his downturned eyebrows.

"I'm not bit," she murmured. "The stitches just didn't hold."

He slumped and turned back around. "Jackson, get us somewhere in the woods away from the population. We need running water."

"You got it, boss man," Jackson said with a tug of the wheel. He steered them from what used to be a main road toward the outskirts of town.

Finn rifled through the first-aid kit and shoved Brandon down the bench seat before jamming a wad of gauze to her back. He clucked behind his teeth. "You've made an awful mess of our handy work. Look at this." A little pluck pricked against her back, and he held a tiny loop of suture in front of her. "Remember how we said to be gentle on them?"

She didn't even have the energy for a snarky retort. Instead, she leaned against the window and closed her eyes against the ache. Everything was so confusing. These life or death situations happened at such a high frequency, she was a little desperate to even out for a day.

Just one day where someone wasn't almost killed, or where needles and thread weren't needed to put the team back together like a pack of Frankenstein monsters. One day where all of the medical buildings they hit went to plan. Where Sean picked a temperature — hot or cold.

On they drove until the early evening light turned to dusk and the dirt road Jackson found was lost to piled leaves from the coming fall. The drive seemed to have subdued the others, who didn't talk as they exited the Terminator and did a perimeter search of the area.

"Is there any point in re-stitching you?" Finn asked, shoving the sliding door in the back of the eighteen-wheeler up to reveal a level, if not sanitary, surface for her to lie down on.

"Probably not," she muttered, plopping onto her belly and dangling her arm off the side.

Boxes had slowly but steadily filled up the back of the truck, which now neared capacity. They'd be going home soon, and the relief of the approaching end was a satisfying warmth that spread through her. She just had to live a couple more days.

"There," Finn murmured after a few minutes. "I did you up tight with butterfly bandages, but you still have to be careful with them."

With a lazy salute from the comfort of the dirty bed of the truck, she said, "Will do, Finneas," as he walked away with a shake of his head.

The needles on the evergreens made a pleasant swooshing sound as the wind caressed them. Evening light penetrated the foliage and cast mottled shadows across the forest floor, and she lifted her fingers to touch the breeze. Without the bother of switching positions or hunting up a more comfortable headrest, she fell asleep with her boots crossed at the ankle and her shirt pulled up to invite the touch of that cool wind against the heat of the injury.

A moment later she woke up, or at least that's what it felt like, but the sun had had time to sink, and a mystery hero had covered her body with a thick blanket. She didn't want to get her hopes too high, but it smelled like Sean had when he'd held her earlier today.

She closed her eyes and inhaled noisily, trying to place the smell for certain.

"Are you okay?"

"Aaahhhh!" She lurched forward and flipped off the back of the truck where her arm had retained its dangling position through the duration of her nap. With a thud, she landed in a pile of pine needles, which offered no cushion whatsoever, and she groaned as she tilted her head to find Sean himself, standing over her with a twitch to the corner of his lips like he was trying to hide a smile. He really was lovely to look at from that position, and as soon as she caught the wind that had been knocked out of her, she would ogle him more thoroughly.

"Were you just sniffing my blanket?"

Okay, maybe she could pretend she couldn't get her breath back for the rest of her life. She eyed the underbelly of the truck and debated log-rolling under there and not coming back out for the rest of the night.

Sean was already bent down, offering her a hand up though, and she didn't want to be rude. Besides, she was a fighter, not a runner. She would've told him so, but he hefted her up like a bouquet of dandelions, and she nearly toppled into him. Steadying her elbows, he frowned and took a step back like she had some disease that was catching.

"What gives?" she asked, narrowing her eyes.

"I don't know what you're talking about."

"You seem to like me one minute, but then I gross you out the next. Why can't you just treat me like the others do? At least until we get back to Dead Run River, and then we can go back to never speaking again."

Cocking his head slightly, he opened his mouth but was interrupted.

"Dinner's on!" Finn called from the stone-encircled fireside.

Sean slid an angry glance toward his second-in-command and then gave her a smile that didn't reach his eyes. "Dinner's on."

Dinner, as it turned out, was a new dish that, according to Jackson, Finn had mastered a few supply runs ago. Grease hissed and sizzled into the fire from a spit impaling five small, skinned animals.

"Please don't tell me you killed someone's pet Fifi," she said through a careful mask of ambivalence. If they admitted to cooking up cats, she was going to be sick.

"We're having squirrel," Steven said. "And if this is the part where you admit to us you're a vegetarian, know in advance, we're not hunting down a salad for you."

Squirrel? Okay, definitely a little less nasty than barbecued kitty.

"How are we supposed to eat them?" Brandon asked. He sat on his backpack beside the fire, and his shoulders slumped as he stared suspiciously at their meal.

When the only answer the boys offered was a noncommittal and very caveman-like grunt from Jackson, she helped him out. "I'm going to go out on a limb and say you eat them with your fingers."

Steven pointed to her and said, "Ding, ding, ding, we have a winner." He held up a stick like a microphone and said, "Jackson, why don't you tell her what she's won?"

Jackson answered by pulling one of the tiny animals from the spit and handing it to her like a hot potato. The grease was fire against the palms of her hands, and as quickly as she could manage, she gingerly set the tiny meal on a log someone had dragged up beside the campfire.

"I'm going to do a perimeter check," Sean said and left the light of the flames.

Finn watched him go with a thoughtful look, and then his dark gaze slid to her. "You need to let him be."

She checked behind her, but the only one sitting in the immediate vicinity was her. "Me? What did I do? The man doesn't even talk to me, so if you're looking for someone to blame for his gnarly mood, you can point your judgy Sasquatch finger elsewhere."

She balanced the squirrel on her fingertips and blew the steam from the meat. Finn could glare at her all he wanted. It wouldn't change the fact that Sean's attitude was his problem, not hers.

Squirrel was her new favorite meal. It tasted good enough. Finn had known just when to take them off the fire to keep them from drying out, and the simple salt and pepper seasoning worked just fine for a camp dinner. The best part of the whole fifteen minutes it took to pick her meal clean, however, was watching Brandon try to eat it. Hopeless and entertaining all at once.

"I miss video games," Steven said. "The first-person zombie-shooting games? I miss those."

"Why? Because you get unlimited life as long as you have a bucket of quarters and no one behind you in line?" she asked.

"Well, yeah. But all the chicks in that game dressed sexy and were a lot less mouthy than you." His baiting grin was obnoxious.

"Oh, you want me to dress sexy while I'm running from Deads and trying to save your sorry life? I'll be sure to pack my stilettos next time I need a go-bag, you jack-wagon."

He shrugged like her offer was acceptable. "That's all I ask. And maybe a little makeup wouldn't hurt. A little lip gloss so we have something pretty to look at, you know."

She chunked a miniature, cleaned leg bone across the fire, and it bounced off his forehead. "Parasite," she muttered as he and the boys chuckled like they were the funniest things to ever grace the planet.

"Where are we supposed to sleep tonight?" Brandon asked over the noise. "There isn't enough room in the back of the truck anymore, and we can't just sleep out here in the open."

"Yes we can. We'll take turns on watch," Jackson said. "Not much choice for it at the end of supply runs unless you want to all sleep together in the cab of the Terminator."

"I'm not doing that," Brandon said, plucking a tiny piece of meat from his mostly intact dinner. "You idiots can go to sleep out here like an all-you-can-eat buffet for the night walkers, but I'll take the left-over space in the back of the truck. I like my liver intact, thank you."

"Great," she said. "I'm tired of listening to you talk in your sleep anyway. It's weird."

His lip curled up in offense. "I do not talk in my sleep."

"No? 'Oh, Mercedes. Come closer, Mercedes.'"

His face blanched with heat as it crept up his neckline and landed in his cheeks. "Shut up," he muttered. "I was talking about the car."

"Mmhmm." She threw the bones into the fire and wiped her hands on a tuft of grass beside her.

"I'm not the only one making noises in their sleep, Vanessa." He spat her name like a curse. "You're over there moaning and groaning all night too."

His words sounded venomous, but they had little actual sting. She shrugged. "Yep. Nightmares are a bitch, and I've been stabbed a couple times this week. It hurts to move."

"I can make you some of the tea Doc sent with us if you want," Finn offered. "It'll take the edge off."

"Thanks, but no. I may be sleeping up in a tree tonight, and I need my head on straight so I can strap myself in without hitting every branch on the way down."

He pulled his canteen from his pack and washed down the last of his meal. "Carpenter, you take first watch. Rookies have to pay their dues."

"What?" Steven groused. "I'm not the only rookie here. Don't tell me you're favoring her because she's a girl. She's the one always saying she wants to be treated like the rest of us."

Finn waited with a dark, arched eyebrow raised. "You done?"

"Yes. No. She already got a nap. Now I'm done."

"Carpenter," Finn said with an unhurried drawl, "count your injuries."

Steven cleared his throat quietly, pointed to a tiny cut barely even visible in the firelight on his finger, and said, "One."

Vanessa leaned forward and squinted. "Do paper cuts count?"

"No," Finn said. "Vanessa needs rest, and we take care of our own. If it was the other way around and it was you who was injured, Vanessa would take first watch." His gaze traveled over the campfire to her. "But if I had to guess, she wouldn't be complaining like you're doing. She'd just offer."

Hmm. Maybe Finn was starting to understand her after all.

"Now, Vanessa, I want you to take all of our dishes and go find some running water to wash them in."

Or maybe not.

The corners of his lips turned up, and his eyes danced with reflected flames. "That was a joke. You should've seen your face though. I think you have steam coming out of your ears."

Irritation blasted heat into her cheeks, an odd sensation with the bitter chill that was seeping into the breeze.

"Vanessa," Sean said in a quiet voice from just outside the firelight. "Come here. I have something to show you."

Jackson whistled, but Finn jabbed him in the ribcage with an audible thump.

"Um, sure." Slinging her rifle and backpack across her shoulder, she shuffled into the woods behind Sean with her flashlight beam dancing across the ground. Why did she get the feeling he was leading her far away to yell at her? She sifted through a mental catalog of inappropriate things she'd done and said throughout the day, but the others had done and said worse. Okay, maybe not worse, but at least in the same boat, surely.

"Look, if this is about the small penis jokes with Jackson, I'll dial it back to thirteen or fewer jabs a day."

Silence.

"Twelve and that's my final offer. I mean, he named it Thor, so it's almost a call of duty to make fun of him, and besides, he knows I'm just joking about—"

"Vanessa. I'm not reprimanding you. Do you ever just listen? I mean, table the snark and open your ears. What do you hear?"

She frowned at the back of his head and dragged her flashlight across the area. Leaves fell from a black walnut tree to their left in a constant stream under the wind's urging. Little creaks and groans sounded from the trees as their branches were brushed with the invisible force of Mother Nature's breath, and some distance away, a bird called and another answered. No groaning, no gnashing of teeth. Just peace. And then a sound so subtle touched her ears, and she turned her head to the side so she could better hear. The soft babble of a stream talked happily in the night as it rippled over rock and felled tree.

"I hear water."

He waited for her to catch up and tipped his head. "I thought you could bathe tonight, after the boys are asleep, if you wanted. You'll have to remember your way to and from it though. Do you think you can?"

The prospect of a bath was at once exhilarating and terrifying. It was colder than a polar bear's nipple, and that water would likely be the consistency of a slushy, but oh to be clean again. It was tempting to wait the extra two days until they got back to Dead Run River where she could finally take a hot shower, but not tempting enough. She wanted to feel untarnished and human again. She liked to think she'd out-matured the consuming-vanity phase of her life, but very little compared to feeling clean.

The stream pushed its way around boulder and tree to wind through the woods like some giant serpent.

Sean sank onto a giant rock and rubbed a seemingly irritated hand over the stubble on his face. He'd been doing that more and more lately.

"Are you okay?" she asked.

"I'm just ready to get home." He graced her with a self-deprecating look. "I miss my kid."

She searched the woods. Sean had never been so candid when he spoke to her, and her curiosity to know more battled with the urge to heft her rifle over her head and high-knee it out of here. Squeezing her eyes closed and releasing a long sigh, she sat down beside him against her better judgment. His closeness was just as dangerous as a Dead's. Both had the power to inflict irreparable damage. "Is this the longest you've been away from her?"

"I used to head up most of the supply runs for my colony, and I was used to being away from Adrianna. It was like traveling for work or being deployed. It hurts less if you're used to it, you know? She's older now though, and she started asking me not to go, so I stopped for a while. I'm all she has."

"I thought you were the colony leader of Denver. Why were you running supplies?"

"My life isn't any more valuable than anyone else's. The other men on my missions had families and loved ones back home too. If I went with them, I could give them a better chance of making it back to them in one piece."

"Yeah, but anything could happen out here. I heard about you. Your life was more valuable because you were the youngest colony leader, and you had the best survival rate."

He rubbed his chin on his shoulder as he searched her face. "And now I have one of the lowest. My entire colony was compromised. The tragedy of all those people—those women and children, and good men who'd survived the outbreak—that's on me. It always falls on the leader's shoulders. I should have seen the betrayal of my second long before he had time to plan what he did. He'd been unreliable from the beginning, but I just wanted to trust him so badly. No one else but him was up for the job of taking care of the colony when I was on runs."

"I knew people at your colony." The admission made her throat tighten up as she remembered the faces of her friends. "I asked Laney to give you a list of people I knew, and you told her you hadn't seen any of them in the room of survivors."

"That was you?"

She nodded.

"I remember some of those names on the list. They were good people. I'm sorry."

"Stop apologizing for things that are out of your control, Sean. You couldn't help them, and shouldering all of those ghosts is a poison."

"I want to know what happened with Jerry."

Shocked at the shift, she automatically shook her head in ready denial. No way was she in the mood to rehash something she'd been trying to put out of her head for the last few days. "I don't want to."

"And I don't want to hear it, but if you keep that stuff inside, it'll eat at you. Trust me."

"Polite decline," she said, reaching for her backpack.

His hand was warm and firm on her forearm. "Please. I need to know."

"You just said you didn't want to hear it."

"Needing and wanting are two different things."

Anger washed over her like a fiery wind. Talking didn't make anything better, didn't he know that? If she let all the demons loose, they'd never stop coming. So many would be released, she'd never get the door to hell closed again. What right did he have to ask for such a personal piece of her? He might as well hold her soul in his careless hands, and she'd be damned if she was giving anyone the ability to really touch her.

"Please." His voice was deep, soothing, pleading, and it pacified the fury just enough.

"Fine," she gritted out. Maybe if she just said the facts, as unemotionally as possible, he'd be satisfied without her really letting the taint of that day sink into the remaining goodness in her. There had to be some somewhere. "Jerry dressed me up like a doll. He had this old dress he'd found somewhere, and he asked me to fix my hair. He wanted to have a nice dinner to celebrate, so while he made food, I searched for an escape. My options were back the way we came, with all those Deads, or through the door Jerry used. But he was there when I opened it, and I lied and told him I was coming to help him with dinner."

Her lip trembled, and she bit it as punishment. "I gagged when I saw the plates with chunks of raw meat, and he was angry I couldn't eat it. Over and over, he'd say, 'I won't hurt you. I won't hurt you. I don't need to eat you. I don't need to eat you.' But his eyes would go vacant, and he'd watch me like a bucket of caviar sitting on the buffet table. He started repeating everything he said, like he was trying to convince the monster half of him that I'd be more valuable alive. And I was shaking so bad—shit." She leveled him with her gaze, begging. "I can't do this."

Sean slid his hand over her knee, and he squeezed it. "You have to finish it."

Her voice hitched, and she took a long, sobering breath. "He said he'd just bite me a little, and then I could come back, and he'd save me like he did himself. He'd give me all the medicines, and then I'd be able to eat what he made for me. Like that would justify it. He paced for an hour, maybe two. I don't know. Just talking to himself and picking at the skin on his face. Jerry was insane. The stuff he said? The things that came from his mouth? They were horrifying. There was very little man left in him. Still. He's the first man I've ever killed."

"He doesn't count as a man, Vanessa. Whatever he did to himself didn't keep him human."

A warm tear slid down her cheek, and she gave her gaze to the river so he wouldn't see. "He was human enough. Between rants, he would apologize and talk about a girl he used to love. When the hospital fell, he'd been trapped inside but carved out this little life for himself. He experimented on the Deads and after he was bitten, on himself, and he worked for years on a cure so he could save the world." She let Sean see the agony that consumed her. "He couldn't even save himself from a hundred pound woman with a hidden knife."

Sean couldn't hold her gaze and let his drop to the leaves beneath their feet.

"Afterward, I got lost in the hospital. I couldn't think straight. My mind just kept playing the last moments over and over like it was my punishment for what I'd done. The sound of the end of his life was—" She swallowed hard. "The sound of the end is something that'll stay with me. He screamed and then begged me for help. And it felt wrong to let him die alone, so I sat there beside him while he babbled about how maybe it was better this way. The monster wasn't there at the end. Just the man."

His whisper was ragged. "Vanessa—"

"Don't. Don't let me off. I had no choice, but still, I ended a life. You shoulder the lost lives of your colony. This one is mine to bear."

Sean's gaze dropped to her lips in the half moonlight in the quiet of the woods. When he lifted them to her eyes once again, they were tortured. "I shouldn't have left you there. We walked out the front door knowing you were in danger, knowing you would have to make that decision. And when time went on and on, and you weren't back, I wanted to burn down the damned city to get back in there to you." He rocked back in a tiny escape attempt that didn't pan out.

With a tortured sound, his lips crashed onto hers. His kiss had the violence of a tornado behind it. Like he couldn't stop himself if he tried. So unexpected was the warmth of his lips, she froze for an instant before she closed her eyes and let the tide of relief wash over her. For this moment she didn't have to think about Jerry or Keeter or all of the near-death experiences of the last week. She could just let go.

He kissed her harder, urging her mouth open until she gave in and his tongue grazed hers. A jolt of adrenaline and lust and something deep and warm inside pushed her closer. With her hands around the back of his neck, he pulled her hips into the safety centered between his knees. So powerless was she under his capable command, she didn't protest when he lifted the hem of her shirt with a frustrated growl, or even when he brushed her bare ribcage with his thumb. She would melt into him at any moment and cease to exist, and for the life of her, she couldn't find a single thing wrong with it. It was so natural to disappear after everything. So potently good to be under his attentive hands after feeling the sting of Mitchell's rejection for so long. "Sean," she pleaded against his lips.

His response was immediate. His hands dropped to her hips, and he lifted her onto his lap with a strength that rivaled iron. Under his uncompromising grip, she slid against him like she was made to be there, cradled in his embrace. How had she lived so long without this? His warmth seemed as important as breathing, and she gasped as he dropped his kisses to the base of her neck. Arms snaking around her, he pulled her tightly against him until she could feel his hardened response to her between them. His arms were smooth, taut, and strong under her hands, and she eased back long enough to pull the shirt over his head.

Moonlight reflected from the blue fire in his eyes—reflected from a revering hunger like no man had given her before. Gray light touched the flexed planes of his chest and disappeared into hollows between each muscle, and she traced the map of his body with the tip of her fingernail until he closed his eyes and shivered under her touch. When he opened his eyes again, she could see it. He'd let go. The reserved, controlled Sean wasn't here anymore. All that remained was this alluringly built man who saw nothing but her, wanted nothing but her. She pressed against the urgency of his need, and he leaned forward and grazed his teeth against the tender skin of her throat.

She'd give him anything in that moment.

If he asked, she'd give him everything.

"Laney," he whispered against her neck.

Chapter Twelve

Vanessa consumed him like fire. Sean was lost in her scent, the feel of her silken skin against his fingertips, her hair entwined around his fingers, the sound of her pleading sighs when his lips touched her flesh. He'd kept his physical attraction to her in check, but her inviting him in, allowing him to see her cry, and her sharing the dark secrets of the day with Jerry had done him in. He was helpless against his need now. He was burning.

"What did you just say?" she rasped.

The question was strange and unexpected here in the dark of the woods. He hadn't said anything.

Lips against her throat, he murmured, "Nothing." Wrapping his arms more tightly around her, he pulled her closer to his hips. God she felt good against him.

She eased her head back and glared at him. "You just called me Laney."

Jerking back, he searched her face for humor. Surely he hadn't. He'd been here, with Vanessa. Laney hadn't been on his mind but a handful of times since they'd left Dead Run River last week. "No, I didn't." Why did her accusation seem to niggle at him in such an uncomfortable way though? Had he?

"Yeah, you did. Why would I make that up?"

What could he say? The more he thought about it, the more him saying Laney's name felt familiar. Oh God.

Vanessa pulled back and slid from his lap. The chill from the absence of her body against his was a physical ache. "If I did, I'm sorry. I didn't mean to."

She sat on the rock beside him with wide, vulnerable eyes. "Are you still in love with Laney?"

Reaching for her and holding her hand, he shook his head, but when he opened his mouth to explain how wrong she was, nothing came out. Was he still in love with her? Had he ever loved her, or had she just been something he couldn't have and that much more alluring for it? Had she just been a way to fill the void after Aria, or was it something more? "I don't think so."

If he hadn't seen how tough Vanessa was firsthand, he would've sworn her eyes were rimming with moisture. Maybe it was just a trick of the creek water, but she pulled her gaze away before he could be certain. "I don't know what this is, or even how I feel about you," she said softly. "But I made a big mistake with a man last year, and I don't want to do it again."

He was too risky for her. The somber tone of her voice all but sang it. How could he have been so lost in the moment to utter Laney's name to Vanessa? She'd allowed him to see her vulnerability, and he'd repaid her by hurting her. The scruff of his week-old beard rasped against the palm of his hands as he rubbed his face and wished for talent with words — for a way to soothe what he'd done. He'd pulled this crap with Laney too. It was like Aria had ruined him. He'd let the dead parts of her infest how he treated people he cared about, and he was so damned tired of failing. Of hurting people who deserved so much more from him. He didn't deserve Vanessa. He didn't deserve anyone's affection. "Do you still love Mitchell?"

"Not enough to say his name when I'm here with you." She stared at the river for a long time before she spoke again. "Mitchell was never mine. Even if Laney didn't exist, we didn't fit somehow. It was jerky when I was with him. Like him, hate him, like him again. I wasn't his type, and maybe he wasn't mine. It had just been such a long time since I'd connected with anyone, it was nice to feel wanted again, you know?"

"Yeah." She couldn't even guess how much he understood that relief.

"It's okay. At least we can see this won't work early on so we can just avoid each other."

Jerking his head toward her, he demanded, "What? Vanessa, I like you. I messed up. I messed up bad, but I don't think it means we're doomed before we start."

"Then why did you call me Laney? Me—the actual flesh and blood woman you were kissing and touching?"

"I don't know. I was just in the moment, and you do something to me—I can't think when I'm around you sometimes, and I made a mistake in the heat of that moment." Desperate to redeem himself so she'd understand how completely into her he was, he tried to explain. "The only time I think about Laney is when you do something funny or strong that reminds me of her. You're a lot alike and—"

"I remind you of Laney?" Her delicate eyebrows flew nearly to her hairline. "Is that what you're telling me?"

"Maybe that came out wrong."

"I remind you of the woman who ruined the last year of my life. Of the woman who got the man I cared for?"

"What? Laney didn't mean to ruin anyone's life. She's not like that."

"I know, Sean! And I even kind of like the skank now, but it doesn't change the fact that she got something I wanted. I've been so lonely! I've had to raise Nelson on my own, with no help, knowing that I was a poor substitute for our parents. We spent the first year just the two of us running, and it was up to me to get my little brother somewhere safe. And the second I decided there was a man I could share my concerns, my burdens, my life with, he couldn't love me back. And now I'm kissing a man who is hung up on the same girl who got him? Hell no to all of this." She stood and snatched her backpack. Whirling, she spat, "I'm nobody's replacement Laney."

"Vanessa, wait! I didn't mean it the way it came out." He ran after her and grabbed her elbow in desperation. She had to listen until he fixed this. Until he let her know he couldn't stop thinking about her, watching her, dreaming about her. Vanessa filled his head every moment of his life, and now she was getting this wrong because he couldn't find the right words.

She flung his arm off and spun around with fire in her eyes. "Don't talk to me anymore, Sean. Don't tell me stories to get me addicted to you. Don't make me care for your daughter. Don't involve me in this effed up love triangle you've created. I'm not battling Laney

Landry in a round two. History proves she wins, Sean. Unless it's an order for this mission, don't talk to me anymore."

Nope, he hadn't imagined the building tears, because right at that moment, when she revealed how much his mistake had really hurt her, two matching drops of crystal pain rolled down her flushed cheeks and made tiny pings against the dry pine needles below them. Clenching his hands in an effort to relieve the hurt those tears churned inside of him, he whispered, "I'm sorry," as she retreated into the woods and away from him.

He hadn't been with anyone since Aria, hadn't been affected so wholly since Aria, and what did he do? Pushed Vanessa away before he even had a chance to make her happy. Damn it! Squatting down, he watched her steady retreat into the dark woods. Maybe this was it for him. Maybe this was some bigger force telling him he wasn't the type of careful man who could nurture a woman the way she needed. Perhaps being a soldier and a father were the only two successes he could expect in life, no matter how long or short it was.

He'd have to learn to be okay with solitude. To wear the loneliness that followed him like a badge of honor because it was his lot in life. The faster he accepted that, the happier he'd be.

Vanessa took a detour in the woods and came around on the other side of the truck. Even if she'd thoroughly dried all of her tears, her cheeks would be flushed and her eyes puffy, and she'd rather swallow a sticker patch than listen to the guys' jabs on this one. This little disaster was her secret shame.

She shouldn't be so upset. It's not like she didn't know he had feelings for Laney. The sadness in his eyes that first day, when she'd seen Mitchell again and he'd seen Laney, made it obvious he was still into her. A week with her wasn't going to change his heart. Love wasn't magical or logical. From what she'd seen of love, it didn't even feel good as much as it hurt. Hopping into the Terminator, she yanked the door closed behind her and turned her back to the men laughing around the fire outside.

Tonight she'd be pathetic and nurse her wounded pride, and tomorrow she'd pretend that little intimacy party with Sean in the woods hadn't even happened. At least she found out now and not months from now, so there was that.

Why did her heart actually hurt? It was hard to breathe without a nagging, stinging pain that only served as yet another layer of annoyance over the entire situation. She'd only known the man for a second, and he'd ignored her for most of it. Screw him and his perfect body.

Laney. *Pfft*. She couldn't believe he freaking called her *Laney*. It would probably be funny in the morning. Or at least a year from now when she compared worst boy stories with Eloise one future night over shots of Ricky's rotgut.

The door to the truck opened, and Finn stuck his head in.

"You don't have to worry about Sean and me anymore, so spare me the lecture."

His dark eyes were steady and worried. "Are you all right?"

She meant to laugh, but it came out a sob and then a defeated sigh. "Yeah. I will be. Thanks."

"Yep. You'll spell Carpenter in a few hours so get some shut eye, okay?"

She nodded, and the closing door rocked the truck. For the next two hours she tried to do as Finn had suggested, but only managed to stare at the back of the bench seat in front of her and replay the night over and over. For a moment, she'd had him before Laney took him back. She'd felt so good and warm and wanted for an instant. Now her stupid heart hurt even more at the absence of a man. Homesickness warred with the uncomfortable anticipation of seeing Mitchell again. She didn't feel the same about him anymore. Maybe she had Sean to thank for that. He'd shown her she could feel something for another, and it was time to move on. Way past time. Still, she didn't look forward to the awkwardness around the others who thought she was the rejected one who deserved the pitying looks. Those were the worst.

With a growl, she sat up and kicked the door open. Steven stood droopy-eyed against a tree, scanning the woods around camp, and she gave him a little wave as she headed for the river. With a mental pat on her back, she straightened her spine at the fact she hadn't even spared a glance for where Sean was sleeping.

The call of the river beckoned her, but she listened for more. The woods seemed darker somehow without Sean beside her, and she flicked her flashlight in an arc around her. It seemed to take a lot longer to reach the water and by the time she got there, the feeling of complete aloneness was an overwhelming weight in the darkness. One last look around and she stripped out of her clothes as fast as she could. No way was she hanging around splashing like a little fish kabob for any Dead who felt like a midnight snack. Goose bumps rippled across her flesh as the cold wind bit into her, and before she could change her mind, she cast herself into the gentle waves. Clamping her lips together to hold the scream of shock at bay, she dunked her head and stayed under as long as she could hold a breath. When she emerged, she scrubbed her body with rose scented soap from a woman at Dead Run River everyone called the Cleaning Lady.

She closed her eyes and dragged gentle nails across her soapy scalp, giving the moon her neck. Her fear had disappeared with the realization that she had somehow managed to procure a moment of private time. The team was great, but good grief she was enjoying a few minutes away from the pepper of fart jokes.

Her body had become used to the cold of the rapids, and now the air outside was the offender, making her sink lower into the water.

A twig snapped.

The flashlight was on the beach in the front pocket of her waiting backpack, and to retrieve it, she'd have to streak naked. Water lapped at her chin as she tried to make out any shape in the dark. "Sean?"

Another twig snapped, and the brush just behind the treeline moved. Her heart pounded so hard, surely her chest was making those tiny ripples in the water. "Finn?"

A shadow moved from the forest and lumbered toward the shoreline. Toward her. It stumbled in the dark, and she couldn't make out anything except that the Dead was big. And dressed in — Steven's clothes?

"Steven? What the hell are you doing out here?"

He stopped just shy of the waves lapping at his boots.

"Hellooo." She waved. "Did you hear me?"

Something wasn't right. Steven stood there frozen, and the gray of his eyes stared unblinking at her. She couldn't even tell if he was breathing. Fear slithered up her spine as she imagined Keeter's steel grip around her. "Steven?" she squeaked.

A soft groan came from his lips and broke her heart. Oh no, no, no. Had the others been attacked in their sleep too? There had been no gunfire, and surely they would've put down Steven before he turned. If they were alive.

"Steven," she pleaded. "You're scaring me." She paddled up the current, and he followed along the shoreline.

He'd been awake when she left, so how could he have been bitten unawares? Oh Steven, that half-lazed idiot. How had he let this happen? And now she was going to die by a Dead she'd known as a friend. What a sad fate for both of them.

"Oh my gosh, oh my gosh," she chanted, swimming harder. Fear thickened in her veins until she panted with panic.

His boots scattered loose pebbles and scuffed the earth clumsily as he followed her along the shore. Deads didn't like moisture—wasn't that what Sean had said? But she couldn't tread the near-frozen water all night. He'd wait her out until she drowned or got close enough for him to reach her. Then her friend would eat her just like Keeter had tried to do.

Maybe if she called out, someone from her team would hear. It was a long shot because they were so far away, but maybe. Or maybe her screaming would alert every Dead in the area. Maybe her entire newly turned team would show up on the water's edge to eat her alive.

Think, think, think.

He didn't want to get in the water—that much was obvious—so she swam closer to the other shoreline. He stopped his pursuit and stayed lined up with where she was in the water. When she hit the beach she ran straight back through the trees until the shadows covered her. The ground was unforgiving against her tender, bootless feet, and the air bit into her unclothed skin with such a bitter vengeance, her teeth chattered uncontrollably. Huddling in on herself, she hid in the darkness and watched Steven-the-Dead. He stood just where he had been, watching the area where she'd disappeared.

Okay, she would travel back down river and cross at a safe distance. Then she'd run for her bag and get the heck out of Dodge. Tiptoeing through the woods was a pointless endeavor, of course, because everything there was trying to kill her and sounded like cannon fire under her clumsy, frozen feet. Every bramble reached for her bare legs, and every blade of tough autumn grass cut at her ankles. Every rock jutted out just in time for her to step painfully on it. She found every branch to snap in half, but Steven remained where he was, patiently waiting for his meal to return to him. Stupid Dead.

The wind picked up and whipped the tree branches around her as if it were telling her to flee and live. Or maybe it was warning her of what was to come. She picked up her pace and peeked her head around a large evergreen. She couldn't even see Steven-the-Dead anymore, so she padded to the shore and sank quietly into the waves. Swimming as fast as she could, she reached the other side and looked up in time to see the Dead's dark figure ambling up the shoreline toward her. Shit.

She bolted for her bag. She needed a weapon and warm clothes if she was going to survive this. Her legs prickled like they were falling asleep, and her fingers were stiff as she slowly froze. She reached her backpack before he did, but not by much. It was better this way. She couldn't live with herself knowing she'd let him go to survive as a Dead. A sob wrenched itself from her throat as she fumbled for the Glock in the dark.

She was about to shoot her friend. No, he wasn't her friend anymore. Steven had died when the Dead bit him. She couldn't think of him as human now. Not when her time had come to pull the trigger on a teammate.

He picked up his clumsy pace, and a string of slurred of nonsense left his lips as he bore down on her.

The cold metal of the Glock was a solid weight in her hand as she lifted the pistol to his head. She aimed and put her finger on the trigger. "I'm sorry," she sobbed. "I'm so sorry."

A movement rushed from the woods, and it shocked her into stillness. Just as she was about to pull the trigger, Sean tackled the Dead and hit the pebbled beach head on. Both figures collapsed onto the rocky shore, and Vanessa stood shaking like a leaf as the Glock rattled in her grip.

"Don't shoot him!" Sean yelled. "Don't shoot! He's sleepwalking."

"Wh-What?" She sagged to her knees into the earth that was absorbing her warm tears.

"Look." He gestured, sitting up. "He's asleep. He's not a Dead. He's asleep."

"I almost shot him. I had it aimed at his face, about to pull the trigger!"

"But you didn't. You didn't. He's okay. You're okay."

"I'm not okay!" she yelled as she stood and barreled down on the snoring moron.

"Vanessa, he's pretty far under if that fall didn't rattle him, and I don't think you're supposed to wake up a sleepwalker."

She straddled Steven and leveled Sean with the most deadly glare she could muster butt-naked and shaking from the cold. "Maybe that rule applied in fancy-dancy times before the outbreak. Nobody gives a shit about sleepwalker's hurt feelings in a forest full of Deads." And then she raised her fist and socked Steven in his slack jaw.

He lurched forward with a yelp and looked frantically around like his eyes needed to adjust. When they landed on her, he ogled her exposed body and then frowned. "This is happening? Did I fall asleep while we were doing it?" His eyes landed on Sean. "Oh man this is getting weird."

"We aren't having sex, you idiot. When you're out on missions, did you not think it was pertinent information to let your team know you're a freaking sleepwalker? I almost shot you!"

"Here," Sean said in a deep, exhausted voice. His gaze was averted as he handed her a pile of clothes he'd retrieved from her backpack.

The emotional upheaval she'd endured between his rejection and almost offing a friend were just too much. "Awesome. Are you offended by the sight of my body, Sean? Well, I know I'm not hideous because Steven here won't stop staring, so you don't have to pretend." Her anger boiled over and filled her head with shards of red fury. She gripped Steven's jacket and pulled him in to lay the least intimate kiss on his lips that had ever existed. In fact, his mouth was likely bleeding. Then she stood, snatched the clothes from Sean's outstretched hand, and jammed a big fat middle finger in his face before stomping off.

"Now, that's a woman," Steven murmured as she left, and she fought the urge to turn and hurl rocks at the both of them.

Chapter Thirteen

One more day. One more day of scavenging medical supplies, and they'd be on their way back to Dead Run River and she could pretend Sean-sexy-face-Daniels didn't exist. She would get back to normal, where she didn't feel as if she could cry or laugh at any second, and she'd be back with Nelson. Once she crossed those colony gates, she'd be back to her old, unafraid self again. Just twenty-four more tiny hours.

"V," Finn scolded. "Are you paying attention?"

"Finneas, answer me this." She ignored his groan and scanned the street in front of Saint Francis Medical Center for the hundredth time. There was nothing but a bold rat digging through debris. "Am I the only one who wasn't told about Steven's sleepwalking problem?"

"For the fifth time, I said I was sorry. He came to me with it right after he was picked, and I thought I told everyone. I didn't mean to leave you out."

"So if I would've pulled that trigger, if Sean hadn't been fast enough, all of the guilt I lived with for the rest of my life would be your fault."

"Yes. I made a tactical error thinking the problem wouldn't be as bad as it got. I'm sorry I put you both at risk. Though, as I hear it,

Carpenter's *not* sorry because he seems to have gotten an eyeful of you last night."

"Yeah, roughly half of our team saw my goodies last night, so next time he goes around bragging on it, please remind him he's not so special."

"Sean said you knew people in the Denver colony. Back before it fell."

She narrowed her eyes at him. "Does Sean tell you everything?"

"I just wanted to give my condolences. It was my home, and I lost a lot of people in that uprising too." He stretched his thickly muscled neck like his sweater was suddenly too tight. "And no, Sean doesn't tell me everything, but I like to think he tells me a lot. We've been friends for a long time."

"How long is a long time?"

"Uh, since about six months into the outbreak. I met him when he was looking for a place to set up a colony, and I helped him build the gates to the one he eventually chose. I was the first one to congratulate him when his daughter, Adrianna, was born, and I was there when his wife was taken. V?"

She'd grown more and more uncomfortable during the touchy-feely speech Finn was giving, and she twitched suspiciously under the moniker. "What?"

"Go easy on him. He's been through some really hard times."

"Yeah, well, it's the apocalypse, Finneas. Everyone's been through hard times. Take that guy." She gestured to a perfectly cleaned skeleton draped elegantly across a cracked curb. "He probably came in here for a routine colonoscopy and came out as someone's lunch. Now that's some hard times."

Finn didn't say anything for a long time, so she pointed her attention back to her post. The others were inside, trying to find anything that would fill the last couple of boxes they could fit into the back of the Terminator.

"Three and a half years you've known him, and that's a long time. Isn't that crazy?" she asked. "That three and a half years is a long time these days?" Every single thing had changed after the outbreak. Sometimes it still hit her just how much.

"Three and a half years is a lifetime now," he agreed. "Days seem longer when there's not much hope, so the weeks and months drag on."

"Did your best friend Sean tell you he made out with me and then called me Laney?"

Finn's startled gaze snapped to hers, and he muttered an oath under his breath. "I didn't think he liked her as much as all that."

"Hmm. Would you approve of me if I were her?"

"That's not a fair question, and you know it. Laney is good people. Sean is good people. They were not good people together though. They were like oil and water, always fighting each other, always keeping each other at a distance. He had no business going after anyone in the state he was in after Aria."

"What happened with Aria?"

"That is something Sean is going to have to tell you if he ever tells anyone."

"Never mind then. I'm not talking to Sean after this is over. He makes me crazy and not in a good way. Besides, I have a strict I-don't-date-boys-who-stab-me-and-call-me-by-other-women's-names policy. Keeps the creepers away."

Movement across the street had both of them lifting their rifles to better see out of their scopes. Just another rat joining the first. The day had been so quiet, she almost itched for a little action just to rid herself of the humming tension that ran under the surface of her skin. She sank back against the painted side of the Terminator, flipped one of her blades up in the air, and caught it by the hilt as static crackled on the radio.

"We're about done here," Sean said. "Are we still clear out there?"

"Yep, we're clear," Finn murmured into the speaker. "Come on out whenever you're ready."

He lifted the sliding door to the truck, did a perimeter sweep of the sides of the building, and joined her again. "And just so you know, Sean isn't a creeper. He's a good guy. I know, because I saw him with Aria."

She sighed and closed her eyes against the ache of denial. "That was three and a half years ago, Finn. A lifetime, remember?"

A shot echoed from the building.

"Sean?" Finn radioed.

Static was the only answer.

"Sean!" Uh-uh, screw that radio.

"Vanessa!" Finn yelled as she blasted around the truck and through the front doors.

Rifle up and finger at the ready to pull the trigger on whatever had caused the fear of loss that clung to her gut like moss, she barreled through the door and ran into Sean who was headed the opposite direction. She would've been relieved he was still upright if not for the sagging weight of Steven on his arm.

Sean's eyes looked somber and angry, and she moved out of the way as he brushed past her. "Load up, Summers. Deads will have heard that shot, and they'll be on us soon."

Jackson growled as she nudged her way in front of him and asked, "What happened? Is he okay?"

"Ask Brandon back there," he offered without missing a step. "And before you kill him, remember we need him to save Steven's life."

The rifle clacked as she slid it to her back and dropped under Steven's other arm to help drag him out. When she looked down, his dark sweater was wet. No, no, no.

Finn stood ready beside the sliding door, and Sean barked for him to go grab the other two boxes in the supply room. "Be quick about it," he advised.

Between her and Sean, they got Steven laid out across the backseat, and she eased his head into her lap before yanking his shirt up to expose a perfect entry hole. Bile rode a wave of dread and threatened to gag her. "Steven," she said a lot more calmly than she felt. "We need to see if you have an exit wound. Help us roll you over."

Jackson fired a shot at a Dead running around the corner of the building and Sean fell back to help fend them off. Brandon took his place.

Her voice shook with anger. "What did you do?"

His face was pale to match Steven's, and when he opened his mouth to speak, his lips trembled. "It was an accident."

"Please don't tell me you were messing around with your gun in there and shot one of your own team."

Air snuffled loudly to and from his nose as he looked like he might pass out. "I didn't mean to," he squeaked.

The color of his eyes drew heavenward as he swayed, and Vanessa slapped him cleanly across the cheek. Without a moment's pause, she clutched the front of his shirt and brought him face to face with her. "If you don't save him, I swear, I'll kill you to avenge his death."

He swallowed hard and nodded vigorously.

With Brandon's help, she rocked Steven on his side and lifted the back of his shirt. There it was. Right at the mouth of a red stream, the exit hole was buried and leaking. The bullet had mushroomed the second it hit Steven's skin and the hole in his back looked much worse than the front. She could only imagine the kind of damage it had inflicted on his organs as it smashed through his body.

"It's bad, isn't it?" Steven asked.

Vanessa inhaled a great gust and set his head on the seat so she could retrieve the first-aid kit. Gunfire peppered the air around them. Where the heck was Finn with the last of the boxes?

She spared a glance for Sean, who'd moved a ways off from the truck and was picking the growing numbers off one by one. His focus was complete and unwavering—he was a stone among the chaos.

Ripping the red backpack open, she shoved it at Brandon and took over putting pressure on the shirt he'd found to push against Steven's wounds. There was so much blood. How could anyone survive losing so much?

Brandon tore through packages of medical supplies she couldn't even guess at, and after giving him an injection of some sort of clear fluid, he pulled a pair of latex gloves over his hands and tossed her a pair too. While she pulled hers on, Brandon stuck his finger into the entry wound and felt around, eliciting a pained scream from Steven. With all of her weight, she held his shoulders down.

"His liver is definitely nicked. Dr. Mackey is equipped to handle that kind of patch up, but we don't have the supplies here. We have to get him back to Dead Run River, and we have to do it now."

"Sean!"

"Yeah?" he shouted between rounds.

"We have to go, now!"

Finn jogged through the front hospital doors with two oversized boxes stacked in his giant arms. Under Sean and Jackson's cover fire, he secured them in the back, and the door to the Terminator made a metal grating sound as he slid it closed. Jackson hopped up into the driver's seat just as a trio of Deads reached that side of the truck and clawed at the freshly closed door. Finn and Sean piled into the passenger side and slammed the door, but not before Sean had to kick a scrabbling arm out of the way.

As Jackson hit the gas, Sean spun around. "How bad is it?"

Her silent answer seemed good enough for him because he leveled her with the saddest look swimming in the depths of his eyes.

The truck jostled and threw them as Jackson ran over any Dead in the way of their escape. The grille was definitely going to have to be scraped clean after this little joyride. "Where to, boss man?" he asked.

"Home. Get us back to Dead Run River as fast as you can." He sunk into the cushion of the front seat and rubbed his eyes. "Brandon, you better hope you can keep him alive until we get there."

Vanessa was a warrior. Tirelessly, she'd held her finger against a nicked artery in Steven's open wound. The common iliac artery, Brandon had called it. Even long after Steven had passed out from the blood loss, she'd worked to keep him alive. It ripped Sean up to see her so scared. Loss came with this life, but every instinct in him cried to protect her from the unfairness of the world.

The muscles in her arms jerked and twitched, and her back spasmed visibly from where she leaned over to apply pressure. The trip back had taken hours. Steven had been shot in a hospital down in Colorado Springs, where they'd dipped to find the supplies they couldn't get in Denver. They'd tapped it out and had to go further for the things Dr. Mackey needed—unfortunately for Steven.

Vanessa's skin had paled to the color of her dying friend's by the time they pulled up to the colony gates.

"Welcome back, sir," the guard who opened the giant wooden barrier greeted.

"Grady, I need you to make a call to Dr. Mackey right away. We have a bad injury."

Grady's eyebrows lowered, and he leaned in closer. "What kind of injury, sir?"

"Not a bite. He's been shot. It's obvious, entry wound and exit. He's in bad shape."

"Yes, sir." He jogged a small distance away, and his murmured order floated across the clearing.

"Bite check," Ramirez, an older guard, barked into the cab of the truck.

"We don't have time for this," Vanessa gritted out.

Sean jumped out with Jackson and Finn and pulled off his shirt. "There's no time to argue. We can't get in without being cleared, and we're losing precious seconds."

He'd done a gate check a hundred times. Still, for some reason it bothered him to be so exposed in Vanessa's direct line of sight. Cleared, he yanked on his pants and jumped the step into the Terminator. "Brandon and Vanessa, you guys are going to have to keep that pressure on while we take him in. There isn't a road to Dr. Mackey's that the Terminator will fit on, so we hoof it from here to the ATV the guards are bringing around. You ready?"

Both nodded wearily.

Between him and Finn, they managed to get Steven's limp body out of the truck without cutting his lifeline in Brandon and Vanessa loose, but it had taken time. Time the fading man didn't have.

Waiting for Vanessa and Brandon to pass gate check was a test in patience, but thankfully Grady was the one up for the job, and he seemed to sense the urgency of the situation because he lifted their shirts and checked their legs and every other square inch of vulnerable skin by lifting clothes, not making them strip. Not exactly protocol, but fitting considering. Grady asked him not to tell Mel, and he assured him he wouldn't.

Finally loaded into the bed of a small trailer hitched to a four-wheeler, they jostled and jounced until they came to the medical cabin. Dr. Mackey was waiting.

"I need everybody out so I can work," Doc said in a somber tone.

With Steven on the operating table in the small and poorly-equipped operating room, Vanessa finally pulled her finger away from the warmth of his slick injury. She stood there, white as a sheet and nearly as flimsy, with blood smeared up to her elbows and her bottom lip trembling as the door closed behind her.

"Doc will let me know as soon as he has anything to tell us," Sean promised, gripping the radio to stop himself from gathering her up in his arms and hugging her until she had color in her cheeks again.

She dragged wide, shocked eyes to his and gave a curt nod. Her crimson forearms lifted under the window light as she stared at the drying color. "I need to clean up."

"Sure," he said, dropping his hand. When had he even reached for her?

She turned and ambled out the door, leaving a bloodstain on the handle where she'd let herself out.

Brandon leaned heavily against the operating room door, and Sean rounded on him. "Don't you leave here until you know something either way. You radio me the instant you have news. Whether he makes it or not, you call it in."

"Okay," Brandon murmured.

He wanted to see Adrianna. To hold her and let her know Daddy had come home safe and that she was protected. But on runs where there were injuries and deaths, other matters had to be seen to first. Keeter's wife would already be looking for him, as the news of their arrival would spread like a grass fire on a windy day in drought season. He had to find her before she found out about her husband's passing in some callous way.

Steven didn't have any family, or even a girlfriend that he knew about, but he'd have friends around Dead Run River who deserved to know he was fighting for his life. The man could use every ounce of positive energy from his loved ones they could muster.

Adrianna would have to wait until the painful chores were done. He wasn't really back yet. Not until he tied up all the loose ends of the jumbled knot that had been the supply run.

For the tenth time in an hour, Sean turned the radio off and then clicked it back on and checked the channel. Still no news on Steven.

"Daddy?" Adrianna asked as she flipped a handmade fly into the stream again.

"Yes, baby?"

"I asked Laney to be my mommy, but she said I have lots of moms. Her, and Mel, and Eloise. She said I'm lucky because everyone wants to take care of me. Maybe it's okay if I have lots of mommies because Mel makes me cookies, and Eloise teaches me about flowers, and Laney shows me how to fish, and she even promised she won't be too busy for me when her baby comes out of her tummy."

His mouth was hanging open, so he snapped it closed and counted to five before answering. "Why did you ask Laney to be your mommy? I thought we were doing okay, just you and me."

The fly made a tiny sound against the surface of the bubbling stream. "Oh, we do good, Daddy, but sometimes you have to go away and sometimes I want to stay with one mommy instead of three."

Sean stood from the bag chair he'd been settled into and crouched down in front of her. With gentle hands against her fragile shoulders, he searched her dark eyes. "Honey, getting a new mommy isn't as easy as all of that. Your mom was so special to me that when she passed away, it made it hard for me to find someone who would make me as happy. I can't promise you we'll have a family like you want, but I can promise we'll do the best we can, just like we always have, okay? And whenever you need girl time, Laney, Mel, and Eloise are always there to talk to. Just let me know what you need, and we'll get you to 'em, okay?"

She nodded. "'Kay."

He frowned at the fishing line, tugged by the current and waves, but nothing else. "We haven't caught any fish, Ade. I don't think they're biting this late in the season."

"Oh, I know, but Laney told me I need to keep practicing with the fly so I'll be a fish denominator come spring."

"A fish dominator?"

She pulled the line in. "That's what I said."

"You need to stop growing, Ade." He scooped her up and tickled her face with his whiskers. "Stop it this instant. I demand it!"

In a fit of giggles, the little girl placed her tiny hands on each side of his face and graced him with a smile that mirrored his own. "I missed you, Dad."

"Oh, I'm Dad now? No more Daddy?"

"Nope." She burst into another round of laughter as he tickled her ribs.

Her laugh filled the forest, reverberating off giant pines and landing in his heart. God, he'd missed that sound. It rubbed layers of angst and uncertainty from him. That tinkling sound made everything clearer and brighter somehow.

He set her upright and folded up the chair before sticking it in the hollowed-out tree stump where it belonged. How many hours had he and Adrianna sat in this very spot while she honed her fishing skills? How many times had he tied flies and helped her with her swing, and unhooked tiny cutthroat trout from her line? This was what surviving the outbreak was all about. Life was hard when you were the rarest species on the planet, but this was the point, wasn't it? It was all about having this completely happy moment with someone who fought the darkness with you.

She shouldered the fishing pole and slid her little hand into his as they headed up the trail toward their cabin.

Movement up the trail had him shoving Adrianna behind him before he had a thought. He'd probably do that for a week before he settled back into the safety of Dead Run River. That's the way it had always been when he went on supply runs.

Laney hiked the trail toward them, visibly rounder than when he'd seen her the week before. How had she grown so much in such a small amount of time? Her walk seemed uncomfortable, and she kept her gaze downcast at the trail she approached. Something in him stirred, but it wasn't what he thought it would be. Instead of a pang of loss or lust, there was just relief. Relief to be home to see people he knew out on a trail he walked. Relief to see someone who cared about his daughter. Relief at seeing a friend. But most of all, he was relieved that he saw her as he was supposed to see her. Like he saw her before she left with Mitchell all those months before. No longer did he feel like he'd lost out or missed the boat. She was just Laney. Not Laney-the-one-who-got-away — just his friend, Laney. The week had changed his heart.

No, it was more than a week off from the regret.

Vanessa had changed him.

Laney waved as she caught sight of them. "What're you doing this far up the mountain?" he asked.

Her breathing was heavy, and she stopped and waited for them to reach her. "I came to say welcome back and to see how the supply run went. Also, I wanted to tell you all of the stuff we did that you wouldn't approve of before munchkin over there did so I can explain myself before you explode."

"Ha! Okay, spill the beans, ladies."

"I shot a crossbow," Adrianna offered.

"I can deal with that as long as you only do that with Laney or Finn."

Laney shot a conspiratorial grin at his little girl. "She got to carry around a pocket knife when she was around me or Mel." She handed him a small red Swiss Army Knife. "It's hers. Mitchell and I picked it up for her at the last colony we were in."

"You know this isn't a toy, right?" he asked.

Adrianna nodded with wide, serious eyes riveted on the tiny weapon in his hand. "Laney taught me all about how to use the tools, and I even cut my finger once, see?" She held up a nicked finger as proof. "I know how to be real careful with it."

"Mmm," he said, eyeing the tiny cut. "If you prove you can be responsible with it around me, maybe in a year or two, you can carry it on you all the time."

"Also," Laney said slowly, "I took her to work with me two days this week."

"Work?" he asked as a panicked feeling sank into his gut like a stone in the river. "Work, like with the cattle? Outside of colony gates? Are you testing me?"

"A little," she admitted. "Mostly, Eloise was sick, and Mel was up to her eyeballs in colony business, and my workload is light on account of—" She gestured to her expanding belly. "Plus it was a big adventure for her, and she got to feed a late spring calf, and Mitchell and Guist were both on guard duty there, so she was completely protected. And yeah, maybe a little piece of me wanted to see if you'd flip out like the old days because I'll tell you, this new zen Sean is kind of freaking me out."

With his eyes closed tightly shut, he counted to ten before he opened them and smiled (some would call it a grimace) at her. "No more of that. The other stuff is fine, but I don't want her outside of colony gates unless I'm the one who takes her."

Laney's dark eyebrows arched. "That's all? No yelling? No mental mind bullets fired my way?"

"Please don't test me with her anymore, Laney. I want to keep trusting you with my daughter, but that was crossing the line."

"I understand. And I swear I won't test you anymore. Ow!" She doubled over and gripped her belly.

Hunching, he held her elbow in case she went down. "Laney, what's wrong?"

"Oooh, it's the baby. Doc says it's just those false labor pains because it's way too early, but dang it they hurt. Whoo!" She straightened but didn't remove her hand from her stomach.

"How far along are you?"

"Only seven months. If this is what I have to look forward to all through the last trimester, this is super lame."

"I remember Aria getting the false labor pains, but she didn't get them until later in the pregnancy."

Laney had a faraway look and a slight frown when she said, "Maybe if I eat again, I'll feel better."

"Okay, let's get you to the mess hall. I have nothing in the pantry at the cabin."

"Ew, Dad, feel how tight her belly is," Adrianna cooed with her hands plastered on the front of Laney.

Nope. No way was he pushing that boundary. He'd just learned he didn't have the intense feelings about her he used to. He wasn't tempting his heart to soften to her mothering side. "I'm good."

Static crackled over the radio. "Sean?" came Brandon's weary voice. "Sean, are you there?"

"I'm here. How is he?"

Brandon sighed. "He made it through surgery. Doc says if he lives through the night, his chances are good."

"Good," was his only reply. He wasn't thanking the little prick. He was the one who'd shot Steven in the first place, and honestly, Sean had counted down the days to when he didn't have to be stuck on a mission with Brandon and his hundred daily complaints. Next time Mel asked him to tack a civilian onto his team, he was flat out refusing. If he hadn't learned his lesson the first time, he'd sure learned it this go 'round.

"Someone's hurt?" Laney asked.

"Uh." He frowned at the radio. "Yeah, this supply run was rough. Lost a man, and now we might lose another."

"Oh, I'm so sorry. I didn't know."

Shaking his head, he led them down the trail toward the mess hall. "No use apologizing for something you didn't have a thing in the world to do with."

"I'm not apologizing for that. I just know how hard you're being on yourself for not getting your entire team back here, and it makes me sorry it happened."

"Laney, please. I don't want to talk about this." Huh. That was a lie. He just didn't want to talk about it with her. Vanessa was the only one he could think of to balm the ache of loss and fear.

Maybe there was hope for him yet.

Chapter Fourteen

Vanessa finally felt human again. It only took an hour of scrubbing in the shower until her skin was raw and prickled and the water ran cold, but it was worth it. Sean hadn't sent word if Steven was going to live or not, so she was taking matters into her own hands. A quick trip to ask Dr. Mackey herself wouldn't be too pushy. She had a right to know, after all.

Stalling as long as possible, she'd dressed in a cherry red, fitted sweater and even applied makeup for the first time in weeks. Her blond hair, usually hidden into a ponytail for guard training, was allowed to dry in sloping waves and left down for the wind to caress.

Nelson had welcomed her home but had only stayed for half an hour before running off to plans with his friends. The week apart had done wonders for his independence, but she had to admit, it stung a little when he left so soon. What if she'd died out there? She almost had on several occasions. Maybe he just didn't understand the gravity of her job.

The leather of the holster squeaked as she tightened the belt around her waist, and as she slid her Glock into place, a soft knock thrummed against the door.

Sean stood on the other side when she opened it, and the shock of seeing him here, at her room, left her with a skittering feeling of panic. His face was shaven clean, and he smelled crisply of soap and shaving cream. She fought the urge to reach out and touch where his beard had been this morning. When she lifted her gaze back to his, she was helpless to look away. His expression was so penetrating and consuming that she was unable to do anything but hold his stare.

He cleared his throat and looked every bit as taken aback as she felt. "You look beautiful. Nice. You look nice all dressed up and with your hair like that." He tossed a glance heavenward and cleared his throat again. "Look, Steven made it through surgery, and I thought we could go see him together. I brought you this." In his hands were two metal plates of food. "I saw you weren't at dinner, and we hadn't eaten yet either."

"We?"

One side-step revealed his dark-haired daughter peeking out from behind his legs.

"Hi," the girl said with a shy wave.

"Hi." Vanessa cast an angry glance at Sean for throwing the temptation to invest herself more deeply into his life and squatted down in front of the girl. It wasn't the child's fault her father couldn't follow directions. "What's your name?"

"I'm Adrianna Joy Daniels, and I'm four years old."

"Four? That's the perfect age, did you know that? I'm Vanessa Dawn Summers, and I'm twenty-four," she offered with a grin. "I don't know if you remember, but last year I painted your nails while you were spending the day in the cabin a couple of doors down."

"I remember. I picked bright red like your shirt. Do you shoot guns? Because Laney and Finn are teaching me to shoot guns and crossbows, and if you don't, then I can teach you."

A little pang of something green and jealous nipped at her insides, and she spared a short look for Sean. "I do shoot, but probably not as well as you. Are you going to come with us to visit Dr. Mackey?"

"Yes. One of Daddy's friends got shot up, and he needs to see if he's okay."

What a sad thing for a child to say offhand. Before the outbreak, children worried about Halloween candy and misplaced stuffed animals. Now, the cruel reality was that children learned about death almost from the moment they were born.

"Let me grab my jacket, and we can go, okay?"

Adrianna poked her head into the room as she pulled her black, fitted winter coat on carefully, so as not to pull her still tender injuries from the week. "You want to come in and see it?"

"Can I, Daddy?"

"Sure," Sean said, looking decidedly uncomfortable.

Begrudgingly she   offered, "You can come in too if you like. It's not much, so it's not like the tour will take that long."

The room was tidy for the most part. Adrianna fingered the endless drawings and lists that dotted her table, and showed Sean a picture Vanessa had drawn of the inner workings of her Glock. The sketches weren't anything to write home about, but Sean held it and looked at it for a long time.

"Can you draw me a horse?" Adrianna asked.

"Sure." She tore off the bottom half of an unfinished list and sketched a cartoon horse under an apple tree with a happy sun and smiling clouds.

Across the bottom, she scribbled:

To: Adrianna-the-Gunslinger
From: Vanessa

The little girl stared at it with wide eyes before breathing a thank you and folding it lopsidedly. She shoved it in her pocket. Vanessa couldn't help the satisfied smile that played at the corners of her lips, though she tried. Sean was watching her with the most disconcerting look on his face, like he'd just witnessed her surf the English Channel on the back of a polka-dotted porpoise or something.

How did the man fill up the entire room? Sure he was six-foot and muscled, but not overly so. He wasn't thick like Finn. He was lithe like a panther, and his eyes slanted slightly in a very jungle cat like fashion. The man wasn't born to be anyone's prey. His presence felt bigger than her eyes perceived, as if his force of personality stretched far beyond the confines of his flesh. Those unnervingly blue eyes followed every movement she made and did so with no apology. Just frank curiosity, like he was trying to figure out the end of a mystery movie.

The thick, delicious scent of him filled the small space and penetrated her mind until she imagined she couldn't breathe without wanting him. Without a word, she stepped out the front door and took a long drag of cold, cedar-scented mountain air to clear her drunken head of Sean's effect on her.

Her stomach clenched, like the loss of his scent left some unattainable craving she couldn't comfort.

"What's wrong," Sean said in a low rumble from just behind. She would've jumped if she didn't want him that close so blasted much.

"The walls were coming for me."

He stood there, just behind, and so close, she could feel his warmth. Electricity floated just above her flesh like blue lightning had struck somewhere nearby and the current had settled into the space between them. She'd give anything to feel his lips against her neck right there, in that moment.

His fault. She'd asked him not to torture her, and he hadn't even listened for an entire day.

"Vanessa," he whispered against her neck.

"Don't." She spun and lowered her voice. "I told you before — I'm no man's second choice. I asked you not to pull me any closer, and then you bring your daughter for me to fall in love with. Backhanded tactics, even for you, Daniels. Let's go."

She would've maintained her anger too if Adrianna's little hand hadn't slipped into hers on the trail. The child was like this magical anger tamer, and Vanessa threw one more mental curse into the sky for Sean. If he kept it up, she'd be playing mistress to the man in love with another in under a week. At the thought of Sean's voice against the back of her neck, warmth pooled inside of her. She couldn't trust herself around him. And the worst part? He probably had this effect on all women. Oh, she'd seen the way the ladies of the colony basically launched their pheromones his way when he passed. And the man didn't even seem to notice! A sure sign that he could have, and probably did have, any woman he wanted. She'd liked a man like that once, and he chose another. Heck no was she playing second fiddle to other options again.

She felt as if she were catching fire. Like the whole forest was going to burn around her because of the tidal wave of gasoline-soaked flames that licked at her body when he was around her, looking at her like that. Like he couldn't help himself.

Stupid man was going to be the death of her sanity.

A million years later, when they opened the door to Dr. Mackey's medical cabin, it was abundantly clear they'd waited too long. Steven sat weakly on a bed, slurping down chicken broth of his own free abilities. She'd wanted to be there when he woke up.

"Hey," he croaked in a tired voice. "Summers, you look hot. And are you wearing makeup? Doc, I thought you said I lived. Clearly I didn't."

Dr. Mackey scribbled away on a desk in the next room. "Heaven wouldn't hurt so much, Steven, remember?"

Steven winced. "Good point. I feel like I've had someone's finger stuck in my abdomen all day."

Sean was setting up a table in Doc's office for Adrianna to eat, and Vanessa took the seat beside the bed.

Steven's sandy brown hair was mussed and sticking up in all directions, and his twinkling hazel eyes had lost some of their vigor to the weakness that wracked his body, but he was still breathing, and that was good enough for her.

"You scared me today," she admitted.

"I scared me too."

"I swore to Brandon I'd kill him to avenge you if you died, and I thought you were really going to make me follow through with murdering that dork."

A short laugh turned to coughing and obvious pain, and she squeezed his hand. "I haven't eaten yet, so I'm going to give you some space. Yell if you need anything, okay?"

"Yep," he said with a gray pallor smile and a flimsy nod.

Sean passed her in the doorway. "The plate by Adrianna is all yours."

"What are you going to eat?"

"Whatever Ade doesn't eat. She's finicky. It'll be plenty."

She eyed his physique as he disappeared into the room, and she privately disagreed. A man built like that needed more than just the leftovers from his kid's plate. The first thing she did when she sat down was split the beans down the middle and pull half of the cornbread apart to save for him.

The quiet drone of deep-voiced conversation carried on long enough for her to finish and for Adrianna to leave her seat to play with a model skeleton Dr. Mackey let her borrow. Scraping all of the food onto one plate, she took it to Sean and sat in the only open seat in the corner.

"I have something I wanted to talk to you about since you're both here," Sean said. He'd leaned forward to rest his elbows on his knees, and his triceps bulged through the tight black shirt he wore. Geez, was the man trying to make her ovulate?

"Well, what is it?" she asked irritably.

"Both of you did excellent in the field, and I've already talked to Mel about you graduating immediately to full guard duties. Finn seconded my opinion. You've probably already figured out that you are graduating as that was part of the deal, but I wanted to formally tell you how impressed I am. I couldn't be prouder of two new recruits with how you handled yourselves in impossible situations and went above and beyond what could ever be expected of you. I trust both of you with keeping this colony safe and have no problem recommending your immediate promotion from the training program to full guard so that you can start your careers."

There it was, there it *was!* That was the news she'd needed to get her out of whatever funk the last week had pulled her into. She'd worked so hard for this, and there had been moments she thought she couldn't do this job after all, but she'd persevered. She'd gone the harder route and proved herself, and now she'd be a guard. That accomplishment was something no one could ever take away from her.

Her goofy grin was mirrored by Steven, and she laughed at the jubilation on his face. It wasn't until she saw the smile on Sean's face that she sat stunned. He was such a serious man on the supply run, but not there in the medical cabin. His smile was a work of art. Straight, white teeth stood stark against his olive-colored skin, and his smile lines were a personal map to a deep contentment that resided within her at seeing him happy. Even his laugh was alluring. Deep, easily offered, soothing to a tainted soul. The smile had reached his eyes and made their brilliant color even brighter somehow.

Happiness lingered around his lips as he spoke, and she couldn't seem to take her focus from the sensual way his mouth danced around words. "I don't know if you've ever been to a guard graduation," he said, "but they are small events. Finn will host it, and since we'll likely need to have it in here, you'll be allowed to invite a guest." He was looking at her with such seriousness when he said, "Maybe two. After graduation, Vanessa, you'll start guard duty wherever you're assigned, and Steven, you'll start when you're cleared by Dr. Mackey. Vanessa, do you know what area you'd like to guard?"

"Eventually I want to be a personal guard. Maybe for Mel, if I can prove myself. Until then I'm good with wherever I'm needed. Cattle gates, garden gates, front gates, supply runs, doesn't matter."

"You'd do another supply run after this one?"

"Not right away, but I think I would again with the right team. Yeah. We did important stuff out there, Sean. It didn't suck to be a part of that."

Adrianna drifted in with droopy eyes and crawled up into Sean's lap. He pulled her against his chest and rocked gently. "I better get this one into bed. Let Finn know who's invited by tomorrow morning, and he'll get the cooks on making you guys a special meal afterward. He'll do the ceremony here, tomorrow night at six."

"Wait," Steven said. "Aren't you going to be there?"

"Nah. I don't go to the graduations. You're Finn's until that day. After that, you're mine," he said. He stood and on his way out of the room said, "Good night, Vanessa," quietly enough for only her ears.

"Night," she mumbled as he carried his daughter through the front door.

He'd meant it as a threat. *After that, you're mine.* Darn it all if it didn't sound like the most enticing offer she'd had in a while.

Chapter Fifteen

Nelson. And Eloise. Or Sean. Sean? Crap, when did he become a viable option for Vanessa's short list of important people? If she invited Sean to the graduation, he'd act weird, and apparently, she was so attracted to weird. No Sean.

She did an about-face and launched herself back down the trail and away from Sean's house. It was an ungodly hour, and really she had no business marching up to his front door in the near dark that preceded dawn anyway.

But—

If she didn't invite Sean, she'd spend the entire five-minute graduation ceremony thinking of how different it would be if she had asked him and Adrianna to come. Wait, Adrianna now too? They probably wouldn't give two blinks whether they were invited to her boring graduation or not. Just because it was a huge deal to her didn't mean it was a huge deal to other people.

But—

When she imagined the tiny ceremony, she wanted him there. She turned again and hiked faster up the trail. Hopefully he was more of a morning person than he had been on the supply run, because

Freight-Train-Vanessa was coming, and his cabin was smack dab in the middle of her tracks.

She'd give him the speech along with the invitation. The Let's-Be-Friends-Without-Benefits speech, just to ease some of the tension that had kept her awake and borderline crazy all night. It was becoming painfully clear she couldn't just cut him out of her life. He was simply too intriguing, and they'd been through way too much together over the past week to go back to polite nods in the mess hall.

Friends. She could do just friends. They could target practice together and talk about the people they were dating and definitely never kiss again. She tugged the hem of her jacket a little lower and glared at the cabin that appeared over the hill. This would be easy.

A small sniffle brushed the breeze, and she froze. The sniffle accompanied the frail sob of a child, but she couldn't see well enough in the dark to tell where it was coming from.

"Adrianna?"

"Who's there?" came the small reply.

Stalking forward, she called, "It's Vanessa. Where are you, honey?" She paused again and listened for the answer. There she was.

The child hovered against a woodpile twenty yards away from the cabin in a pair of purple footy pajamas. A pink bunny in a floral frock was clutched to her tiny body. She shook like a leaf, and from where Vanessa stood, she could hear her teeth chattering. Stripping off her jacket, she bolted for the girl and wrapped her close to her chest. "Baby," she whispered as alarms went off in her head. "Why are you out here?"

"It's Daddy. I hate when he screams."

Vanessa's heart stopped. Nothing moved in the woods. Not a leaf, not a branch in the wind. Slowly, she turned her head toward the house. Wrongness wafted from the open door like a fog.

"I don't want to go back in there," Adrianna sobbed in a broken whisper as another fat tear slipped down her pale cheek.

"Adrianna, I won't let anything happen to you. I swear."

"Like Laney?"

"Yes. Laney protects you. I'll protect you just the same, do you understand?"

The child nodded.

With a small grunt, Vanessa hoisted her to her hip and clutched her jacket tighter around Adrianna's shoulders. "I have to make sure Daddy's okay, but I can't leave you out here."

"Okay."

The first slate rays of dawn light were making their way through the heavy trees, but the growing illumination didn't syphon the eeriness from the woods. The porch stairs creaked under her careful boots, and she set Adrianna by the door. Pulling her weapon, she brushed the cracked door with her shoulder.

The inside of Sean's cabin was shrouded in darkness. It was the first time she'd ever been to his place, and she hadn't the foggiest idea where he kept his lanterns. Reaching behind her, she took Adrianna's outstretched hand and pulled her protectively beside her.

"He's in there," Adrianna said in a terror-filled voice as she pointed to a closed door to the right of the living area.

A short yell rattled the house, and she nearly jumped out of her skin. Adrianna whimpered as Vanessa turned the doorknob and threw the door open.

A window above Sean's bed illuminated him just enough to show him in the throes of some terrible nightmare. His body was rigid, and without a shirt to shield him, Vanessa could make out every strip of muscle and edge of bone. A frown of pain brushed his face into an unrecognizable mask, and the sheets that should've been protecting his body from the cold autumn air had failed in their duty and sat in a tangled pile around his feet.

"Adrianna, did you already try to wake him?"

"Yes, but he wouldn't wake up," she cried.

The child didn't need to see this, so Vanessa pulled her into the living room and searched the small kitchen for a lantern. One sat on the counter, and she lit it with trembling fingers before turning it up as high as it would go and setting it atop the fireplace, out of Adrianna's reach. "I'm going to fix Daddy," she said. She tucked the child onto the couch with her jacket and an extra blanket and bolted back for Sean's room. "Stay there, and I'll be right back."

Closing the bedroom door softly, she padded over to Sean and tried to gently shake him awake. "Sean, you have to wake up. Sean." She tried again a little harder, but his arm was a cold stone statue under her touch. "Aw, for chrissakes." She straddled him and slapped him like the palm of her hand was made of steel. Steel that stung like the dickens when it met his skin.

"Ahh!" he yelled, just before his hands wrapped around her throat.

The blue of his eyes exposed the devil in him. Open and empty, they were the windows to a soul that hadn't awakened with the rest of his body.

She gasped and tried to pry his iron grip from her neck. "It's me," she rasped. "It's Vanessa. Sean, come back to me."

The change was slow, subtle. The hardened planes of his face softened to that of a fallen angel once again. His muscles lost their tension, and his hands left their purpose. "Vanessa?"

"I'm here," she gasped, clutching her neck like it would put her strangled esophagus back together.

Instead of scrambling away from her, he pulled her into his bare chest and clung to her like a life raft. "I'm sorry," he whispered. "I'm so sorry."

"Shhh," she cooed, rubbing the smooth, taut skin across his back. "It was just a dream. It's over."

"Adrianna! She gets scared when I do this. Adrianna!"

"I've got her. She's cuddled up in the living room."

"Daddy?" The little girl poked her head through the doorway. Her dark eyes were rimmed with tears that threatened to spill over at any moment.

Well, this was awkward. Sean didn't seem to remember she was straddled across him like a lover and clutching him in an intimate embrace. Nor did he seem the least bit embarrassed that his daughter saw him in such a compromising position. For all she knew though, Sean had a lady over to the house every night. Maybe Adrianna saw this kind of behavior all the time. Why did that make her want to storm out of the house?

"Come here," he said, and the little girl scampered across the wooden floor boards and hopped onto the bed.

Vanessa slid off and made her escape to the side of the mattress nearest the wall as Sean gathered his daughter up into his arms. "Were you scared?" he asked.

"Mmhmm," Adrianna said with wide, chocolate brown eyes. "I couldn't wake you up and then Vanessa came and said she was going to fix you."

"She did. I feel all better now, okay? You want to go get the pastries Mel made you out of the pantry?"

A tremulous smile dotted her mouth, and she slid from the bed and disappeared into the other room. Sean rubbed rough hands through his hair over and over like it was a gesture done more out of self-deprecation than of habit. His eyes stayed on the window and beyond with a faraway look.

"She was out by the woodpile when I found her. How often does this happen?"

His throat worked as he swallowed, and he looked down at his hands which were clenched across his knees. "Probably a dozen times in the past year. Here," he said, pulling his dark blue comforter up and across her lap. "You're shaking."

Somehow this felt more intimate than if they'd just slept together. Sitting on his bed together, sharing the comforter, and so close she could reach out and trace the strong lines of his shoulders. It was the most affectionate moment she'd ever been a part of, and they weren't even touching.

"Have you told anyone about the dream?"

Awake and fully functioning, Sean was a stunning man. Half asleep, mostly dazed and in the vulnerable state before day readiness, Sean was devastating to the defensive walls she'd been building so high.

"No."

"Maybe you should."

"I don't want to talk about it," he said, rocking himself out of bed and padding to the washbasin that decorated the back wall of his room. He busied himself with menial things while she watched him with confusion. He brushed his teeth and washed his face. He took a year to dry it before he faced her again. "It won't help anything."

"It's poison, just like you told me when I spoke of Jerry. You've kept it in, and it keeps trying to leak out of you when you are defenseless and asleep. You're giving the dreams power by hiding them, not the other way around."

"Oh yeah? Are you an expert on dreams?"

His hard tone stung in ways she'd never admit to him. The man wielded more power than he knew and it felt imperative he never discover it. Quietly, she said, "I have experience with this kind of dream is all."

His crossed arms fell limply to his side, and his frown eased. "Damn it, Vanessa, I'm sorry. I didn't know."

Clad in only a pair of loose, cotton sweatpants, he leaned back against the washbasin and had her mouth feeling drier than a mason jar of desert sand. It was hard to stay angry with him when her eyeballs stayed so chronically happy with the vision of his body. His chest was toned, and his nipples had pulled taut against the cold morning air. His stomach was flat and ridged with the type of muscle she'd seen in an anatomy book once. Two strips of muscle wrapped around his slim hips and delved beneath his low-slung pajamas in the most tantalizing way.

Holy crap. She was staring at his crotch, and Sean's obnoxious grin was growing wider by the milli-moment.

Clearing her throat, she said, "Can you put your damned shirt on? And some real pants, if you please?"

"You don't like what you see?" he asked a little too innocently.

Of course she liked what she saw! He was a freaking Ken doll come to life but with all the working man-parts and better hair. "Fine. Do as you like." She tried to escape the tangle of his covers and failed, and when finally she flopped from his bed, to straighten her shirt in a very dignified way, she said, "Have a good day." Then she gave a tiny salute and marched for the door.

"Aria," he said.

Seriously? "First you call me Laney, now Aria?"

"No, the dream. It's about my late wife, Aria."

"Oh." She looked around awkwardly, unsure.

He folded onto the bed, and the wooden frame groaned underneath him. Patting the spot beside him, he pleaded with the sadness in his eyes.

"I'm afraid if I tell you, you'll run for the hills and never look back."

She snorted. "Now that's just stupid. We live on a hill, and besides, I've come to the conclusion we should be friends. And friends tell other friends about dreams no matter how weird or perverted or whatever. I read it in a magazine once. The article even included a test to use at a slumber party about which type of boy you'll end up with. I remember questions three, four, and seven if you want to know."

"You want to be friends?"

"Unless you don't. In that case, fine, my friend card is full enough."

"No, no, no. I do. We can be friends."

"Why are you smiling like that?"

"Like what?"

"Like you just won the lottery but aren't announcing it to moochy acquaintances and family yet."

He arched an eyebrow. "Do you want to hear the weird, but definitely not perverted dream, or not?"

She sighed and threw herself backward until she was comfortable on the mattress and staring at the wooden posts of the ceiling. "Paint me a picture."

"I have to preface the dream by saying everything in it actually happened, and it's more like a memory that won't leave me alone. Last year, when I lost my colony, we had to escape in the night, and we ended up on this old gas station roof. My wife followed us there."

"Wait, you left your wife in the colony?"

"No, Aria was turned almost three years before, right after Adrianna was born. We got in this stupid fight, and she left — anyway. Every day she'd come to visit the Denver colony gates, the one I was working on when she'd died, so I thought there was something left in her mind. She remembered me, you know? So when she followed us to the gas station, I thought she didn't want to be away from me, from our daughter. But Laney, she told me she wasn't following us for sentimental reasons. She was hunting us. That she was attuned to my smell, like other Deads were to their family and friends and old homes. And Laney held a gun up and asked to shoot her, and the biggest part of me just wished she would. Wished she'd just put us both out of our misery, but I just couldn't let it end that way. I wasn't strong enough."

Vanessa sat up on her elbows as his voice grew thick with emotion.

"So I asked Laney to use her blood to bring my wife back before I killed her so I could say good-bye."

"Wait, what do you mean about the blood? Laney has powers?"

"No, not magical powers. It's chemistry. Whatever makes her immune improved her sense of smell to be aware of Deads, and when they bite her, they die their final death. And when they taste her blood, their mind comes back, like that little piece of her kills the infection in their brain and gives them human thoughts again. I'd seen her do it to her brother the night before, and even though I saw how that ripped her up to see him like that, I asked her to do it again for me anyway." He turned his head and gave her the saddest look. "Who's the real monster now?"

"Sean—"

"It's okay. I know my faults, and I'm working on them. So, I bullied her into doing it. I was there, restraining Aria as her groans of hunger gave way to groans of pain. Her body was three years decayed, and I'd pushed to put her mind back into a corpse. When she came to, she was so frightened and kept looking around like she couldn't understand what was happening, even after I'd explained. She kept saying how badly it hurt, and she begged me to kill her. It was an instantaneous regret. I should've put her down years ago, and I'd let her exist in this horrible life. She asked if she'd eaten people, and I couldn't bring myself to lie. I just sat there, beside the shell of my wife, wondering why I hadn't been able to love her enough to do the right thing. I told her about Adrianna and how special she is, but I don't think she could hear me anymore." Sean drew his knee up to his chest and dangled his other leg over the edge of the bed. His back was to her and his shoulders lifted with a long sigh. "When I put the gun to her temple, she whispered, 'Move on from this, Sean. Live.' And then I pulled the trigger."

She sat up and brushed his arms with hers. She was so close, his warmth radiated through her sweater. "Is that all in the dream?"

"No. The dream is just the conversation. Sometimes it's the real one, word for word, and sometimes it's one I've made up where she says the most awful things."

"Like what?"

"Like I'm a terrible father. I was a terrible husband. I don't deserve anyone to protect. She wished she'd never laid eyes on me. On and on and on it goes, and I can't escape it. And then the shot echoes through my bones and the dream is over."

"Sean," she said as she placed her hands on either side of his face and let him see the seriousness in her eyes. "You are a wonderful father. You deserve someone to protect, and Aria loved you. You gave her a life even after the outbreak, and I know she never regretted that. And you probably didn't suck as a husband."

A grin cracked his face. "Probably didn't, huh?"

"Well I'm an honest kind of soul, and I've never seen you as a husband to anyone, so I can't say for sure."

His eyes dropped to her lips, and the smile faded from his face, only to linger on the edges as he leaned in. Powerless under the hand that slid around her waist and gripped her shirt, she waited, frozen and panicked until the moment his lips touched hers.

Okay, it was just a kiss. She'd kissed a dozen people, and some of them she hadn't even liked. None of them were like this though. Sean's mouth moved against hers, gently asking for more from her, and when he pulled her closer and closed the space on the bed between them, a little helpless sound escaped her throat. He pulled her hand until it rested on his neck and then reached to cup the back of her head. The pad of his thumb made tiny trails of fire as it rubbed a path down her cheek, and her body responded by matching that heat in her middle.

It wasn't until his tongue brushed the inside of her lips that she lost it. She opened for him, begging for more, and she squeezed her eyes shut tightly as she rode the wave of being wanted by a man. How could anything in this messed up world feel so good?

"Daddy! I can't reach the cups!" Aria called from the other room.

Vanessa jumped like she'd been shot and flipped over the side of the bed in an escape attempt. Sean sat with his arms still held out toward her, and his laughter filled the small room when she peeked her head over the edge of the mattress.

"I don't think she saw you," he said in a teasing tone.

She stumbled up and brushed off her jeans. "Well, that's because I was so lightning fast."

The smile on his face was breathtaking. "Come here," he said, holding his hand out.

"'Coming here' is definitely a bad idea," she hissed. "We are in the friend-zone, remember?"

"Scout's honor, I won't kiss you." Standing, he pulled her into his chest and hugged her. Into her ear, he said, "Thank you for listening to my dream. I feel better than I thought I would. It's nice to share that burden with someone else for a change."

She wrapped her arms around the strength of his back and absorbed the blanket of complete safety she hadn't known since the outbreak. Until this moment, she hadn't known such a feeling had existed in the world anymore.

"Stay for breakfast with me and Adrianna."

"Is that something friends do?"

"I don't want to hear any more of this friends crap. No more rules to our friendship. We'll make our own from here on out, okay?"

Some niggling voice in her head wanted her to fight, but she couldn't quite remember the reasoning behind that small instinct to flee. Not when Sean was holding her so close and sharing his warmth with her in such a delicious way. "Okay, but the second you call me Laney again, our friendship is terminated, murdered, kaput—"

"I won't."

"I made breakfast!" Adrianna announced from the doorway.

This time Vanessa didn't jerk away like she'd been caught snogging a forbidden eighth-grade crush under the bleachers. Instead she smiled at Adrianna and asked if she could stay and eat with them, to which the little girl adamantly agreed.

Chapter Sixteen

That morning had started as the worst ever, thanks to the dream, but as Sean sat there laughing at the breakfast table with Vanessa and Adrianna, something had shifted in his soul. He could be good for a woman as long as he kept making strides to improve what he knew needed work. And Vanessa was strong. Much too strong to allow him to bowl her over. No less woman would be able to handle him.

Her long, blond hair was down and shone in the morning sunlight that drifted through the kitchen window. Her full lips parted often in a ready smile, and the warmth in the blue-green depths of her eyes had his body physically responding nearly every time she graced him with a glance. He'd been wrong to compare her to Laney. They only thing they had in common was their strength of character. He'd been a fool to miss it. She had a smart mouth that bordered on crass, and she terrified him with talk of going on more supply runs, but she'd help him grow where Aria hadn't been able to. He hadn't been ready then, but now? Vanessa made him want to be a better man for her.

She was a guard now, and as much as it scared him that she'd be in more danger than the average civilian, he'd seen her in action. She was deadly, ruthless, and capable. He'd have to learn to let go of his protective instincts so she could be happy with her career. With her life. With him.

"So, were you just passing through, or did you hear me screaming all the way from your cabin down the mountain?" he asked as he pinched another piece of flaky pastry off and took a bite.

"Oh, I forgot. I actually came here for a reason." Her cheeks turned the most attractive shade of pink as she blushed. "You totally don't have to go, and I would understand if you have plans already, it's just—well."

What had flustered her so much? She never hesitated in what she said. Granted it was usually insults she flung into the world, but the people on the receiving end of those usually deserved it, more or less. "What is it?"

"I wanted to invite you and Adrianna to the ceremony." The words tumbled from her mouth like a boulder down a mountain.

Inhaling slowly so he wouldn't yell his answer right away and scare her off, he smiled. "Ade, do you want to go to Vanessa's graduation today, and then eat dinner with her?"

"Uh huh," his daughter said with a big head nod and solemn, slow-blinking eyes.

"We accept."

"You do?" Vanessa asked. "I mean, you do. Good."

Static crackled over the radio, and he frowned at the thing flung carelessly onto the hand carved coffee table in the living room. "Hang on. Let me see what's going on."

"—ean?—an? Sean?" Mel asked. Her voice was laced with panic or fear, or maybe both. Never since he'd known her had she ever sounded scared.

Button jammed, he said, "Mel, I'm here. What's wrong?"

"—aney." *Crackle, crackle crackle.*

"Mel, I can't hear you. Press the button hard and slow down."

"Laney's had the baby."

"What? It's way too early."

"Sean, are you around your weapons?"

"I'm still at home, so yeah."

"Bring them. Bring them all to Dr. Mackey's, and get there now."

Vanessa had gathered Adrianna into her arms and said, "I'll take care of her."

"Are you sure?"

"Yes! Just go!"

He bolted for his closet and threw it open. Behind a hidden panel was a small armory. Two handguns in holsters and an AK slung over his shoulder and he was running for the door. "I'll be back as soon as I can," he called as he flew down the porch stairs. What could have Mel so worried that she'd asked him to come weaponized inside the colony gates? The baby wouldn't have survived at seven months gestation. It wasn't like the old days where there were equipped Neonatal Intensive Care Units just waiting for a baby to save. Times were different now. Only the strongest under the best circumstances survived.

He pushed himself harder, faster down the trail until his feet barely touched the ground. The angry wind whipped his face as he raced it, as if it were telling him to go back home, back to Vanessa's easy smile, where it was warm.

Dr. Mackey's office came into view much sooner than it should have. Hordes of people were gathered around the small log building, and their angry voices carried up the mountain. Shoving his way through the throngs, weaving in and out of the maze of angry bodies, he bullied his way until he reached the porch. "Hey. Hey!" he yelled before putting two fingers in his mouth and blowing an ear piercing whistle. "What's going on?"

"The baby is a monstrosity!" cried a woman. "It cannot be allowed to live."

"It's all right!" a man yelled. "Sean's here. He'll take care of it in a minute flat, and nobody'll have to worry about it anymore."

What the hell was going on? "I want everyone settled down while we figure out what is happening, okay? I promise we'll fix whatever is amiss. Please, just stay out here while I check on what's going on in there."

When he opened the cabin door, he came face to face with the barrel of a gun. Mitchell's gun. "Sean, I know you, and you're good people. You have this sense of honor, and a need to protect your people, but you don't have to protect them from us."

Sean shoved the gun away from his face and dodged around Mitchell's stiff figure to the room where Laney lay exhausted and pale. "You okay?"

She gasped a sob. "Sean, they're going to kill us."

"No one is going to kill you. I won't let them." He sunk onto the edge of the bed and squeezed her hand. Her cheeks were pale and splotched from crying, and her lips trembled as her eyes filled. "Did the baby live?"

"Mmhmm, but something's different about her. Dr. Mackey wants to run tests on her to see the extent of the problem, but Davey Cummings came in here to get his hand stitched up and saw the baby when Doc was bathing her, and he told everyone in the whole colony."

None of what she was saying made any sense at all. Carefully, he pulled the blanket aside from the bundle she held. He kept his face completely still and emotionless as he looked at the little creature.

Laney hadn't had a baby. She'd had a Dead.

The child's skin was so pale it was translucent, and a network of veins could be seen under her skin. Her nose and lips favored Laney, but her eyes favored no human. They were so light blue they were almost white. Her pupils dilated strangely when she looked at him, like she was much more developed cognitively than a normal infant. And her hair? She had a full head of platinum blond, silken tresses atop her tiny head, colorless to match her eyes. The child was striking and beautiful in an otherworldly kind of way, but she was part Dead, and no one could deny that.

"Doc, how'd this happen?" he asked the solemn man in the corner of the room.

Dr. Mackey adjusted his baseball cap and pushed his glasses further up his nose. "The best guess I have is that Laney's immunity passed to the child. But she still has the virus in her blood. It's been there all along, and when the baby was developing, a war was going on in there between the immunity and the virus. Both won, I think. She's a hybrid. Likely the first and only of her kind."

"Can she spread the disease?" Sean asked, pulling the blanket back to her chin again.

"Don't know. We'd have to do extensive tests to answer any of these questions, and those tests take time. The crowd outside won't give us that time. They see the child as a Dead inside the colony gates."

"Laney, has she eaten yet?"

She nodded, on the verge of tears.

"Tell me, what does she eat?"

"Milk. She nurses. Hasn't spit up even once, not even when we burped her. The milk satisfies her. Sean," she pleaded, grasping his sleeve. "I love her. She's our child, and they'll have to get through me to get her."

"Me too," Mitchell said with such an eerie calm, his words couldn't be anything but truth. "She's not some monster. She's our daughter, just a baby with a birthday and a name."

"What's her name?" Sean asked.

"Soren. Soren Mitchell," Laney said with a proud smile.

"It's beautiful. Perfectly suited to her."

"Sean," Laney said. "Think if Adrianna had been born this way. What mountains you would've moved to save her. Soren deserves to live. She's human, too."

He knew exactly what he would've done if anyone had come after his baby for any reason. He'd have burned them all and spat on their smoldering ashes. The child had to be given a chance at life—a chance at proving the human side of her was in control.

"I need to talk to the masses before they light this place up with us all in it. Mitchell, it's probably best if you're there too." He squeezed Laney's trembling hand once more. "We won't let them past the door. You and Soren are safe."

Waiting around wasn't going to work for Vanessa. It wasn't her style and probably never would be. With a firm tug of Adrianna's jacket zipper, she steered the girl toward the door and shut it behind them.

"I brought an apple to share," Adrianna announced, holding out the red, and slightly bruised, delicious offering in her mittened hands.

Oh, it had been so long since she'd bitten into the sweet skin of an apple. "Where did you get it?"

"Daddy helps people in the colony, and they give him treats to pay him. Mr. Forester gave him three shiny apples for helping him rebuild his cabin when a tree branch fell on it. I've been saving this last one."

"Tell you what, how about you eat as much as your little belly wants, and I'll eat what you can't finish? And I'll carry you down the trail so you can eat it on the way, and I don't have to worry about you choking. Sound good?"

"Can you do it piggy-back style?"

"Sure. Hop on." She bent down and loaded Adrianna up like a pack mule carrying a squirmy pile of boulders.

Adrianna was light for her age. She remembered when Nelson was this age, and he'd been a solid young boy, with the benefit of all the food he could want. Were all children destined to be petite from here on?

The child munched happily on her treat as Vanessa hauled her down the hill toward the medical cabin.

"Whoa," she murmured as the growing number of seemingly angry residents were piling around the porch and vying for the best view.

"What's going on?" she asked the first person who wasn't busy grumbling or yelling their complaints. Martha Baynard chewed on her lip with a worried set to her delicate eyebrows.

"They're going to kill a baby. And everyone's so riled up no one will listen to reason."

"What?" Her stomach dropped to the floor, and she set Adrianna down to pull her in close.

"Shh," Martha said, pointing to the opening door of the medical office.

Sean stepped out, followed by Mitchell.

Both men looked somber, but it was Mitchell who held her attention. His dark hair had never been out of place, but there in the morning light, he looked downright disheveled. The grim set of his mouth was completely at odds with his chronically happy demeanor. Oh, this was bad.

"Listen up," Sean barked. "The child is as you say, but more than that, she's human too. Her name is Soren, and she takes milk from the breast, not blood or steak — milk, like any other babe. She hasn't been sick on it even once."

"She's an abomination!" yelled a man, seconded by another.

"She's a product of Laney's immunity, that's all. Developmentally, she looks just like any other infant."

"That's a lie!" yelled Davey Cummings. "I saw the little devil with my own eyes. She looks just like a Dead!"

"No she doesn't!" barked Mitchell. "Her coloring is pale, and her eyes are lightened, but her skin is warm and alive. She's human!"

"Dead!" screamed a red-faced Davey. "You know the rules well as everyone else. No Deads in colony gates, no exceptions. That monster has to be put down before she bites someone and compromises the whole damned place. She'll be the death of every last one of us!"

A chant of agreement was flung into the surrounding forest by the members of the mob, and the lot of them surged forward.

"If you don't have the guts to protect us, we'll do it ourselves," yelled a man in the thick of it.

Sean and Mitchell fought viciously as the door was besieged. The look on Sean's face was captivating and dangerous enough to send a chill down her spine. He was going to die for Laney and her baby. Blow after blow was swung, and though Sean and Mitchell didn't fall, their faces were cut and running rivers of blood.

She understood why they hadn't drawn their weapons. The mob wasn't the enemy, after all. They were frightened and trying to protect themselves as best they knew. Firing shots into a crowd wouldn't sit well with their ethics.

It sat just fine with hers though.

She took a bite of the apple core Adrianna had handed her and pointed her Glock at a cloud above them. And then she shot it.

The crowd hunched and searched for the danger in panic. Some of the fighters on the edges ran for the woods, and she yelled, "Oy!" around a bite of apple. Dragging Adrianna behind, she waved the handgun limply and chewed the fruit as she ascended onto the porch. "'Scuse me, crazy lady with a gun coming through," she muttered to the masses separating like the Red Sea for her.

Sean shoved a man off him and stared at her like she'd just walked through a wall.

"Adrianna, you go on inside with Ms. Laney," she said. "I'll be in there shortly." Sean's way wasn't working, and she needed to jar the mob into listening to reason. She turned. "Okay, people," she addressed the crowd before turning a glare on a man still clutching onto the front of Sean's shirt. She lowered the gun into the general vicinity of his eyeball and said, "Let him go, and get off my porch before you spend the last thirty seconds of your life fighting to be a baby-killer. I'm pretty sure they have a special room in hell for that caliber of sin, mister." As he scampered from the deck she raised her voice. "Or have you all convinced yourself that you wouldn't actually be killing a defenseless baby because of what she looks like? You heard Sean — she drinks milk. Milk! When was the last time you saw a Dead chugging a gallon of two-percent? Hmm? Now, I've listened to both sides of this, and here's how this is going to go. Dr. Mackey wants to do tests on the baby. Let him! Give him time to see if she's even dangerous. Put Laney and her baby in quarantine until then. Brandon —" she gestured to Dr. Mackey's assistant, who leaned against a tree behind the mob "— can you set up a first-aid tent by the mess hall?"

He nodded. "I will."

"Good. If anyone gets a splinter or has a bad case of blue balls or toe jam problems or whatever, go to him over there. Don't come here for the next few days until we've had time to make an educated decision on the fate of the baby."

"Soren," Sean said.

"The fate of Soren," Vanessa corrected. "Because if Dr. Mackey does an autopsy on a little baby you've killed out of irrational fear and finds out she wasn't ever a threat to you, you're all going to have to live with that for the rest of your lives. Now, from where I'm standing, I think you've forgotten the reason you have that little vaccine you are all so proud of. Laney Landry is the source of that. Maybe you don't understand the sacrifices the woman made to get to Dr. Mackey and the toll all of the tests and samples took on her body, but I saw it with my own eyes. The woman is scarred for you. She almost died for *you*. So that you can live. So that your children can live. That child is the product of her immunity. You can't put Laney up on a throne, while at the same time condemning her for a condition that is of direct benefit to you. Don't you think you owe her three days at least to hold her baby before the final decision is made?"

The hum of the murmuring crowd filled the clearing.

"Two days," a man countered.

The mob seemed to agree so Vanessa pounced. "Fine, two days of sanctuary for Laney and Soren. We'll give the decision here, same time, day after tomorrow. Now get back to your jobs. Everything can't just come to a screeching halt around here. We have winter to prepare for, or we're all doomed anyway.

"Sean," she murmured as the crowd slowly scattered. "You still control the guards. Call them in, and give the order to protect this place until the two days are up. No way that worked on everyone. You'll have yahoos out here in the dark on a kill mission, and you can't afford to keep this little protection on them."

Sean shot her a grateful look and paced to the end of the deck to talk into his radio. Mitchell stood wide-eyed and staring. "Thanks for doing that," he breathed.

The apple crunched against her teeth and she gave a full mouth smile. "No problem. I've been looking for an excuse to pop off a round inside colony gates."

"Do you want to see Soren?"

Did she want to see the baby Mitchell had with another woman? Not particularly, but if they were ever going to be on friendly terms, she had to play nice. "Sure."

Sean and Mitchell stayed rooted on the front porch as she opened the heavy wooden door. Laney stood shaking with a handgun in her limp hand, and a baby cradled in the other.

"I thought they were coming in," she said in a trembling voice.

"Nope, just me. Where's Adrianna?"

"I told her to stay in the back room in case they made it past Mitchell and Sean. They'd probably stop after they killed me and the baby." Laney swayed dangerously.

"C'mon. You're one tough chick, yes, but you just had a baby and shouldn't be out of bed."

"I don't feel so well. Will you hold Soren?" Her speech was slurred, and Vanessa snatched the baby before Laney went down. "Doc!"

Dr. Mackey rushed from the back room and helped her to the bed. Vanessa peeked her head around the corner, and Adrianna was sitting on Steven's bed. She didn't miss the gun he held ready over the edge of the pillow. The mob scene outside could've gone very differently, and an ache swelled inside of her when she imagined all she could've lost. "Adrianna, let's go visit Ms. Laney."

She held her hand out and led the child to the other room before settling her in the chair in the corner. When she was comfortable in her own chair beside Laney's bed, only then did she pull the baby blanket away from Soren's face.

"Oh my gosh," she breathed. Soren was definitely part Dead at least. No child on earth looked like her. Even through all of the abnormalities though, she was shaped like a baby and made little hungry sounds like a baby. "She's beautiful," Vanessa breathed, placing her finger in the infant's tiny reaching palm.

Laney sniffled and it looked like the waterworks were on their way.

"Oh crap, Laney, I don't do well with sobbing. What's wrong?"

"I heard what you said out there, and it meant more to me than you'll ever know that you stood up to all those people on my behalf. I know things didn't start off good with us, but I really hope that someday I can repay you for what you've done for my family."

"Well, don't thank me yet, you crybaby. I only bought you two days."

Laney laugh-sobbed. "Still. It's two days more than I thought we had when she came out looking like she did."

Two days. Dr. Mackey had two days to prove Soren wouldn't jam the entire colony onto the extinction list.

Two days and the mob would come for her.

Chapter Seventeen

The woods chirped with the sound of small bugs singing from the safety of their tree bark homes. The night was cold, and Sean flipped up the collar of his jacket to protect his ears and shoved his hands in his pockets. Leaning against a support beam of the medical cabin porch, he nodded a silent greeting to Guist, who carried a rifle stiffly hugged to his chest.

"All clear and quiet," he said in a gruff voice. "Finn said he's going to stay in the back to make sure we don't miss anyone sneaking in."

"Good."

Guist climbed the stairs two at a time and stood beside him. "How do you think this is going to play out?"

The sinking feeling in Sean's gut that had rooted itself there since he saw Soren said nothing good would come of the situation. The two days was just a stall on the inevitable. Even if Dr. Mackey gave the all-clear to Soren, no one in the colony would accept a Dead infant. She'd always be in danger. "Not good," he admitted.

Leather boots that protected Guist's feet creaked as he shifted his weight. "I know you're working on a plan, boss man. You know as well as I, we can't just let them take the baby. That little girl is already part of our family."

"I know, but everything I've got so far only holds off the inevitable. We need something that'll keep her safe long-term."

A twig snapped in the dark, and he lifted his handgun.

"Don't shoot," Mel said from the shadows. "It's just me."

Sean lowered his weapon, and Guist followed suit.

"I brought food," she said as she entered the lantern light. When she had climbed up the stairs, she smiled. "And a plan."

Thank goodness someone had come up with something. His plans all ended with them eventually getting dismembered by the mob.

After she'd disappeared inside with a large canvas sack of what smelled like scalloped potatoes and ham, she returned with a tin cup of the hearty meal for both him and Guist and settled into a rocking chair.

"What's this plan of yours?" Sean asked, blowing on the steaming cup.

"Go home."

He looked at her long and hard. "I hardly think my little cabin is going to keep her safe, Mel."

"Not here, *home*. Go home. Go back to your colony, and take them with you. Rebuild your colony, but do it around the child."

He scoffed and waited for her to say she was joking. When she didn't, he said, "You know that place is overrun by Deads, don't you? Clearing them out would take an army."

"Not an army. You, Finn, Guist, and Mitchell are the best fighters I've ever seen. You as a team? You're unstoppable. Take back the Denver colony, Sean. Provide a home for Laney and Soren, and take back your destiny while you're at it."

"As easy as that?"

"No, not as easy as that. It'll be hard. Like in the old days when you were first building, but you'll have your colony back. You were meant for more than head guard, Sean. You ran that colony perfectly. You are meant to have people under you, not just to play my second."

"Obviously I didn't run it perfectly. There was a take-over, and it was about as hostile as it gets. I lost an entire colony of families, kids. And you want me to rebuild? You've lost your mind, woman."

"Sean," Guist said quietly. "If it keeps Laney and Soren safe, we have to consider it."

"We? It would be me and a new mother and Mitchell to clean out hundreds of Deads. The odds for survival for any of us are zero. The baby dies anyway."

"You wouldn't be alone. I'd go too."

"And me," Finn said from the corner of the house.

"Yeah, and what about Eloise? Huh? She's a month away from giving birth, Guist. You can't just up and leave your pregnant wife here alone."

Guist stood quiet, and Sean rubbed his hands through his hair until the friction of it warmed his scalp. "That plan doesn't work out the way we want, Mel. We'll have to come up with something else."

Mel continued as if he hadn't just nixed the idea. "I can give you an RV loaded with supplies. It's all I can part with going into the winter. I wish I could load the Terminator for all you've done for this colony, Sean, but the people here come first. They always do, and we won't have enough."

"Okay, and what happens when Erhard and his army of moral-less soldiers don't want us to take back the Denver colony?"

"You know as well as I there's no human life there. We've sent scouts three times, and there was no sign of anyone living. Just Deads."

Was he the only voice of reason in this? Sure, he was a good soldier, a good fighter, good under pressure — he wasn't invincible though, and the odds of them making it through this plan still human were terrible. "Finn, those gates are filled with Deads we know, man. All of them walking around in there? They were turned that night we ran. Your brother is in there somewhere. Your friends. You seriously want to go back and see them like that?"

"Yeah! If it means I get to keep the family I've made here safe, then yeah, I'd go see them like that."

"You guys are really serious about this?"

"Yes," Guist, Mel, and Finn said in unison.

He propped his palms on his hips and gave a short, humorless laugh into the dark woods. He shook his head at the sheer stupidity of the idea and leveled Finn's serious gaze with one of his own.

Well, hell.

He was going back to Denver.

Vanessa wrapped her arms more tightly around herself and huddled under the covers a little deeper. The night was cold, and the chill bit through the cabin walls. Even the fire in the small, old-fashioned wood burning stove couldn't keep the place warm enough. Or maybe the chill had just settled into her bones with the sadness.

She didn't hate Laney anymore or even dislike her. Now, she just mourned Sean's heart belonging to her. She'd seen the ferocity on his face as he prepared to fight to the death to protect her and the child. Would he have done the same thing for her if she were the one laid up in the hospital bed? She didn't think so. The history simply wasn't there for them. He liked her as a soothing balm to the ache of Laney choosing another, but not much more than that. She traced the pattern of the wood grain on the wall with the tip of her fingernail. A pity because her heart had already decided to love him.

A soft knock thumped against her door, and she sat up with a frown. "Who is it?"

"It's Sean. Can I come in?"

Perfect, she was busted mooning over him and definitely wearing an oversized green thermal shirt she only saved for the times she needed comfort. She couldn't paint a less sexy picture if she tried for a hundred years.

Defeated, she called, "Yeah. Come on in."

The door opened, and a burst of frigid wind accompanied Sean. He closed it and sat beside her on the bed without so much as an invitation to invade her space.

"Why aren't you protecting Laney?" she asked.

"I am. Vanessa." He grabbed her hands, and his were ice against her skin. His blue eyes penetrated her down to her very soul. "We're taking Laney in the night."

How those words caused such pain to rip through her. Of course he was. It was the only logical thing to do. The child wouldn't survive life in a colony of trigger-happy Dead-haters. "Where?" she asked, trying to keep the heartbreak from her voice.

"We're going to take back the Denver colony and start fresh there. We'll have to find people who are okay with Soren to settle the place."

She swallowed the slashing pain that tore at her heart. "When will you leave?"

"Three hours."

His gaze held hers like a lover's touch. "Vanessa," he whispered. "I want you to come with us."

She floundered under the overwhelming panic at the thought of leaving her home. Of leaving Nelson. Of moving to a place with a man in love with another woman.

"Think of what you're asking me right now."

"I am." His eyebrows furrowed over his glorious cerulean eyes. "We'll be starting completely from scratch, and we'll need someone who knows about gardens."

She cocked her head and narrowed her eyes. "Really? You want me to come so I can run your gardens? No thank you. I like guard duty just fine. And furthermore, hell no, I'm not shacking up in a Dead-infested colony with a kiss-buddy and the woman he loves. That sounds a little too much like the second ring of hell to me, Daniels."

"I'm not asking you for the gardens. I just thought if I gave you enough excuses to come…Damn it, Vanessa, I care about you. I want you at my back, and guard, gardener, or splinter extractor, I don't care so long as you're with me. I don't want to do this, but the thought of doing this without you?" His shook his head. "I can't stand it. I don't love Laney." Through a clenched jaw, he gritted, "You fill my head and make me crazy when I'm not around you because I want to fight tooth and nail for an excuse to see you again. You have to let your feelings about Laney go. I have. I can't promise I'll be perfect or even good at being yours, but I can promise I'll try until my last breath. Adrianna is the blood running through my veins, and you're my heart. There isn't any room for another."

"But, Sean, I just watched you risk your life for Laney this morning!"

"Because she's family! You're more than that. I want you there when I have the nightmares. I want it to be you who comforts Adrianna when I can't. I want it to be you who sees the darkest parts of me that I've kept hidden from everyone else. You scare me in the best possible way."

Oh dear goodness, a man had just professed his desire, and she was the one on the receiving end for the first time in her life. And not just any man either. Sean-Sexy-Face-Daniels, the man women rocketed themselves at for just the chance to be in his bed. If they knew how amazing he really was beneath that demigod face, they'd never give her a chance to win him over. He'd kept it all hidden under that serious façade and the bark of command. He was baring his soul for only her to see, and something about that revelation made her delirious with an unfamiliar warmth.

"Say yes," he said with a slow smile that danced into his eyes. The flames of the stove shimmered and echoed in his brilliant gaze. There it was, that beautiful soul. Slowly he pulled her by the back of the knees until he was encompassed by them. Inch by inch, he leaned into her. "Say yes," he whispered against her neck. "I need you by my side. We work best together, and you know it. I need you on my team. I need you in my family. I need you, Vanessa. Just say yes." His strong hands snaked around her waist, and he rubbed the bare skin just under the hem of her shirt.

Her breath came in needy pants, and she clutched the front of his shirt in desperation not to lose the warmth of the safety he brought. His lips brushed her skin, and she closed her eyes to the world. It was only her and Sean in the glow of the flames.

Desperately, she clawed at the bottom of his shirt and tugged it upward. His chuckle was deep and touched places inside of her she hadn't known existed until this moment. She breathed for the sound of his contentment and it rumbled deep in his throat as she grazed her teeth against his neck and trailed tiny kisses to his lips.

He took his time, unrushed by the coming deadline or his duties outside of the room. He pulled the oversized sweater from her, and his hungry gaze dipped to her breasts. Gently kneading one, he lowered his lips to the other and lapped at her skin until she arched against him. His fingers pulled her panties until her legs were free of them. She lay in front of him, unclothed and vulnerable, and the most heartbreaking smile crooked his lips as he drank her in. She sat up and ran her palms down the hard planes of his chest and stomach, and then tugged at his jeans until they joined her clothes on the floor. His gaze never left hers.

"You're so beautiful," he whispered, and suddenly the cold was banished from the room. Sean was simply too consuming and too warm.

She lay back against the soft mattress, and he followed as if he couldn't help himself. Nudging her knees apart, he kissed her, sipping at the seam of her lips until she rocked her waist toward his in a silent request. With her hands on his lower back, she could feel the muscles in his hips flex as he slid into her. With a gasp at the intense pleasure, she bowed against him, and he eased back and pressed into her again. His languid pace increased until she shattered around him as he whispered her name with his own release. He cupped her head and kissed her in the tenderest way a man ever had as she pulsed around him. Her skin melted into his like fired iron that never wanted to let go, and their souls threaded together until all that remained was a blinding light where the darkness had been.

Time drifted by as she lay there, connected to him and wishing she could be this close to him always. Under his adoring gaze, she was happy to just be. When he finally pulled out of her, a tiny pain jutted through her chest at the loss of their skin touching, but he softened the ache by pulling her in close to his side, and kissing her forehead.

Sated and shaken from the metamorphosis she'd just undergone, Vanessa lay contentedly on his shoulder as he studied the ceiling with a lingering smile. Tracing the outline of his puckered nipple with a light fingernail, she tried to imagine not going with him.

She'd be a guard here at Dead Run River, and she'd be with her brother, who, despite his newfound independence, needed her. Nelson was all she had left from her old life. It had always been the two of them against the world and imagining abandoning him like that wasn't something she could live with.

"Sean," she started, so quiet as not to disturb the peace of the perfect moment.

He sighed. "I know." The words rumbled against her eardrum and cheek. "You have a life here, and I have no right to ask you to leave it." Stroking her hair, he said, "I had to try though."

"Will you ever come back?"

The silence stretched on and on like a great ravine between them. "I don't know."

Chapter Eighteen

Peeling himself away from Dead Run River, from Vanessa, was an impossible task. After the intimacy they'd just shared, all Sean wanted to do was remain in the sanctuary of her arms. A sick, dark wave washed over him every time he thought about pulling the loaded RV out of the front gates. Every mile he put between them would batter his soul like hurricane waves against a rocky shore.

"Daddy, where's Vanessa?" Adrianna asked as he hoisted her into the door of the camper. She clutched her little pink bunny and looked at him with such beseeching brown eyes, he almost couldn't stand it.

"She can't come, baby. She has to stay here with her brother. She has to stay and protect this colony."

Her little bottom lip poked out, and her eyes filled with heart wrenching tears. "I know how you feel, kiddo. We'll get along okay though. And you'll have Laney there—"

"And Eloise," the waddling redhead called from up the trail. "Don't leave without us."

"What are you guys doing here?" he asked in shock.

"I just got my best friend back, so heck no am I hanging around a colony that exiled Laney. Besides, rumor has it you could use my husband's special skills."

Guist shook his hand roughly and helped his wife into the escape vehicle. He carried three backpacks and a duffle bag loaded with supplies. Maybe, just maybe, they'd survive this little adventure after all.

Mitchell sat in the passenger seat with a flashlight, pouring over a map, and Laney sat on a bench seat in the back beside a scrambling Adrianna. The whole gang was there. He scanned the woods for the last time. Well, almost all of them.

The metal of the door handle was cold in his grip.

"Wait!"

He jerked his head at the imagining.

"Wait for me," Vanessa called breathily. Like an angel, she appeared out of the shadows. If angels carried copious amounts of luggage and dragged a pink, four-wheeled suitcase through the woods.

Her fair hair hung in front of her face, and her cheeks were flushed from the exertion of toting the heavy load such a distance, but she was here.

"Vanessa?"

"Yeah I know. It's a lot of luggage, but it's not all for me. Look." She ripped into the suitcase and pulled out a small burlap bag. "Seeds. I snatched them from the storage shed in the gardens. I prepared most of the danged things so I think I'm entitled to some. Dead Run River will have plenty for next spring, even without these."

He wrapped her up in a hug that lifted her from the ground, and she giggled against his neck.

"I couldn't imagine you leaving without me. I talked to Nelson, and he said I can go as long as I come back for him when we are all set up."

He inhaled her feminine sent and buried his face in the space between collar bone and neck. "I promise, if we survive this, we'll come back for him."

"Okay then," she said pulling back to look at him. "I've got your back then. Always."

Kissing her would never get old, but time wasn't on their side. He made quick but thorough work of it and patted her firm little backside as she climbed into the back with the others.

"Whoa," Eloise murmured. "You and Sean?"

"Nah," she said with a wink into the rearview mirror. "I'm just playing with his mind for a little while."

"You can play with my mind as long as you want," he muttered as he pulled the RV onto the road that would lead out of the Dead Run River gates.

The next time he looked back, Finn was sitting in Vanessa's place with a stern look. "Aw crap," he said as Finn strong-armed Vanessa up to the front.

"What is it?" Mitchell asked, twisting in his seat. "Oh man, Finn looks pissed. Escape tactics," he muttered, dodging the angry giant headed their way. "Evasive maneuvers!"

"Thanks for the backup," he sang as Finn plopped Vanessa in between the seats.

"Any time," Mitchell said from the safety of the bench seat in back.

"Once upon a time, a few days ago, we had certain rules set in place that got us home alive."

"Not all of us," Sean argued.

"My point," Finn growled, "is you mess with each other's heads and right when we're headed for a freaking rattlesnake den of Deads." He sighed. "I'm not trying to be a dick, and Vanessa, stop glaring at me like that because I'm actually happy for you guys. But Sean's tactical mind is imperative to this mission. It's why I didn't want you guys going after each other like rabbits until we got back to Dead Run River."

"Finn, what do you want us to do? Just never be happy because of missions? There has to be life in between."

He pointed at Vanessa with an excited arch to his dark brows. "Exactly. Between missions, but right now, we're all in big trouble. We're low on manpower, and half of our team is out of commission or they're children. The odds of survival aren't exactly stacked that high in our favor if you haven't noticed. Vanessa, graduation ceremony or not, you're a guard, and what have I taught you all throughout your training?"

"Keep my head on straight in the thick of it."

"Yep. And do you think you can pay attention one hundred percent of the time while you're making googly eyes at Sean? With your friends' lives in jeopardy?" He lowered his voice and hissed, "With Adrianna's life in jeopardy, do you think you can function without thoughts of Sean tripping you up?"

Vanessa stared at the vents with such a troubled look.

"And, Sean, this mission is heavily on your shoulders. Now, I've never envied you for having to bear the burden of so much, but no one has been given the natural ability or instinct to get your team to safety like you, so it's yours alone. We'll back you up, and do everything we can for our cause, but the big decisions will fall to you. Can you say with certainty you can make the decisions that are best for the team with Vanessa factoring in there? I'm not asking you to hate each other until we're safe. I'm asking you to cool it so Sean can lead us in taking back this colony. Without his full focus, this mission fails, and we walk as Deads by morning."

"He's right," Vanessa breathed. "Sean, I saw it on the supply run. You shoulder us. If you aren't focused, we put the others in danger. We put Adrianna in danger."

Sean pulled the RV to a stop and threw it into park. "Finn, you're a dick. We're past the point where we can turn it off and on, and the same argument could be made for all of us. Guist has Eloise to protect, I have Adrianna, Mitchell has Laney and vice versa on all of us. You're going to have to give us more credit than this. And if I have to hear your pointless lectures all the way to the Denver colony, I'm going to throw you off this bus myself. You're dangerously close to stepping over the line. Have I ever lost my head while on a mission? No? Your point has been made, now lay off." He spun in his seat. "I need a minute."

Pulling Vanessa out the door with him, he strode for the nearest tree that would conceal them and pressed her against it. "Damn it, I can't do this. I just got you, and I don't want to go back to keeping my distance. That cock-blocking Bigfoot has a point, but it's impossible now." He focused on the pattern of the tree bark behind her shoulder as he tried to imagine going back to the way things were. "I can't go back to pretending you're just another teammate."

"Then don't. I know you. You'll make the hard decisions, and you'll be fair. It's what makes you a great leader, Sean. We can focus on the mission, and when we get Denver situated, we'll pick up where we left off. Hey," she said, placing a gentle hand against the side of his unshaven face and dragging his gaze to hers, "I'll wait."

Pressing his forehead against hers he squeezed his eyes tightly shut. "I want you to be the one protecting Adrianna when I can't. The others can help, but I want her under your care."

A look of such tenderness washed over her face. "I'll protect her with my life."

"I know," he said against her lips just before he pulled her to him and drank her in one last time.

He was a professional at being professional, and after this stolen moment, he would put all of himself into leading the team. But for right now, she was warmth and serenity and home.

Lacing her fingers with his, she leaned into him once more as he placed his chin on top of her head and glared at the woods beyond. Nothing in him wanted to retreat from her touch. It felt so damned good after so long depriving himself.

"I like you," she whispered against his chest.

The words filled him with a warmth that started in his torso and spread to his limbs. He knew what she meant—she just wasn't saying it yet. "I like you, too."

A quick honk from Finn elicited a delicately placed middle finger from Vanessa, and they trudged back to the waiting RV with a painful distance between them. He'd better get used to it or make a valiant effort to get them settled as soon as humanly possible.

When Vanessa stepped back into the RV, everyone was staring at her.

Sparing a dirty look for the team, she asked, "What?"

"Uh," Eloise said with a hint of a smile. "Your hair."

With a quick glance in the rearview mirror, she smoothed the tangles back down. When had Sean even roughed it up? If that wasn't embarrassing enough, her cheeks were set aflame by the attention of the others. "Well worry not, comrades. No more blatant public displays of affection until we get settled, thanks to Finneas-the-Demon-Cupid over there."

The RV lurched forward, and she sprawled into Guist's lap.

"Sorry," she moaned and rolled off to sit in the space between him and Laney.

"That sucks," Laney sympathized.

Her saying that actually made Vanessa feel a lot better for some reason. "It's not so bad. I understand that we both need to focus, and we aren't going back to ignoring each other completely. I just don't like outsiders meddling with my love life. This is all so new to me. Finn says I mess with Sean's head too much and he's known him a long time. If he's worried, I guess we should be more careful."

Laney lowered her voice. "Vanessa, that's a good thing. I haven't ever seen Sean act the way he just did with anyone."

"Not even with you?" The answer mattered more than she'd admit.

"Heck, no. He never acted like that with me. Until we decided we worked better as friends, he acted like he borderline hated me."

"Huh. That's good." She squinted at the back of Sean's headrest. "I mean, sucks for you, but good for me."

Soren fussed and flailed her tiny hands out of the baby blanket. With a quick check of the cloth diaper swaddling her little bottom, Laney frowned. "She must be hungry again."

By the time Laney settled her to her breast, the newborn was in an inconsolable fit and took a while to latch.

"Adrianna," Vanessa said. "Tomorrow is a big day, and you need to be well rested. Come lie over here, and try to get some sleep, okay? We'll be there in the morning."

Sleep would likely elude her, but she could at least get the little girl settled. With Adrianna's head resting on her lap and a blanket pulled snuggly over her small frame, she rubbed her back until Adrianna drifted off.

Mitchell and Guist played a quiet card game at the small table, and Eloise tried to get comfortable in the twin bed in back among piles of supplies.

Vanessa turned her head and rested it against the cool window glass. It was full dark outside, but the moon lent some of its light to the woods that lined the dirt road they traveled. A lone Dead stood stunned by the road, hunched and limping. He opened his mouth in a silent bellow and started hobbling after the RV, much too late to catch up. The sight of him in the dark would've scared her witless before the hunting trip with Finn and the supply run. Now, the monster stirred nothing in her. Just an apathy that said if she were on the ground, and he was a threat, she'd not hesitate to end his miserable life. Who would've thought a person could change so much in the course of not even two weeks?

She dragged her gaze to the back of Sean's headrest again.

Certainly not her.

The RV bounced, and her head flew forward, awakening Vanessa to an early dawn streaming through the windows. Laney and Eloise had been sleeping on the bed, but were looking around with the same confused expression she likely sported, and Mitchell was changing Soren's tiny diaper on the end of the bench seat. Adrianna still slept soundly in her lap, but Guist had already hopped out of the side door of the RV and Sean and Finn threw their doors open too, letting in twin streams of gray light.

"What's happening?" Laney asked.

"Have to refuel," Mitchell said, pulling his newborn daughter to his shoulder. "Plus there's a road block that we need to clear before we can get over this little bridge. We've been driving on the shoulder for a while, but even that runs out sometimes." He handed Laney the baby and checked his handgun. "Be back in a minute. Vanessa, up on the roof to do some recon." He twitched his head upward.

Now usually she wouldn't take orders from someone, and especially a man who'd wronged her in any way, but this was Mitchell's way of accepting her new guard position. It was a terribly wrapped gift, but a gift just the same.

Gently, she laid Adrianna's head on a folded blanket on the seat and stretched her back. With her rifle slung across her shoulder, she shimmied up to the top of the camper and lay on her belly. The wind whipped her hair all around, so she pulled it back into a band and yanked a radio and small pair of binoculars out of one of the cargo pockets of her dark pants. Clicking on the walkie, she tested it. "Can you hear me?"

"Loud and clear," Sean crackled over the air waves. Oh, that voice settled something turbulent inside of her.

It didn't take long for her to figure out what the problem was. Mitchell stood in front of the RV, pouring various fluids into it, but behind him, Finn, Guist, and Sean were working on a traffic jam. To the side of the bridge was a deep creek that posed a ninety-eight percent chance of the RV getting irreparably stuck if they tried to ford it. The bridge had to be cleared before they could proceed. Most of the cars seemed to be unlocked and were thrown into neutral and pushed off to the side easily enough. Some of the cars, however, had been locked from the inside and still had the remains of their inhabitants in them. Deads had probably tried to claw at them for days, unable to open the door, and not quite smart enough to use their combined force to break the windows. Vanessa swallowed a lump of bile as Sean leaned over a body still buckled into the driver's seat. What an awful way to die. But then again, every way was an awful way to die these days. Nobody went painlessly anymore.

She scanned the road behind them as far as she could see, but nothing stirred except what the wind picked up. The woods around them were quiet beyond the song of moaning branches, complaining of the wind's unsavory treatment. Even the birds had fled the eerie woods to find shelter from the storm clouds that churned overhead. A fat snowflake landed on the fiberglass roof in front of her, and she glared at it. Great. Just what they needed was the first snowstorm of the season to lay all of their plans in a grave. Movement pulled at her eyes, but it was just the boys, pushing another car into the ditch.

Wait.

She focused the binoculars onto a spot in the distance. The cars ahead seemed to be moving. No, not the cars. Heads above the cars.

"Sean," she said into the radio. "We've got Deads up the road. They're headed this way."

"You have a head count?"

"They're still a ways off. At least five. No." She squinted. "More than that. Too many for us out in the open."

Sean slid out of a car and faced her. "ETA? We have four more cars before we have a shot at moving over this bridge."

"Five minutes if you're quiet. They're walking."

He spun his finger in the air and said something to Finn and Guist that didn't reach her ears, and she pulled herself over the front of the RV. "You done refueling, Mitchell? We're going to have to dodge some Deads here shortly."

He eased the hood down and wiped grease onto a rag before he squinted behind him. "Stay here and keep a rifle trained on them. I'm going to give them a hand so we don't cut it too close." He jogged up the road with long, deliberate strides.

Sean wrapped a rag around his elbow and busted out the driver's side window to an old sedan. Three cars left.

"Come on, come on, come on," she chanted as she watched the herd of undead make progress. They seemed to be speeding up.

Two cars left.

The team was scrambling, and an old Dodge pickup seemed to be the holdup. Guist tried to get it into gear and then Mitchell tried. Finally the truck lurched, and all four of them pushed, muscles straining against the massive weight of it until it was rolling.

It wasn't a figment of her morbid imagination. The Deads had heard, or smelled, or seen them, or all three, and had picked up the pace to a sprint. "Time's up," she barked into the radio. "It'll have to be good enough."

The engine roared to life below her only to sputter and die. Just as she swung through the side door, Laney tried again, pumping the gas.

"Oh, this is a terrible time for engine trouble," Vanessa said in a voice much calmer than she felt.

The engine roared again and dropped to nothing, and Laney muttered an oath before she ripped the engine again.

"It's that crap they use for fuel," Vanessa said. "Sometimes it takes a few minutes to get her going again. This happened on our supply run a couple times. Keep trying!" she exclaimed as she hopped back out the side door.

The first pepper of gunfire lit into the growing horde as Guist turned and covered the others' retreat. A Dead sprinted out of the woods on a straight-line warpath for the RV. She pulled the Glock and fired. Miss.

Aw hell, she didn't need to be wasting the ammo anyway. "Oy!" she called around the side of the camper. The Dead flew toward her as fast as a corpse could with a snapped shin bone on one side. His hair was thin and stuck out in all directions, and gray liver spots coated his pallid complexion. His rolling eyes were sunken deep into the recesses of his rotted face, and he bellowed through a mouth that no longer had lips. She lifted her boot and thrashed it against his chest, launching him backward. Her carefully placed knife was in his skull before he could right himself.

The engine died again.

Hell was coming for them.

Sean running full out was a work of art. Each step was more powerful than the last, and the intensity on his face rivaled the grace of his stride. She stood for them, popping off round after round into the brains of the closest on their tails until they'd all piled inside. Sean's strong hands pulled her in by the waist just as the monsters reached the RV. The body of a Dead blocked the door, and she kicked viciously at it while Sean hacked mercilessly at the ones trying to take advantage of the opening.

The engine finally roared and kept going, and Laney hit the gas just as Sean was captured in the unrelenting grasp of a monster. With the strength of inhuman hunger, he pulled Sean to his jagged teeth just as the RV lurched forward.

"No!" Vanessa screamed and pulled her gun up. The shot echoed through the cab, and cold moisture spattered against her face.

The Dead went limp, and Sean shoved the freed door closed before pulling her back.

"Hold onto something!" Laney screamed just before they barreled into the last remaining car, a dark SUV.

The impact sent Vanessa reeling, and she hit the corner of a cabinet.

Sean had reached for her a moment too late and flew into the back.

Dizzy, she pulled herself onto all fours and retched at the pain in the back of her head. The RV thumped and bumped as Laney ran over any Dead in their path and pulled to the shoulder to avoid the dense traffic of abandoned cars.

The chaos in the RV blurred in and out of focus. Finn pointed animatedly from the passenger seat while Laney maneuvered the oversized getaway van. Mitchell clutched Soren protectively. Guist had thrown his body across Eloise to keep her in place. Adrianna sat on her knees crying and clutching her bunny by the sink, and Sean lay limp near the bed in back.

"S-Sean?" she slurred. Why did her voice sound so far away?

Afraid to try to stand up, she crawled until she reached him. Her hands felt funny as she shook him, like they were detached from her body. Her ears rang from the pain that spread across the back of her skull, and she closed her eyes against another dizzy spell.

Crimson ran in a stream down the side of Sean's face, and she touched it with a frown. Red coated her fingertips and terror snaked down her spine. That was Sean's blood on her hand.

"First aid, Finn!" she screamed, aggravating her headache until it felt like a fire alarm in her face. "Get me the first-aid kit! Sean," she sobbed, shaking him again.

Guist was closest, and he checked his pulse and then pressed against his spine with a faraway look in his eyes. "I don't think it's broken. I think he just got a nasty bump on the head. Here," he said, holding a hand out for the red backpack stuffed with medical supplies.

Gentle hands tugged her shoulders. "We need space to work," Mitchell said calmly. "Go on up by Laney so we can fix him."

The edges of her vision were blurred as she stumbled forward. Finn gave her the passenger seat, and she rolled down the window for some fresh air. Up ahead, a lone Dead stumbled toward the road, and the closer they got, the first inklings of an awesome idea took shape.

"Vanessa, close the window," Laney said.

"Nuh uh. Watch this."

The cars on the left of the RV were bumper to bumper, and Laney had no choice but to drive on. Vanessa hung out the window and spread her fingers out like a little star in the whipping wind. And when they were close enough, she leaned farther out and smacked the Dead's outstretched hand.

"Shit, Vanessa!" Laney yelled, yanking her hair until she was no longer hanging out of the window.

Vanessa frowned as she watched Laney roll her window up and put on the child lock from her side. And then Laney looked down at her hand with a furrow to her perfectly arched eyebrows. The palm of her hand was covered in red. "Mitchell," she said in a strange tone.

"Yeah, babe? You okay?"

"I'm fine. Something's wrong with Vanessa."

He pulled away from Sean's still limp body and rubbed a sheen of sweat from his face with a forearm. "What do you mean?"

"I mean, she just high-fived a Dead."

He gave his wife a look that said she'd lost her mind. "What?"

"I mean, she leaned out the window and slapped happy palms with a freaking Dead, and then there's this!" She held her crimson palm in the air before grabbing the wheel again. "She's hurt, Mitchell. Can you help her?"

Three long strides was all it took to reach her, and he yanked the hair band out of her tresses before parting it down the middle. "You split yourself like a peach, kid. Stay here while I get something to fix you up."

She narrowed her eyes at the unsavory nickname. "Don't call me kid," she said as seriously as she could muster while the world spun on its axis. Sex goddess or warrior woman or some other such name would fit better. At least that's how Sean made her feel. "Where's Sean?"

Laney squeezed her hand and left it there. "He's going to be okay. Mitchell doesn't seem worried, so that's a good sign. He probably just got a bump on the head like you."

Vanessa's stomach dropped out of the bottom again. "Adrianna?" she asked, the edges of her vision clearing slightly with the effort to focus. She felt like a drunk trying to sober up too fast.

She stumbled toward the child and slid onto her knees. She couldn't go any farther without passing out. "Come here, sweetie. Daddy's going to be all fixed up soon."

The little girl slumped, sniffling into her arms, and she held her as tight as her twitching muscles would allow. The soothing words she offered didn't make a lick of sense, but the child didn't seem to care as she buried her head into Vanessa's shoulder.

A murmured voice asked a question, and Guist answered. "She's okay. They both are."

"Where are they?" Sean asked.

Guist moved to the side, and Vanessa got the first glimpse of Sean's brilliant eyes, filled with worry and pain. Something heavy and suffocating lifted from inside of her, and she smiled. Or at least she thought she smiled. Her body wasn't really working like she told it to at the moment.

Mitchell cut off her view and held a needle the size of a miniature saber and a small length of sutures. Oh good. She was wondering when she'd be stabbed again.

He squatted down behind her and told her to sit still before he started sewing humpty dumpty back together again.

Against the pain, she pursed her lips and tried to concentrate on Sean. He was moving his legs, and Guist helped him sit up. She fought the urge to gag each time the thread pulled through the flesh of her scalp, and when it was done, she nearly died of relief.

"I think you need to go lay down," he said. "Or wait. Guist, if she has a concussion, is she supposed to sleep or no? I can't remember."

"No. Don't let her sleep."

Sean frowned but winced as the expression pulled at new stitches. "Vanessa, come here."

She swayed with the effort and then shook her head. "I can't."

Mitchell half dragged, half carried her until she and Adrianna sat next to Sean, and then he went to take Soren from Eloise.

"Let me see," Sean said. He prodded the soreness with tender fingers and shook his head. "I tried to reach out to shield you, but I didn't have enough warning."

"I know. Neither one of us was going to get off uninjured when she had to run through that SUV. It couldn't be helped."

Guist handed Sean a bowl of water and a rag.

"What's that for?" she asked.

"Your face. You have that last Dead all over you."

Gross.

With tender strokes, he cleaned her, and when he was finished, he drank in her face like he was taking inventory. "You're a fierce woman, Vanessa."

She nearly glowed around the edges with pride. In fact, she was quite surprised she didn't look like an actual giant lightning bug. That was until she noticed Finn's glare of impatience. Him and his stupid made-up rules. Clearing her throat, she held out her hand for a shake and gritted, "Finn's going to taser me if I don't leave you alone."

His warm hand slid solidly into hers, like they were created to touch. A devastating smile touched the corners of his lips, and he shook her hand gently. Oh, Sean could tell Finn to go jump off a bridge if he wanted to. There was no question who was leader here, but he seemed to be enjoying the game. Finn probably didn't even realize he was just pushing them closer together with his challenge, the oaf.

"Thanks for saving my life," Sean murmured in that deep, rich voice she'd come to adore.

"Thanks for saving mine." With a naughty grin and a stolen glance at the back of Finn's head, she leaned forward and kissed Sean on the cheek before moving off. Sean's smile expanded until it reached his eyes, and she'd do just about anything to be the cause of adoring looks like those.

Chapter Nineteen

Vanessa checked the knot of Laney's baby sling again. "Is it too tight?"

Laney turned her neck from side to side and checked the weight of Soren, cradled snugly against her chest. She couldn't defend herself or her daughter with no hands, so they'd had to improvise with a sturdy sheet. "It's good. Thanks."

"Eloise, how you feeling?"

"Still pregnant. Not even a single false labor pain. I think this kid's going to stay in here forever."

Vanessa huffed a nervous laugh. "We don't need forever. We just need until we can clear out Sean's old headquarters." She gestured to the pistol in her friend's limp hand. "Remember to take the safety off before you pull that trigger."

They'd parked the heavily damaged RV a quarter of a mile outside the Denver colony gates so the noise of the engine wouldn't draw the Dead's attention. Surprise would be their best weapon against the monsters trapped inside. Guist unzipped a black duffle bag and passed out rectangles of Teflon with Velcro strips hanging from them like vines.

"What's this?" Vanessa asked.

"Here, let me show you." He strapped it around her forearm and tightened the Velcro until the armor stayed firmly in place. "If you get in a jam, deflect their bite with this. They won't be able to get through it."

"Whoa, this is freaking awesome," Mitchell said. "When did you make these?"

"I've spent the last year making as many as I could. I brought a pair for each of us. Even a small pair for Adrianna. Patent pending," he said with a wink.

The second arm guard chaffed the half-healed knife wound Finn had given Vanessa, but the discomfort would be worth it if it saved her life. She bent down and strapped Adrianna in and zipped up her jacket. "You stay by me the whole time, do you understand?"

The child nodded solemnly.

"We don't separate. I'm going to protect you, but you have to be near me and Daddy at all times. Follow right behind us, like a shadow. Do you know how your shadow always goes where you go? Stick to us like that."

"Okay. What about Daddy?"

"He's going to carry you as long as he can, but he might have to do different stuff, and then you'll be with me. When he goes off, I'll be there to keep you safe."

"Promise?"

Vanessa smiled and hoped she lived to fulfill the oath. "I promise."

Sean watched them openly. Not even Finn dared to reprimand him, as he'd said not a word since she'd kissed his cheek. His face was a beautiful mask of determination. Serious Sean was back, and though she missed the easy smile he saved only for her, she understood the need for him to turn off his emotions. It was up to him to get them from the bottom of the lake to air.

"Everyone, check your weapons one more time, and then we need to head out," Sean said.

She had more than usual to arrange. Two pistols, her trusty M16A2 strapped across her back, cargo pockets overflowing with bullet-filled spare magazines, and after learning a valuable lesson on the supply run, she wasn't running short on knives. Six sharpened blades were slid snuggly into notches in the back of her belt.

She was cold, but a jacket would hinder her movement, so she wore nothing but cargo pants weighed down with the cold metal of

Dead killers, and a fitted black thermal shirt that fit over her arm guards. Her boots creaked as she leaned forward and planted a kiss on Adrianna's forehead.

Sean handed Adrianna a small, red pocket knife. "After what you see today, you'll be big enough to carry this with you all the time. Put it in your pocket for now. You do exactly as Vanessa says. If she tells you to do something, you do it immediately. Be listening for her to give you instructions."

"I will. I'll help. I'll tell you when the monsters are coming up behind us."

He ruffled her hair and she snuggled against his leg. "Good girl."

"You ready?" Vanessa asked her. After hoisting the little girl onto Sean's back, she took off with long strides behind him and the others.

"Hey," he said with a quick glance around. Pulling Vanessa to a stop, his serious and steady gaze ensnared her. "Be careful." His hand came up to rest on her waist, and his thumb brushed just under the button of her cargo pants.

Her response, clenching flames and weak knees, was immediate. How could a man draw such a reaction from her body? From her soul? His kiss was short, but soft. A gentle promise that if they made it through today, he'd reward her with tender affection and expect nothing less in return.

And suddenly she was terrified, watching Sean's long, easy strides and Adrianna clinging so tightly to him. She had everything to lose now, and her most prized possessions were being thrown to the Deads. A fierce anger roared through her at the monsters who threatened her family, because that's what they were. Supply runs and missions — they didn't make lifelong friends. Such experiences forged bonds of fiery steel that welded survivors together and bound their spilled blood until they were brethren. Laney, Guist, Eloise, Mitchell, Finn — they'd die for her and she for them, but Sean and Adrianna clutched onto her heart until it threatened to burst. Since they'd come into her life, her defenses had been chipped away while she wasn't paying attention, and now she was raw and vulnerable again.

She'd burn the whole damned world to keep them safe.

She stood on tiptoes to rest her cheek against the rasp of his. "I will."

Sean picked up his pace, and she stayed back to run beside him, scanning the woods while they caught up little by little. By the time they reached the others, the looming cinder block and stone walls of the Denver colony peeked out through the trees. Dark storm clouds swirled above it, and lazy snowflakes fell from the sky. The place was haunted—there was no question about that. Now if they could just rid the place of its ghosts.

Laney held her hand over her nose and looked positively green. One of the unfortunate side-effects to her immunity was her sensitivity to Deads. It was as if she'd jumped an evolutionary notch, and her body had learned to fight the virus as well as sense the danger coming at the same time. The rest of them didn't have natural weapons like hers. Only metal ones.

"I was hoping the gate would still be open from when Erhard let the Deads in last year," Sean whispered.

The looming wooden gates to the right were tightly shut. No such luck.

"Finn and I will hop the walls near the gardens and try to divert the numbers to the back of the colony before we open the gates from the inside. Stay here. Stay quiet. If Deads come, and you can't off them without ammo, you head up a tree and wait for us. No noise." He eased Adrianna off his back, and the girl clung to Vanessa's leg.

"And if you don't come back?" Laney breathed.

Kneeling down, Sean pulled loops of climbing cable from his backpack. "If we don't come back in an hour, Mitchell calls the shots." He gave Vanessa one last lingering look before he jogged off behind Finn.

That hour lasted days, and the longer time dragged, the more eerie the woods behind them became. It would only take one bawling Dead to attract others, and they'd be trapped here between teeth and a stone wall. Desperate for a plan B, she scouted the nearest trees with Adrianna's tiny hand clenched in hers and picked the easiest ones to scurry up in a pinch. Laney seemed to be doing the same.

An explosion rattled the woods, shaking pine needles and cones to the earth as the team ducked against the unseen danger. Well, if that wasn't going to pull Deads from the woods, she didn't know what would. Their timeframe had just been limited substantially.

Jerking his head toward the gate, Mitchell led them, gun at the ready, until they stood inside the gargantuan doorway. Smoke billowed, piercing the sky and blanketing everything with the scent of ash. Minutes drifted by as they stood in the shadow of the wall.

Vanessa's body shook with adrenaline as she pressed Adrianna further into the safety of the corner.

"Here they come," Guist murmured. He didn't mean Sean and Finn. The woods crawled with nightmares.

"What do we do?" she asked, trying to suppress the panic in her voice. "Do we head for the trees?"

"If we get up a tree, we'll have a horde of Deads between us and the gate," Mitchell murmured. "We'll be cut off and trapped. Sean and Finn will get us in the gate. They have to. Stay still. Stay quiet. The smoke will mask a lot of our scent and hopefully buy us time."

Snaking wisps of smog crept through the trees and filled the forest until Vanessa's eyes burned. She pulled Adrianna's jacket over her nose and covered the child's eyes with her hands to protect them.

The bulk of the Deads seemed to be headed farther down the fence line where the noise had originated. One, however, was headed straight for them at a slow lope from further up in the woods. He'd pass right by them. Pressed back, she froze against Laney. The smoke was making it hard to breathe, and she stifled a cough that filled her suffocating lungs. And still he came, the unfocused Dead with the emaciated body and gaping sores. His ribs protruded to match jutting hip bones, and so sunken were his cheeks, the outline of his snaggled teeth could be seen through them. He was going to pass them right by without noticing they were there.

As he passed, he flicked his head to the side and slowed. Snuffling air through his nostrils, he backpedaled slowly. Mitchell tensed on the other side of Laney, and as the monster approached, he hunched down and searched the shadows with film covered eyes. Closer and closer he came until Vanessa wanted to scream. Her fear smelled acrid and bitter, even to herself, and she waited for any sign to break formation from Mitchell. *Come on, Sean!* Where was he?

If they moved to kill him, it would draw the attention of every Dead within sight and not enough of them had moved farther down the fence to make a fair fight yet. Laney tensed back into the smoky doorway as he sniffed at her.

Vanessa flicked a glance down at a slow movement. Mitchell had eased a pistol up under the Dead's jaw without the thing noticing. One wrong move and the creature would be fertilizer for the forest.

He sniffed and snuffled at the squirming bundle strapped to Laney's chest, but even when Soren let out a little whimper, he didn't attack. Leaning back, the Dead gave one more unfocused look around the doorway and lumbered off.

As one, they exhaled slowly and relaxed against each other.

"Naaaaaaaaah!" the Dead bellowed as his face appeared around the corner.

Eloise screamed in terror, and Mitchell put a hole in him so wide, Vanessa could see a stream of daylight through his face. They were in it now.

"Stay here behind Laney," Vanessa ordered Adrianna, and she pulled slightly in front with Mitchell and Guist.

The woods erupted in the rattle of gunfire as they downed the front lines of the attack. "Sean!" she screamed.

The number of Deads that rushed from the woods wouldn't be held for long.

"One shot, one Dead," she chanted. They couldn't afford the ammunition to miss.

Laney's relentless fists banged against the gate in rhythm with Vanessa's pounding heartbeat, and beside her, Guist dropped an empty magazine and slid another one in.

A flash of blue took the corner of her vision as Laney's Mini-14 sent a pepper of staggering gunfire into the Deads approaching on the left. Soren cried, but the noise didn't matter now. Every Dead within a mile knew they were here, easy pickings if only they waited until the weapons ran out. Losing ground, she backed closer to Adrianna and reloaded, only to be pushed forward by something solid. Confused, she spared a glance for the culprit, but the only thing there was the door. The door!

"Inside!" she yelled over the noise of battle.

Pulling Adrianna by the arm, she handed her to Sean through the opening Finn was creating with arms that strained against the weight of the wood. She stood guard as Laney and then Eloise disappeared into the colony, and with Mitchell's head twitch as her only order, she slid in just before him and Guist.

"Close it!" Sean barked.

A row of handles lined the wooden doors at chest level, and she pulled as hard as she could. The others did the same, but it wasn't moving fast enough. Deads leaked through the opening. "Vanessa," Sean said. "Clear 'em."

Gladly.

LOVE AT THE END OF DAYS

She pulled her Glock and brushed the trigger before kicking the body viciously out of the way. The door gave a little, and she did the same to the next. And the next. With a thud, the door clamped closed, and Finn and Guist rushed to put the wooden bars in place.

A second wall that mirrored the first stretched up in front of them. "This way," Sean said, scooping Adrianna onto his back. He loped to the left down the length of the impediment like her weight was nothing.

Vanessa ran alongside them. "You tell us if there are any Deads behind us. Okay, sweetie? We'll do teamwork."

The child clutched her tiny pocket knife. "Don't worry, I will."

Sean's arms had to be burning by the time they reached the next gate, which had been thrown closed haphazardly, but he didn't even register the pain on his face. His steely focus was on the next barrier. He set the girl down as Finn and the others pulled on the towering gate. Teeth gritted, Sean's eyes went wide as the door opened, and he ducked back out of the way of the first clawing arm. "They're here," he said with a significant look at Finn.

"Close it back and give me a minute," Finn said, spinning to sprint the way they'd come.

Vanessa threw her weight against the door with the others as Dead after Dead hurled their wasted bodies against it. Inch by inch the Deads gained ground. Finn ran a hundred yards back down the lane between primary walls and pulled the pin on a grenade. Launching it over the barrier, he yelled, "Get down!"

Surprised by the tremendous, bone-rattling explosion, Vanessa lost her footing momentarily before she threw her body weight back at the gate. The pressure became less, and when Finn reached them, he pulled a machine gun from his back and ordered, "Open the gate!"

Little effort was required. Vanessa stood back with the others and readied her rifle. The commotion of the blast had syphoned off some of the Deads in the back, but the ones in front had smelled them and wouldn't be put off.

Adrianna clung to her leg and beside her, Laney lifted her Mini-14 with a look of absolute murder for the Deads that fell out of the opening. "For Jarren," she murmured, lighting them up.

Welp, it was decidedly a good thing they'd fastened plugs in Soren's little ears. Laney was a warrior, and mother or not, she didn't hesitate to down the droves.

With a clearing made, Sean motioned them through the final pair of gates. No turning back now. The scene inside was a slice to her innards. She'd been to the Denver colony before, and never in her wildest imaginings would she ever have pictured it like this.

Bodies littered the entry, and piles of skeletons decorated front doorsteps of dilapidated buildings. The stink of death clung to every air molecule, and the light snowfall did nothing to warm the place up. Abandoned and uncared for, the colony had dried up into a ghost town crawling with the reanimated corpses of its inhabitants. Buildings and cabins stood lopsided, like the frames had failed, and glass was busted out of nearly every dust--laden window. Much of the colony had burned, and the charred remains of old homes dotted the ground. Roofs sagged, and doors stood open, flapping slowly in the wind with an eerie creaking soundtrack, like the bones of the undead. A great plume of smoke billowed from the back of the colony where Sean and Finn must've blown something up as a diversion.

It had only been a year since the takeover, but the colony looked like it'd been abandoned the day of the outbreak. It matched all of the other sad cities and towns ravaged by the virus that ended the world.

None of that mattered when she saw the look on Sean's face. Sadness pooled in his eyes. Maybe he hadn't noticed what his colony looked like in his haste to get to the gate, but in that moment, she could almost see something dying inside of him.

"Later, Sean," she said, pulling his arm toward the hole in the coming Deads the others were running for. "We'll fix it later!"

"We can't fix them," he said, lifting his rifle to a Dead dressed in the same guard garb she was wearing.

Blind idiots had followed Erhard straight to their doom. She'd met the Denver colony's second once, and he hadn't exactly rubbed her right. Arrogant to a fault and not all right in the head, she hadn't been overly surprised when she heard of his betrayal.

"Monsters are coming," Adrianna said in such an innocent voice, such hideous words sounded wrong coming from her lips.

Vanessa hadn't time to even aim before Sean let off a pepper of automatic weaponry across the trio of Deads running behind them. Swinging Adrianna up onto her hip, she pushed her burning legs to catch up with the others.

"Get to the main house like we talked about. It'll be the strongest building against the horde. It's about two hundred fifty yards due west.

That way," Sean said, pointing across a clearing. Over the gunfire he yelled, "If we get split up, try to regroup there!"

His rifle clicked empty, and he slid it to his back before pulling a pistol. They were using too much ammo. The snow fell harder, and the wind whipped around them in a furious embrace.

Eloise was slowing ahead, and Guist grabbed her arm. She cried out, and he holstered his weapon and folded her into his arms. "Cover me," he said and ran with his wife in his arms.

Adrianna was dead weight, and she wouldn't be able to hold onto the child for much longer as her muscles burned to numbness.

The grappling fingers of a Dead scratched her shoulder as she blazed past, and she stifled a scream at the risk of being captured and toppling onto Adrianna. Lashing out, she backhanded the Dead with the armor that encased her forearm, and he slowed enough to allow her to pass.

"I see it," breathed Sean as a looming building appeared over the hill. "Go, go, go."

She didn't have a gun hand anymore. Both were required for carrying Adrianna, and running weaponless beside Guist required absolute trust in her team. Mitchell, Finn, and Laney led them, with only a moment of thought for each Dead that dropped just as it was about to reach them. A behemoth crashed in front of her, and she hurdled the body, stumbling on the dismount and barely keeping her balance. Deads were all around them, desperate for a meal they probably hadn't had in months.

The steps to Sean's front porch were the end of what Vanessa's body could handle. Exhausted, she lurched up them as Mitchell pushed on the door handle.

Nothing.

He rattled it and muttered, "What the hell? It's locked!"

"They're coming," Vanessa sang. They didn't have time for this. "Just kick the damned thing down!"

"Then it won't keep them out once we're in!"

Sean spared a shocked glance for the door and shoved his way past. With a thunderous knock on the door he screamed, "If anyone is alive in there, we need sanctuary!"

There wasn't time to get around to a back door or another opening. The undead were pouring from both directions. She shoved Adrianna up to Sean and pulled both pistols. Mitchell and Guist knelt beside her and together they battled the horde, popping round after round until the empty chamber echoed on her first gun, and then her Glock.

Sean was yelling something behind her, and she couldn't see her teammates anymore but if this was it—if this was her place to go, she was taking as many of those rotting bastards down with her as she could. She backed up and pulled a knife, launched it into the face of a Dead. She threw another, and another.

Ready for the screaming banshee that leapt up onto the porch with her, she drew the gleaming weapon but froze when she saw its face.

Leslie Bertrand. When she'd been human, she'd been a good friend.

The hesitation cost her, and she toppled backward under the weight of Leslie-the-Dead. The knife! She pushed against the Dead's chest with her armored arm, but couldn't lift it further than that. The creature stretched its head toward her throat, and she scrabbled for the knife that had fallen somewhere under her. Where was the blasted thing?

Gunfire sounded from above her, but she couldn't see a thing through the Dead's filthy, stringy hair surrounding her face. She was losing purchase as her exhausted arms failed, and her hand hit nothing but wooden porch deck. Gritting her teeth, she growled and turned her face to the side as she fought to keep the snapping teeth away from her throat, and just as the pain pierced her neck and cut into her flesh, the Dead flew backward and strong hands dragged her away.

She panted as pain escaped her body through a stream of warmth down the side of her neck. Sean launched himself at the door and locked a series of deadbolts before Mitchell and Guist shoved a desk in front of the door and started stacking furniture on top of it.

The faster her heart beat, the more warmth seeped from her body. Sean leaned against the desk for a moment like he was accepting that they'd all made it safely.

Except they hadn't.

"Sean," she said. Even to her own ears, she sounded scared.

Slowly he turned.

"I'm bit."

Chapter Twenty

One of the biggest shocks of Sean's life had been when Arden Moore opened the door for them. There were survivors from the fall of Denver, and they'd lived here all this time. That revelation was utterly eclipsed by Vanessa's admission.

This couldn't be happening. Not to her. Not now.

"Sh-Shoot me," Vanessa said. "Don't let me be one of them."

Sean dropped to his knees beside her as a helpless sound wrenched itself from his throat. "No," he whispered.

Even in the dim light of the lanternless entryway, he could see the pool of dark growing beneath her. He could smell the iron in her blood. "Vanessa, listen to me." Panic thrummed through his veins. "Listen! Was it a bite or the blade underneath you? I saw a blade! Was it a bite or a blade?"

She shook her head back and forth, and tears streamed from the corners of her eyes.

"Vanessa, please." Emotion filled his throat until each word was thick, like the life that was flowing from her. "Please, tell me you cut your throat on the blade."

She opened her mouth but nothing came out.

"Mitchell! Get me the first-aid bag."

"Sean," Mitchell warned.

"Don't! Just give it to me."

Mitchell sighed loudly and dropped beside him before ripping into the pack and pulling a wad of cloth. Guist shone a beam from his flashlight onto the wound, but all he could see was red. Mitchell wiped it, time and again, trying to get a look at the wound.

"I can't tell. There's just too much blood. I can't tell."

His heart was being ripped from him. Desperately, he squeezed her shoulders and arms like it would bring her back. A tortured sound came from his throat as he wiped water from his eyes with the back of his forearm. "Laney?"

"Don't do that to her," Mitchell warned.

"Your blood will bring her back."

"But she'll rot, Sean!" Mitchell yelled. "She'll watch her body rot away. She'll *feel* it!"

Laney unzipped one of her cargo pockets and pulled out a small black bag. Inside were five needles filled with clear liquid. "I have something better," she said.

"What is it?" Guist asked from the other side of Vanessa's body.

"Dr. Mackey gave me some of the first rounds of vaccine, just in case. They haven't been tested on humans though. We don't know any of the side effects yet or even if it will work after she's been bitten," Laney warned.

Sean could almost feel Vanessa fading beneath his fingertips. Before he could change his mind, he snatched one of the syringes, pulled the cap off with his teeth and jammed it into Vanessa's shoulder. The vaccine emptied into her body, but she didn't even respond to the prick. Her eyes were closed and her skin pale.

"She's bleeding too much," he said. "Hand me a needle and sutures. Hurry!"

"Your hands are shaking too badly," Mitchell said softly. "I need room to work. Guist, keep that light right here."

Sean backed up until his shoulder blades hit the wall, and then he slid down it while the team worked to staunch the bleeding. Laney led Adrianna to another room, and as much as a hug from his daughter would've done him good at the moment, she'd done him a favor. Adrianna didn't need to see either one of them like this.

"Vanessa?" Eloise said in a shaky voice. "Vanessa, honey, you have to come back to us." Matched tears streaked down her freckled cheeks in the thin light that streamed through the boarded up windows. Her lips trembled as she fluttered her hands uselessly over Vanessa's limp body, and he looked away. He'd lose it if he took on anyone else's grief.

It should've been him. Again and again, she'd put herself in danger for precious extra seconds so they could all get to safety. It should've been him lying cold on the wooden floors of his old home. Rocking back, he slammed his head against the wall to try to stop the pain in his mind.

In a whisper as quiet as a breeze, Guist said, "I can't find her pulse."

"Check again," Mitchell muttered as he looped another suture.

"I've checked every spot I know and there's nothing. I'm sorry."

The words were a blow to his gut. It was like he'd swallowed a tiny grenade the moment he'd fallen in love with her, and now the pin had somehow jerked free.

He glared at the door that stood in between him and the horde that had killed his chance at happiness.

"Sean," Finn warned. His second-in-command, the ever logical voice of reason.

With a growl he stood and stalked into the next room, one where he was alone among a myriad of stacked boxes, dust covered books, and office supplies. A room where no one was watching him to gauge his reaction.

The devil took him, and he roared against the restraint of loss. A metal stack of shelves stretched to the ceiling, and desperate to get to the brick underneath, he flung it behind him. He threw punch after punch after bloody punch at the unforgiving stones that were as cold as his soul, and as unmoving as he wished his heart to be. As emotionless as he wanted his mind.

He glared at the boarded window before he checked his ammunition. Finn could probably hear him reloading his weapons, but who cared? He sure didn't.

"Give me your radio," he said to Finn when he came back out.

"You're emotional right now."

"Give me your radio. Now."

Finn slapped the radio into the palm of his hand with a disgusted look. "You have a daughter."

"And I'm about to save her," he gritted out through clenched teeth. "Are you with me, or not."

"I think we should wait."

"Wait for what? Until I'm all better, Finn? We'll starve to death way before then. Are you going to cover me, or am I going this alone?"

Finn didn't move for an entire minute. Not a single muscle twitched on his face until finally he nodded. "I've always got your back."

"This way."

Sean took the stairs to his room two at a time. The window creaked open, and he climbed out onto the roof where an overhang gave shadow to overgrown landscaping. "Snipe from here," he told Finn. When he hit the ground, he rolled and knifed a Dead who'd wandered to the back and seen him. He waited for Finn to lower himself to the roof and pop the scope cover off his rifle.

Sean didn't run. So focused was the red fury in his veins that he didn't panic or bolt. He just unleashed his weapons on anything that moved in front of him. A scraggly, old, bald cypress sat in the middle of his backyard, and he turned Finn's radio on and set it in a hollow place between the gnarled roots. He cranked it up just as the Deads from the front of the house began to migrate to the back. The pepper of Finn's gunfire was constant, and he slid his rifle in front of him to mow down the numbers that stood between him and the house. With a burst of speed, he rocketed up the ivy hanger that covered the wall and slid back through the window. Ripping box after box out of his closet, he pulled out a battery-operated tape player that had meant something to him a million years ago and shoved his own radio against the speaker. With one last significant look at Finn, he jammed his finger against the play button, and the lyrics to "Highway to Hell" rang out.

Shoving the radio and walkie-talkie under the mattress to muffle the sound, he crouched by the window as Finn's radio blared out the chorus from the yard below. Finn's face was an open book of shock.

Deads came from all over, throwing themselves in a frenzied pile over the radio that sat protected by the roots of the earth. Sean pulled a grenade, Finn did the same, and carefully they climbed out onto the roof.

"We're doing this?" Finn asked.

"Hell yeah."

"What if the house falls?"

"She'll hold. On my count."

They pulled the pins and held the striker lever down.

"One."

The pile of Deads grew and grew as the monsters threw themselves onto the noise.

"Two."

Deads writhed and snapped their jaws for a chance at whatever made that sound.

"Three."

Twin bombs rocketed through the air, sailing with a slow motion grace until they landed in the horde. Finn flung himself through the window, and Sean followed just as the explosion filled the colony and rattled the bones of the house.

Vanessa lay in a grave. A shovel full of dirt had been thrown over her face, and the black soil caked her lips. She wanted to cry out, to tell the groundskeeper to stop burying her, because she was alive, but nothing worked right. The hole had to be deeper than six feet. Even standing on someone's shoulders, she'd never be able to escape the damp earth that promised to drag her down and down until she couldn't breathe or see. Until she didn't exist anymore.

Eloise poked her freckled face over the edge of her tomb. "I'm so mad at you for scaring me like that."

Vanessa tried to frown, but her eyebrow only managed to twitch. Improvement though.

"I mean, you've pissed me off to no end over the years, but this time was the worst."

Eloise was the meanest angel ever. And also the only heavily pregnant angel she'd ever heard of. Now, she didn't have much firsthand experience with heaven, but she was pretty sure getting knocked up was illegal or at least frowned upon there.

When she tried to spit the grave dirt from her lips, something soft fell against her cheek. Slowly, she lifted her hand to tug on a pink stuffed rabbit in a floral smock. Not the soil of her tomb she'd imagined then. She blinked rapidly, trying to clear her head.

"Adrianna thought you needed Bunny for protection in case you woke up scared. Now if that isn't love, it doesn't exist on this earth anymore because that child adores that stuffed animal. And after the horrid day she's had and the terrible things she's seen, she went right to bed without it so that toy could keep you safe."

So she'd been dreaming of being buried alive. Or perhaps hallucinating. "What happened?" she croaked, fighting a dizzy spell as she sat up.

"You died, I think. Or you came really close to it. We still can't really tell if you slit your own throat on one of your knives or if you got bitten by a Dead, but the boys couldn't find your pulse for the longest time. You ask my opinion, I think you cut yourself trying to get away from those teeth."

"And I'd do it again. Her breath was awful."

"Laney! Vanessa's awake. Be a doll and bring her some water?"

The sloshing of the canteen was the most beautiful melody she'd ever heard. The torn and stitched flesh of her neck pulled with every drag of cool water, but she didn't care. Laney had rocketed herself up to "tolerable" and at that moment, the woman could've blown glitter in her face and whispered, "You're welcome," and she would've thanked her through a big, dumb, happy grin.

"Where's Sean?"

Eloise shot Laney a dark look and then cleared her throat and scooted her chair closer. "He thinks you're dead."

"Well, go get him and tell him I'm not."

"I would, if he were here. Unfortunately he took your passing a little hard and destroyed a storage room directly before he went bat-poop-crazy and bombed, like, a hundred Deads in the backyard."

"He tore up a storage room for me?" That was the sweetest thing anyone had ever done. "Okay, so he killed a bunch of Deads, and then where did he go?"

"I didn't say he killed them. Just bombed them from the upstairs window like a one-man wrecking crew."

"Two-man," Laney corrected as she leaned against the doorframe.

"Right. Finn, the idiot, has basically backed every kamikaze plan Sean had from the moment Guist couldn't find your pulse to — well, we don't really know where they are now."

"So he didn't kill the Deads?"

"Oh, he did eventually. The grenades only managed to mutilate most of them, so he walked out there like he was Clint Eastwood and had all the time in the world, and he put every last one out of their misery. Didn't waste any ammunition either. And Finn stood there picking off the others that came for Sean, and eventually Guist and Mitchell joined the little hunting party. Except, when our boys came back in, it was without Sean and Finn. We haven't seen them since."

"How long ago did they leave?"

Eloise sighed and sagged against the bed. "Six hours."

"Six hours! Eloise, they could be hurt or trapped. We have to help them."

"You're in no condition to do anything, and neither am I, and neither is Laney. We've got two babies to take care of, and Mitchell and Guist will go after them at first light if they aren't back yet. Sean said there were way too many Deads compared to what he remembered, so there must be a wall down. They went off to fix it and sometimes that kind of work can take a long time."

"In the dead of night? While this place is crawling with night-walkers? They're just going to rebuild a freaking wall?"

"Hey, I wasn't the one who came up with that little gem of a plan. That was your crazy man's death wish. I joke you not, he and Finn tossed a couple of grenades right by the house. See that crack in the plaster?" She pointed to a divot that climbed the wall like ivy. "There's at least one to match in every room of the house. Scared the devil right out of us."

"They're likely treed," Laney said quietly. "I don't think they were bitten because I haven't seen them milling around the house, and Sean would come back here for you and Adrianna if he were turned."

"That's...disturbing."

"They can't help it. Anyone they had attachments to as a human, they want to eat as a Dead. It's the virus wanting to spread. It's sharing with loved ones," she said through a humorless smile.

"Aw, how sweet. That makes more sense of why Leslie tried so hard to take a love nip at my neck then."

"You knew her?"

"Yeah, we traveled together for a while with a few more kids our age at the end of the first year after the outbreak. She was really nice.

You know, before she let herself go and started snacking on people. Why do I feel so dizzy?"

"You lost your blood. No really, it's still sitting in a giant puddle in the other room. That and I'm pretty sure you have a concussion from the RV wreck earlier. You really needed a transfusion, but we don't have the know-how or equipment. Or maybe it's a side effect of the vaccine. Sean gave it to you when we couldn't tell if you were bitten or not."

"Huh. So I guess it works."

"Don't know. If you were knifed, it still isn't tested, and there's no way to tell if you suffered the bite and lived, so Dr. Mackey will just have to try it on a more controlled group."

"Is your sense of smell stronger?" Laney asked.

She inhaled long and deep. "I don't think so."

"You can't smell Deads?"

"Not in this room. Why?"

"I always wondered if the people who take my vaccine will get the same extra kick to their senses. I can smell Deads clear as day in here. Their smell has coated everything in this colony."

"Maybe if you take the vaccine and get the immunity, and then get bitten?" Vanessa offered.

"Maybe."

A tiny cry sounded from the other room, and Laney disappeared from the doorway like an apparition into thin air.

Vanessa pressed her head back into the musty pillow. "What if he's hurt out there, El?"

"He's with Finn. And he's Sean Daniels. If anyone can get himself out of whatever jam he's got into, it's him." She threw a look at the door and leaned forward, lowering her voice to a raspy whisper. "There's something else."

"What?"

"We aren't alone in this house."

A chill crept up her skin like she was slowly sinking into mountain stream water. "Who else is here?"

"You know how the door was locked and Sean was banging on it, yelling for someone to let us in? Well, someone did."

"Survivors?"

"I don't know if I'd call them that. There's thirteen of them, and they've been living all this time in here but we can't find a bit of food."

She swallowed the bile that threatened to gag her. "You think they've been gnawing on each other?"

"I don't want to think that, but whatever they've been through the last year, it took the human right out of them. They aren't right, Vanessa. We gave them some provisions and barred them into the auditorium until we can figure out what to do with them, but for now I think its best you sleep with your weapons close by."

"Where's Adrianna sleeping?"

"In the next room. Mitchell and Guist are taking turns watching for the creepers in case they try to sneak around front."

"Can you get one of the boys to carry her on in here to sleep with me? I don't feel right being separated from her with all that's happening."

Squeezing her hand, Eloise nodded. "Sure. Be back in a jiff."

Cannibals? They were no better than Deads if they were eating other people. Maybe they were worse because even Deads didn't eat their own.

"Sean, where are you?" she whispered.

Chapter Twenty-One

"Anguish trumps instinct," Finn said as they walked through the back door of the house and slid the furniture back into place.

The Deads in the backyard would have to be disposed of, and soon, but right then, more pressing matters pushed them further into danger. Erhard had hired someone to let Deads in the year before, but not this many. There were way too many walking corpses he didn't recognize from his colony, and he'd made a point to know everyone he was protecting. These Deads were strangers.

"Finn, I think a fence is down."

Shoving a recliner in front of the load, Finn sighed. "I think you're right."

"My gut says it's the outer west wall that had taken damage before the colony fell. It was only a matter of time, and I think they're leaking in from there through the inner gate we left open."

"Your gut is compromised, Daniels."

"No, it's not," a quiet voice said from the corner of the room.

Arden Moore had been a guard for the colony before it fell. Robust, easy-natured, and diligent in his duties, he'd been a man Sean had depended on to follow orders and protect the gates. Now he'd wasted to nothing. Ragged, filthy clothing hung from his withered body, and his face was so emaciated, it had taken Sean a moment to recognize the man when he'd let them in the front door earlier. He stood with his back resting against the wall, and slouched as if he hadn't the energy to do much more.

"There's been a steady trail of them in and out of here since you and your team showed up. Ones we don't recognize, and we make it a point to know the Deads running around this place."

"Why didn't you kill the ones inside the gates before we showed up?"

"No resources. We ran out of ammo the first week, and between us all, we only have knives, which we're too weak to use with any real results. We've just been waiting for someone to come along and get us out of Denver. You won't be able to do that if this place fills up with Deads."

"Okay," Finn said. "If the new Deads didn't show up until we came in here, then Sean's right. A section of the outer wall must be down, and they're getting through the open gate."

"Yep," he drawled slowly. "We've learned a few tricks about getting around the colony without drawing too much attention if you'd like the help. I need something from you in return though."

"What's that?"

"My people are on their last legs. We could use any food you could spare, and maybe a couple weapons too."

"Food, we can do. You and your people have been through hell and back, and the least we can do is get some energy in you. You'll need it to escape this place when we're ready to get you out. Weapons I can't do. My team is low on ammunition as it is, and knives are going to be useless to you. We'll have to wait until we get you to Dead Run River to get you set up with the things you lack."

Arden nodded. "Appreciate it. I'll go get Shay. She's the best one of us at sneaking around the colony. She'll get you to the gate and bring you back safe."

The survivors had converted the auditorium into a one-roomed house. For the life of him, Sean couldn't understand why they'd prefer to sleep on camping cots to sleeping in the beds that sat abandoned in his and Adrianna's old rooms, but maybe they needed to sleep near each other to feel safe. There was no telling what they'd seen and gone through together. A year inside the gates of hell would likely have given them a bond stronger than anyone else on earth could possibly understand. Regret and guilt pulled at him. If he had been more, he could've found a way to get them all out. If the scouts over the past twelve months had seen any sign of life in these gates, he would've moved mountains to extract the survivors. He hadn't known, but maybe he should've looked harder.

Sean's feet dragged as he shuffled into the front room to retrieve his backpack. He'd empty it of food and give it to Arden for his people. The dark puddle across the floor was smeared and drying, and he pulled up short at the shock of it. He couldn't think of her. If he let his mind have her, he'd never get off the floor. He'd be useless to the rest of the team. After this was done and everyone was safe, he'd find some place far away and mourn her. He just couldn't afford the suffering now — not with so many people depending on him. Not with Adrianna depending on him.

Pulling his glance away from the stain, he grabbed his backpack.

"You really trust Arden?" Finn whispered.

"Why shouldn't I?" he countered tiredly. "He was one of us not too long ago. He's done well to keep his people alive, and that's what he's doing now."

"Exactly, Sean. He's got people to protect." His eyebrows drew into his hairline as he moved closer. "People do crazy things when they have people to protect."

"Protect them from what? Us? We're their only shot at getting out of here."

Finn frowned and stepped back before admitting, "You have a point."

"Sean?" came a small, shaking voice from the corner.

He jumped. She looked like she'd been standing there for a while, but he hadn't even heard her come in.

"Do you remember me?" she asked.

Oh, he remembered Shay. She'd thrown herself in his path every chance she got after Aria turned. She'd been petite but voluptuous, with a confidence that enhanced her natural beauty. The waif that stood in front of him, however, was almost unrecognizable. Her eyes twitched this way and that, and with the gaunt and sunken set of her cheeks, they looked overly big and frightened. Her dark hair hung dull and unwashed around her shoulders, and the smile lines he remembered on the old Shay didn't exist anymore.

He couldn't wait to get them back to Dead Run River where Dr. Mackey could eventually get them healthy again. "Of course I remember you." What did he say after all this time? Small talk seemed trivial to place in front of a person who'd suffered like she had.

She didn't seem to need niceties though. "Come this way," she said with a small wave.

"Don't you need a jacket?" he asked, frowning at her bare arms.

"Don't need one anymore," she said with a smile that seemed at odds with her face.

"Do you want mine? Really, I'd feel more comfortable if you had something to protect yourself."

"Don't need protection. My body learned to protect itself." Her head twitched. "S-Stop it."

"I'm sorry? Stop what?"

"Come," she said in a dreamy voice.

Finn tossed him a wide-eyed look, and Sean reloaded his weapons. No way were they trusting their fate to this poor mouse.

Guist came down the stairs, holding an armload of sheets, and Sean told him in a low voice, "Just to be safe, bar the auditorium door while I'm away. And tell Adrianna—Well, just tell her I'll be home soon."

"Why don't you tell her yourself? She's upstairs with Laney and Soren."

"Because if I do, I won't leave and this won't get taken care of. Please, watch out for her."

Guist gripped his shoulder roughly. "I will. Be careful."

Shay led them to the office window Laney had snuck through the year before. Carefully, she pried a couple of loose boards down and crouched beneath the sill. Deads streamed to either outside corner of the house like they were being beckoned by something on the other side.

When the coast was clear except for one ambling Dead in a dingy pink dress, Shay slid open the silent window and slipped out.

"What about her?" Sean whispered. "She'll attract the others."

"No she won't. That's Josie. She don't eat people no more."

Josie almost looked familiar. Maybe if she had the bottom half of her face, he could place her. The starving Dead didn't pick up her pace or even veer away from her stumbling destination, wherever that might be. She just watched them escape the house and went on her merry Dead way. It was the scariest thing Sean had ever seen.

An outdoor hallway had been erected a short distance away out of plywood, fence posts, and branches. The space was small and had to be taken sideways, but if Sean removed the rifle from his back, he could fit easy enough. Finn had more trouble and was scraping the wall on both sides with every step he took.

Shay whispered, "The Deads never figured out how to get in here."

Clever.

After half an hour of moving steadily and quietly through the maze, Shay steered them to a fork that led to open evening light. "Not much further," she breathed as she swayed dangerously.

"Are you okay?" Sean asked. "We can rest if you need to."

"No, I'm all right. There's a ladder that'll lead us over the gate right through there. If there aren't any Deads on this side, we can run along the wall without being seen, close it, and re-cross here." The ply board behind her creaked as she fell backward into it.

"Whoa, Shay, I think you should stay here. You aren't in any condition to climb a ladder and run a quarter mile."

"Don't leave me here alone." Desperation touched her tone. "I have no weapons and they'll come for me if I faint. Please, Sean. Just let me come."

He shook his head and leveled Finn with a look.

"She'll pass out on us before we even reach the ladder and we'll be dragging dead weight," he whispered.

Shay sagged and her breath came shakily. She was going down, and the small space wouldn't allow it.

"Hey, is there a place that's safe where we can let you rest a minute?"

"Uh, the old root cellar isn't too far off, but it'll waste time if we stop now. More Deads will get in the gates."

"That can't be helped. It's either rest or we leave you here."

"Please don't."

"All right, then show us the best way to get to the cellar without being seen."

Moisture rimmed her dark eyes, and she pointed with a violently trembling finger. "That way."

Backtracking, they took the opposite fork and walked back into a mouth of the hallway. The cellar stood at a slant against brambles and winter-dried weeds. It used to dwell in the shadow of a large cabin, but the home had burned and only half of the structure remained. Looking around with those ever searching eyes of hers, Shay bolted for the cellar and tried to heft to doors up. She failed, too weak to move it much, but Finn and Sean pulled them as quickly and quietly as they could and disappeared down into the darkness.

It was cold at the bottom of the stairs, and a steady *drip, drip,* echoed off the concrete walls.

"There's a lantern hanging from the wall, and a box of matches on the table," Shay squeaked. The poor woman didn't have much strength left, yet she'd volunteered to help them.

Sean's pile of guilt was growing by the second, like the sand at the bottom of an hourglass.

He felt around for the matches, and the clank of metal said Finn had set the lantern on the table beside him.

A frantic little flame licked the wood of the matchstick as he struck it against the tabletop. Protecting the tiny glow from the cold air with the palm of his hand, he pressed it into the lantern and turned it up.

The click of a metal hammer being pulled back on a pistol bounced off the walls, and Sean froze.

"Hand over your weapons, and do it slowly," Shay said in a steady voice. Her transformation there in the glow of the lantern light was remarkable. She stood at her full height and stretched her neck like staying hunched over for so long had irritated the muscles in it. No longer did her hands shake, and her breath puffed steadily from her mouth in chugs of freight train steam. A small, cruel smile tugged the corner of her lips. "Weapons," she reminded him languidly.

"Now, Shay, I don't know what's going on here—"

The barrel of her gun flicked downward, and she pulled the trigger. Finn staggered forward and held his hand up with a stunned look. It was covered in blood, and the fabric around a well-placed hole, right above his knee, was staining by the moment.

"There's your only warning. Set your weapons on the table, and sit in those chairs." She motioned with a flick of her gun.

Five chairs lined a bare wall, and rope ties dangled from the arms and legs of each. Dread spread through Sean's stomach as a dismal future stretched before him. Maybe if he kept her talking, he could buy them some time. "Why are you doing this?"

"Oh my gosh, you idiots all ask the same questions. It's like, try to be original, for once. God, you're all so boring. It literally takes all of the fun out of this when I can predict exactly what you'll ask next."

Sean slid his rifle over his head nice and slow and set it on the table as Finn did the same. "Sorry."

She sighed and searched the heavens like she was praying for patience. "I'm doing this because Denver is our colony."

"What happened to Erhard?" he asked, setting both pistols on the table with a clunk.

"Ha! He was the first to go."

Something in the way she said it brought a new slash of panic, like a lightning strike had run through his veins and jolted his heart into a galloping pace. "Do you eat people? Is that how you've survived?"

"Gross. Hell no we don't eat people, Sean! Maybe that's what you would do when you got desperate, but we're better prepared than all of that."

He frowned and sank into a chair. "Oh. Well what do you do with the people who've come?"

"We feed them to our pets," she said with a wicked smile.

His blood ran as cold as the frozen wall behind him. Finn limped to the chair beside him, but she waved them apart, and he settled in the one three spots down instead.

She bent down to tie him and that was his chance. If he was going to get them out of this, it was that moment when she was vulnerable. Gripping her neck and preparing to twist, he found the cold end of a knife, poking just into the skin covering his throat.

Shay lifted her head and held him with her emotionless gaze. "See? Predictable. Arden lied about us and knives. We've had a year to practice nothing but blades." She pressed harder, and thick wetness trickled down his neck at the sting. "Don't try that again, or I'll make you watch me slit your friend's throat over there."

The skin at his wrist chafed under the next tight knot she tied. "I told you why my people are doing this to you. I didn't tell you my reasons though." She patted his arms gently. "I saw that baby your team brought in. It looks like a Dead, but it was suckling at the breast like a human. I want it. The others we'll feed to our horde, but the baby will be raised by people who revere it. I don't know how you created a hybrid, but I knew the second I saw those eyes,

I was the one meant to mother it. Arden said I could have it before I even had to ask."

These people were insane. They hadn't survived the last year at all. Instead, they'd turned on their own species and were contributing to human extinction. Like it needed their help.

"Tie your legs," she told Finn with the gun aimed in the general vicinity of his forehead.

"The child needs her mother. What will you feed her with Laney is gone?" Maybe if he helped Shay remember they were human with names and identities. Personalities. Maybe he could appeal to any heart the woman had left.

"Oh, a girl." An absent and dreamy smile ghosted over her lips. "I always wanted a girl. And don't worry. We can keep the mother alive for milk. And when she's old enough to wean, we are perfectly capable of providing for her."

In three quick strides, she was at a heavy wooden door and kicked it open with the toe of her boot. Inside were rows of wooden crates housing quietly clucking chickens.

Shay ran her hand suggestively over Sean's shoulder. "I remember when we looked like you. Do you know how much food it takes to keep up this physique? I'll admit it's fun to look at, but wasteful in the grand scheme of things. Now, you just look weak to me. And you." She threw a seething glare at Finn. "You probably eat what six men need to survive."

"Crazy woman," he said, leaning his head back weakly. "This was how I was born. Even if I starved myself, I'd still be bigger than most. Why aren't you feeding us to your little pets now?"

She clucked behind her teeth. "See what I mean? It's like you don't know how to ration. If we fed the Deads every time we got a new shipment of fresh meat in, they'd be starving in between idiot heroes storming the gates. We don't want them all looking like Josie out there, now do we?"

"Uh, yes," Finn said. "The only good Dead is a dead Dead. And you're a fool to forget it."

If looks could kill, Finn would be a dead man. "You'll feed a hundred Deads. And I'll revel in the sound of your screams." With that, she spun and blew out the lantern before shouldering their weapons and jogging up the stairs. The doors slammed closed, blocking the last wisps of daylight.

Finn's voice cut through the dark. "She didn't even tie my hands up."

Chains rattled across the heavy wood above, and something wet splattered against the doors. The smell of rot and iron wafted down through the cellar and the groaning of Deads could be heard within seconds.

"Because she didn't need to."

Chapter Twenty-Two

How in honey-fried pickles was she supposed to sleep with the creepy people-eaters plotting their favorite recipes in the next building over? One tiny set of barred doors separated them from the boogie men, and nervous energy consumed her body as she bowed to the feeling of wrongness that had taken over since Eloise told of Sean's disappearance.

Vanessa willed strength into her limbs. Her injured body needed to heal, and preferably right now if she was going to be of any use to anyone. Adrianna breathed deeply beside her, bundled up tight and clutching Bunny. She didn't even stir when Vanessa reloaded a magazine and slid it into her Glock.

The floorboards creaked above her and stilled. If the vaccine could've given her some X-ray vision, that would've been fantastic.

The brush of a shoe sounded further down the room above.

Mitchell and Guist had left for a search-and-rescue mission no more than half an hour ago, and Eloise and Laney slept soundly by the baby in the next room over.

The crazies were coming for breakfast.

Vanessa lay back down and pulled her gun under the covers before feigning sleep. It was impossible to relax knowing something terrible was coming. Steadying her breath, she waited.

Minutes stretched on and on until finally the senses that had been screaming since she woke up picked up something heavy in the room with her and Adrianna. The cold tip of metal touched her neck, and a woman whispered, "Where are the weapons?"

"What weapons?" she asked, cocking the gun that now rested against the crotch of the intruder's pants. The advance of the blade stopped. "Take that shank off my neck before I blow a hole in your baby maker."

The smelly woman obliged, but ungraciously. "I'm not alone, you know. Dillon," she called out.

Stupid girl. She'd given Vanessa plenty of warning that her partner was coming in. An emaciated man, Dillon, she'd venture to guess, rushed the corner, and she fired a shot as soon as she had confirmation he wasn't one of her team. He sagged to his knees, and the woman tore at her with a feral scream and a slashing blade.

Ducking out of the way, Vanessa grabbed her wrist and kneed her in the rib cage. With a pained grunt, the woman wrenched out of her grasp and spun, then disappeared around the doorframe.

"Vanessa?" Adrianna murmured sleepily. "I'm scared."

So was she, but the kid didn't need to know that. "I'm right here. Grab Bunny, and let's go check on the others."

The next room was chaos. Soren was nowhere to be seen, and Laney searched the small space frantically. Sobs of panic and agony wracked her body, and she chanted, "They must've taken her," over and over, like it would undo the burden on her soul.

"Vanessa," Eloise whisper-screamed. "Where are you going?"

To get baby soup off the breakfast menu, but Laney probably wouldn't appreciate the word choice. She opened her mouth to say something more kosher, but the creak of an opening door stopped her.

The exaggerated noise chilled her blood, and she gripped her Glock a little tighter. The hairs on the back of her neck stood up, and as she rounded the corner, she witnessed the first Dead step over the threshold.

The crazies had let the monsters in.

"We have to move!" she rasped, and Laney snatched her Mini-14 off the night stand.

Tugging Adrianna's hand, Vanessa bolted for the stairs just as the Dead caught wind of them and groaned triumphantly. Eloise and Laney climbed the stairs in a rush, their clattering footsteps echoing off the growing volume of groaning and gnashing teeth.

Sean's old room was the furthest from the stairs, and Vanessa slammed the door behind them. Sean, bachelor that he was, had furnished the room about as simply as he was able, and after the twin bed was shoved against the rocking door, there was nothing left to stack besides a night stand and a squat three-drawer dresser. A few boxes had been tossed haphazardly to the floor, but none of them looked heavy. Not enough to keep them safe.

"Out the window," Vanessa said, shoving the frame open.

"The Deads outside will see us," Laney said.

"The Deads coming through that door in a few seconds are going to get an eyeful of us if we stay in here."

"Vanessa," Eloise said quietly. "I know what I can and can't do, and I can't go out on a roof that steep." Her green eyes pleaded for understanding.

Vanessa dropped her gaze to the full swell of Eloise's belly. Of course she couldn't. The plan had been thought of in desperation, and while that urgency hadn't changed for her, it could for the others. She squeezed Adrianna's hand. "You're going to stay here with Laney and Eloise."

"But Daddy said to stay with you."

"I know, baby, but you can't go where I'm going." She clacked her extra pistol into Eloise's hand and ushered them into the closet.

"What are you going to do?" Laney asked, pushing Adrianna further behind her in the dark space.

"I'm going to draw them away. Shoot anything that comes through this door. Ade, quiet as a mouse, okay?"

The girl nodded, and Vanessa clicked the closet door closed. Oh, she was about to die and it was going to hurt, but if that little girl lived it would all be worth it.

Out the window she slid as the banging on Sean's bedroom door continued. Sliding the biggest knife from her belt, she lowered herself and loped across the roof until she got to Adrianna's old bedroom window. From there she could see the horde pushing and fighting to get through Sean's door.

It took a couple tries, but she managed to throw a strong enough elbow to break the glass. "Oy!" she yelled, before running the blade up her forearm beside the cut Finn had made two weeks ago. Was it only two weeks since that important lesson on feeding frenzies? A lifetime had happened since then. Now, she was going to die without knowing what had become of Sean. Without knowing who would take care of Adrianna until she was old enough to defend herself.

The *pit-pat-pit-pat* of blood dripped across the chipped white paint of the windowsill. That's all it took. In a rush, the Deads diverted their attention to her. She should not have been surprised by the speed with which they were pulled off Sean's old door. She was basically ringing a dinner bell for the monsters.

Getting off the roof was a problem. Deads on the ground hadn't spotted her yet, but the two-story drop was going to get her a broken leg and definitely not buy enough time for Laney to figure out a way to get them safe. She slipped and slid until she reached the corner of the roof, which hung directly over landscaping that had gone native. A crepe myrtle stripped of all its leaves waited patiently with outstretched branches to catch her, and she broke nearly every one on the way down.

The Deads were coming.

Bolting around the house, she screamed into the doorway and clenched her fist until blood flowed in a steady trickle. She'd give the monsters a trail to follow. They came from behind in the yard, and they filed out of the house like an enraged colony of fire ants. She bolted.

Now, there had been very few moments in her life where things happened that were so important that it felt as if time actually slowed. But there in the colony full of ghosts and zombies and cannibals, sprinting for her life, she could almost touch every single moment. She pushed her legs harder and harder, and her arms pumped to lend any help they could. Her shirt had bunched up at the bottom, and frigid wind whipped at the strip of exposed stomach. There was no time to aim her Glock or throw a blade. There was only time to run.

Something brushed her back, and she gritted her teeth and found more energy.

And just as a clammy hand clamped down on her shoulder, the blast of a bullet whizzed so close to her face, she could feel the momentum of it blasting past her to bury itself in the Dead. The hand disappeared, and another bullet flew by.

She searched for the aid, and up ahead, Guist was down on one knee sniping the monsters on her heels. No, it wasn't just Guist. Mitchell was there too, picking off the closest ones so she'd have an extra few seconds to breathe air.

Mitchell pointed to the left, directing her, and she turned the course of the horde. A small wall had been erected from particle board, posts, and trees, and she ran alongside it like Mitchell had gestured. He and Guist had disappeared, and she was alone again, throwing one foot in front of the other and wondering how many steps she had left in her life.

And then something caught her around the waist and pulled her back with such force, it pushed the air and her ready scream right out of her lungs.

A strong hand snaked over her mouth, and the arm that was looped around her waist pulled her sideways into a narrow space. She was dragged back until the clawing hands couldn't reach her. The Deads couldn't seem to figure out that they needed to turn their shoulders to get inside.

She lifted her gaze to drink in the most intense pair of blue eyes ever, and her heart skittered with recognition of its counterpart. Sean crushed her to him and whispered, "I thought I'd lost you," into her ear. "I thought I'd never see you again."

She wanted to cry and scream and laugh and punch something all at once. Too many emotions fought for headspace, and she sobbed into his shirt as she clutched the material to keep him close. She was supposed to be dead, but instead she was in the safety of Sean's arms, a sanctuary she never thought would envelop her again. His fingers rubbed little comforting circles into the back of her head, and even the sting of fresh stitches being agitated couldn't dampen this moment. He was here. He was alive. He was hers.

Her relief was interrupted by a crashing sound, as the weight of the Deads collapsed the entrance.

Sean pulled his shirt off and wrapped it around her dripping arm. "We'll never find a way out if you keep bringing them to you with the smell."

Mitchell and Guist wiggled down a path that intersected with theirs.

"Where's Laney?" Mitchell asked with an intensity in his dark eyes that rivaled Sean's.

"Safe, all safe the last time I saw them. They were trapped up in Sean's room, but I drew the Deads away so they could get out. Mitchell," she said through panting breath, "the cannibals have your daughter. They took her."

"They aren't cannibals," Sean said, putting a hand on Mitchell's forearm. "They won't hurt her. They worship her because she's part Dead. We'll get her back."

Guist took one look at the red fury consuming Mitchell's face and asked, "Where are they?"

"Best I could tell, they holed themselves up in their little castle to wait for the Deads to eat us," Vanessa murmured. "I took one down which means there's twelve left."

Crunching sounded from the pathway as the Deads made headway toward them.

"This thing won't hold for long," Finn said, sidestepping down the tunnel. "We need to go now before it's nothing but splinters."

"Okay," Sean whispered. "Go that way." He pointed to the left side of another fork and Finn sidestepped toward it. "Try to be quiet about it, and maybe we can lose them."

The mouth of the structure opened up, and Sean's house loomed just ahead. The front door sported Deads who'd thrown themselves onto the tiny red line of her blood that led from the porch to the yard, but Sean didn't seem too concerned. Instead, he pulled a matchbook from his pocket. With a *snick, snick,* he lit one and held it to the sides until the plywood caught fire. The dry wood fed flames that reached for the sky, and they sprinted for a window on the side of the house. Sean opened it and kicked in a wooden screen before helping her through. The rest followed.

One Dead ambled toward them at the bottom of the stairs, but Sean knifed him without so much as a change in expression. The heat that crept up his neck and made his eye color even more radiant said he was pissed. Heaven help the crazies, because the wrath of Sean was about to come down on them like a rain of fire.

Mitchell slid a handgun into his palm, and together they threw off the bar to the auditorium. The door swung wide, and a loosely knit group of surprised faces stared back at them. They'd set up a banquet style table, and the smell of rich food filled the room. A plucked and roasted chicken sat as the centerpiece to their extravagant dinner, and Finn muttered, "What the hell?"

It reminded her of Thanksgiving dinner before the world ended. The food wasn't traditional, but the crazies were all but holding hands and saying grace while her team was thought to have been the appetizer for the horde outside the doors. What the hell, indeed.

She was the last inside the room and immediately searched for Soren. The baby wasn't here. She stepped toward an empty cot with a crumpled blanket as the crack of weaponry sounded and her team aimed their guns.

"I don't think so," a venomous voice said from behind her, and Vanessa was jerked backward.

The cold blade of a knife pressed against her throat. She closed her eyes and muttered a low oath. Subtly running her hand down the hilt of one of her knives, she prepared to defend herself, but the blade bit into her skin and warmth trickled down her neck.

"Where's the baby?" Vanessa asked. Damn the tremble in her voice.

"Not that she's any of your concern anymore, but she's safe in her nursery," the woman who'd attacked her earlier growled against her ear. "She's mine now. Don't you fuckin' move, skank."

"Skank is a little harsh—"

"Shut up! Everyone, put down your weapons, or I'll cut her open right here and cover these floors in red."

Sean's eyes had gone wide, and for the first time since she'd known him, he looked scared.

"Do it!" the woman screamed so loud Vanessa jumped.

"Shay, think about what you're doing," Sean said in a soothing voice. "We'll kill every last one of you if you do this. You're dooming your people."

Mitchell jammed his gun at Arden, who sat at the table with his head cocked as if he hadn't a care in the world. "Let her go, or I'll shoot him. He's the one you favor, right? Take your knife from her throat, or I'll pull this trigger."

Shay laughed. The little demon laughed! "You wouldn't. You're too good, the lot of you. I know your kind. You wouldn't shoot unarmed people. Too weak. Dead chow."

Shay was insane if she couldn't read the seriousness on the team's face. It had been a long day, and it seemed their patience had run out long ago. Mitchell cocked his weapon, and Shay slid the knife into the next layer of tissue. She was going to do it. This was it, the end of the road. The crazy woman wasn't afraid to die if she got to take her enemies with her.

She couldn't let them lower their weapons or they'd all be dead, these people she cared for. And she could already see the defeat in Sean's eyes. He was going to risk everything to try to save her. "Sean," she whispered. "I'm sorry."

"No," he screamed as she reached for her knife. The bite of the blade stung, but she was prepared for the pain.

And then a shot rang out, and she stood straight, still alive and utterly confused because Shay had dropped like a sack of stones behind her.

She turned, and Eloise stood in the doorway, holding the extra pistol in trembling hands. She gasped like she was shocked she'd actually pulled the trigger, and the gun clattered to the floor.

"Get back," Sean yelled as the first volley of gunfire hit the sheetrock walls near Vanessa.

She shielded Eloise with her body and shoved her out of the room just as Sean pulled an oversized wooden table crashing down in front of him.

The sound of gunfire echoed down the hallway where she pushed Eloise. They had to get away from the thin walls, or they could still take a bullet.

"Where're Laney and Adrianna?"

"Upstairs," Eloise said, sounding panicked. "Laney found Soren in some shrine room and Adrianna's crying. I couldn't calm her down. She's panicking, asking for you and Sean. Laney is singing to keep the kids quiet."

Thank God Soren was safe with Laney again. It was surprising Adrianna had made it this far without breaking down. The kid was tough, but she wasn't invincible. "Go to them, and stay there until the shots die down." She checked her Glock. "El?" she said as her friend pounded up the stairs.

Eloise paused and turned, looking so scared. "Yeah?"

"Thank you for saving me in there."

Vanessa spun and ran back for the auditorium before Eloise could respond. Getting all teary eyed now would only hurt her aim, and Sean and the boys needed her.

"I'm out," Mitchell said, and she knelt down and slid her Glock to him. She didn't have much, only three shots left, but it was better than no ammo. Picking up Eloise's discarded weapon, she slid beside the boys, ducking as wood splintered near her face. Lifting up, she took a shot.

Food spattered the floor, and the dinner table had been thrown to the side like the table her boys were using for cover. Pity, the chicken looked decent. Pulling a knife from her belt, she hurled it at a man who lifted his face too high over the edge. A satisfying *thunk* sounded just before the thud of a body hitting the ground. Sean winged another, and the man yelled out in pain. The table hiding the others was splitting apart. She counted four bodies near the door, and threw a silent thank you into the universe that Soren wasn't in here.

Loud twin clicks from empty guns sounded, and Sean gave her a wide-eyed glance. "Now," he yelled, and Vanessa lunged forward with him, Guist and Mitchell, pushing the table forward until it butted up against the other with a clack.

As one, they stood, weapons aimed, and the five remaining men crouching on the other side lifted their hands in the air and dropped their empty weapons. The rest weren't moving, and two stared vacantly at her, as if their corpses blamed her for their bad decisions.

One of the men shifted his weight, and Sean gritted out, "Arden, if you reach for that knife, so help me, I'm going to burn this place to the ground with the rest of your people in it."

A waifish man, Arden apparently, put his hands in the air slowly and huffed a half laugh. "Sean, we can be reasonable about this."

Cold steel interlaced Sean's deep voice. "Line up on the wall. All of you."

At their hesitation, Sean yelled, "Do it!" The command in his voice echoed off the walls.

Arden stood slowly with the rest of his men, hands still in the air. "So what — you're going to line us up and play firing squad? We're unarmed. That's not what the Sean I knew would've done. The Sean I knew had mercy. You don't like what we've become? Then you shouldn't have left us here to rot! We've done what we've done to survive. You would've done the same thing."

Sean shook his head, but his furious gaze never left Arden as they shuffled away and pressed against the wall by the back door.

"There's your proof right there, Arden. You never really knew me at all. You think I abandoned you? I gave every one of you a choice to escape with me a year ago, and not a single one of you came! Don't blame the evil you've done on survival. Do you even have a count of how many people you fed to those monsters outside that door? Do you? You could've helped them, but you killed them instead."

One of the men made a movement so subtle but so familiar to someone who'd practiced it a hundred times.

"If you throw that knife, you'll be riddled with holes before we send you on outside," Vanessa said. "Recent experience says blood only frenzies the Deads, so it'll lower your odds of survival, but it's your choice I suppose. Open the door and leave, single file."

"No, you can't do that," Arden said as understanding dawned on his face.

"Why not?" Sean asked. "You've done it to countless others. You tried to kill our entire team and kidnap Mitchell's child. My second-in-command has a hole through his leg, and you put my daughter in danger. You worship these monsters and feed them human lives like they're your pets. Your friends. Why wouldn't this seem like exactly the right punishment?"

Arden's dark eyes narrowed to slits. "We know this place like the back of our hands. This isn't over."

"Fantastic. Get out of my colony. And take all of your guard dogs with you."

Arden gave a cruel twist of a smile and ripped the bar away from the double doors. "Let's go!" he shouted and led his men into the morning light.

Vanessa would've given her femur to see the look on that crazy man's face when he realized they burned their little escape passage. At least they'd given them a fair chance, though. It was more than those monsters had gifted her team. No sleep would be lost over the destruction of these murderers.

The door clanged closed and the room grew silent as the gravity of the moment settled over Denver. The power had shifted, and the colony was no longer run by the tainted and lost. Sean would lend his strength to this place and make it whole again. All they needed was time.

Finn limped to the door to bar it again, and Guist disappeared to, in his words, "see how far the crazies got."

Laney, Eloise, and Adrianna shadowed the doorway with such a look of relief. Soren squalled and kicked in the cradle of Laney's arms. Keeping the child safe had taken sacrifice and pain, but she'd be worth it. Vanessa just felt it in her bones that Soren's destiny was an important one. They'd eventually clear out the Deads and bring the Denver colony back to life brick by brick and nail by nail. Together.

No one would ever touch the bond they'd created. Vanessa looked from one exhausted and relieved face to another. Every one of these people had implanted themselves so deeply into her heart, she had to swallow the sob that accompanied her smile. She'd never had friends like this. Not ones who felt connected to her, like an extended family.

Laney hugged her and whispered, "Thank you, Vanessa," in her ear.

Shocked, Vanessa stood there with her arms limply at her sides, just absorbing the gratitude of the woman she'd hated for so long. It was like medicine for her soul. Slowly, she put her arms around her, carful of the cradled child, and said, "Any time." And she meant it. If she had to do it all over again, she'd do it the same. She'd been prepared to die to draw the Deads away, but in that moment, she was just incredibly lucky to be sharing in the small triumph with her team.

Her team.

They didn't coddle her or try to control her. They respected her and trusted her to help them out of dangerous situations.

Adrianna clung to her leg, and she stroked the little girl's dark locks. Eloise tugged at the T-shirt bandage on her arm, and Mitchell found the first-aid bag without her even asking. And when she looked at Finn, he was smiling at her like he couldn't be prouder of one of his recruits.

She couldn't help the slow tug of her lips. They'd done it. Against all odds, they'd made it into the heart of the Denver colony, and they'd done it together.

Years from now, when she told Adrianna's children about how the Denver colony came to be, she'd draw on this moment of elation. She'd tell them the importance of the team and of their sacrifices and fearlessness. Of their courage in the face of adversity. She'd tell them she died for a moment, but that a power greater than her wasn't done with her yet. She was meant to be here with these people — to help them, to protect them.

To love them.

Sean leaned against a table with his hands clenched against the edges. Such a look of adoration emanated from his face, he seemed to glow with it. His eyes danced with the smile that played on his lips.

There it was. That beautiful soul he'd shared with only her.

He hadn't been meant for Laney, or Mel, or any other. He'd gone through all of the years of heartache and painful spurts of growth so he could be the man he was supposed to be for her. And she'd been fashioned the same.

Dirt was streaked across his face, and there was a cut in his hairline that wasn't quite closed. His eye was bruised from where he'd fought to protect the people he cared about at Dead Run River. His shirtless body was taut from continuous use and sported the triumphant scars of survival.

He was beautiful.

Pushing off the table, he murmured, "Hey, you," as he approached.

"Hey yourself," she said as he laced his fingers with hers.

Looking up into his eyes, she could see that this was exactly the place she'd waited her whole life to be—she just hadn't realized it until right now, in this moment. Here, she was safe, coveted, adored. Beauty still existed in the ravaged world because Sean lived in it. His existence made everything brighter and more important somehow.

On tiptoes, she whispered into his ear, "I like you."

He eased back slowly with the crooked smile he saved only for her. Resting his forehead against hers, he kissed her tenderly, and with the sweet taste of the promise of forever on his lips, he said, "I love you, too."

Epilogue

It had taken weeks and every grenade and bullet they had in their possession, but the Deads had finally been cleared from the Denver colony. Arden and his band of crazies hadn't made it far, and when they reanimated, Sean showed them a kindness they'd failed to give their victims and put them down. The fallen wall had taken almost three months to repair, but they'd worked hard, and the colony was safe in the confines of the towering fences again.

The colony had changed so much in the past few years since they arrived, just like the people who called it home. Cabins were rebuilt, and the gardens grew strong and tall in the warm months, thanks to Vanessa's capable leadership. She still served as a guard, but no one had the experience with growing things like she did. The colony had enough to eat through the snowy winters, and she was proud to be a part of that.

Roofs had been repaired and leaks patched. The Deads had been disposed of outside of the confines of the gates, and the colony cleaned from wall to wall. Evergreen trees had been planted and allowed to grow so that someday, it would resemble Dead Run River as a mountain paradise. No longer were the doorsteps littered with the bones of the unfortunate. Now, children and families sat on rockers through warm evenings and watched the sun disappear behind the hills they called home.

News of the re-colonization of Denver under the great leader, Sean Daniels, had spread like wildfire, and people traveled far and wide to make a home there. Anyone who didn't accept Soren's presence was sent down the road to Dead Run River.

The little girl had grown and thrived. As a rambunctious three-year-old, she'd grown into a strange, but ethereal-looking child with a sweet disposition and a wisdom beyond her years. Being different did that to people.

Vanessa smiled as Adrianna, now a protective seven-year-old, picked Soren up in that way small children did, and hoisted her onto the bottom rung of a play set Sean had built for the kids the first year they were back.

"The world is hard enough," he'd said. "It's not fair they miss out on all of their childhood."

Eloise had given birth to a son, Seamus, the week after they'd taken Denver, and between him, Soren, and Adrianna, the place seemed to be filled with laughter and hope and purpose. Their lives were more important than they'd ever comprehend.

Vanessa waved as Laney approached the bench she sat on. Her friend was dressed in a tight black T-shirt and gun vest, one that looked similar to her own daily garb.

"Hey, I think Nelson's going to graduate from guard training by the end of next week," she said, sinking down next to her.

Vanessa snorted. "Took him long enough."

Laney laughed and bumped Vanessa's shoulder with her own. "I just got an interesting call over the radio."

"Sean?"

A slow smile spread across Laney's face as she watched their children playing and laughing. "He asked me to send you his way."

"Where is he?"

"He said he's on the wall and that you would know what that meant." She graced her with a dancing glance. "I'll watch the kiddos."

"Ade," Vanessa said. "You listen to Laney. I'm going to go see Dad."

"Okay," the little girl said with a wave before she hoisted little Seamus onto the play ladder. "I will."

"Good girl," she said with the glowing pride she always felt when she was struck with what a decent little person Adrianna was growing into. Despite everything she'd witnessed in her short life, Adrianna was thriving under Vanessa and Sean's care.

The Denver colony weighed heavily and directly upon Sean's shoulders, but he bore the weight like it was air. He cared for his people, listened to their needs, and led them fairly. Determined not to invite betrayal like he had done with Erhard, he stayed home from supply runs more often to be present for the people who depended on him to keep them safe. Having Finn as his second-in-command also helped.

She lengthened her stride, impatient to see him again. He'd been working since early that morning, and her heart always hurt a little if she didn't see him often enough. That was the burden of love—of being devoted to another and their happiness, but she'd gladly bear it until the day she died because she'd experienced more happiness in the last three years than she had in her entire life. Impressive claims during an apocalypse.

He watched her approach with an unfathomable expression, and she squinted against the light of the tired evening sun behind him. She climbed the ladder and took a seat beside him atop the wall. It was the fence he'd built with his own blood, sweat, and sacrifice. He'd lost family and friends for this barrier. He'd lost part of himself in the early years of giving everything for a chance that others would survive the impossible odds the outbreak had thrown at them.

He scooted closer with an easy smile and looped his pinky around hers. They didn't say anything there in the fading light, but they didn't need to. It was their place, overlooking the tiny kingdom Sean had given to her and Adrianna and their loved ones.

They could see everything from that place. Deads trolled the woods behind them, waiting for the chance that they'd slip up some-day—a chance Sean wouldn't give them. But inside those gates it was a different world. Finn and Steven ran new recruits, including her brother, down a hiking trail. Mitchell and Guist stood guard at the front gates, and their laughter over something carried on the wind until it reached her ears. People, oblivious to the ever-present danger just outside the walls, talked in small groups and walked home from various jobs around the colony. Stalks of corn swayed in the wind in the gardens, and cattle bawled from a pen against the wall. Chickens ran free, clucking and pecking around their coops, and the children ran around the playground with heart-happy laughter.

Sean watched her intently and wrapped an arm around her shoulders before drawing her close into the warmth and safety of his body.

He'd provided a sanctuary, an escape, for mankind.

Because of his devotion to others, life went on.

Because of his devotion to her, love transcended the end of days.

Acknowledgments

A slew of zombie lovin' people deserve credit for this book reaching its readers. Elizabeth Harper for her amazing vision for Omnific Publishing and for taking a chance on this series. Lisa O'Hara for always answering my silly questions and for working so hard to get this book to air. A huge thank you to my content editor, Robin Lonscak, for working her magic on this book, as well as Sean Riley and Kimberly Blythe. The editing team Omnific put together for both of these books has been phenomenal. Also, if I searched a hundred years, I wouldn't find a better publicist than Traci Olsen. That's a fact. I adore working with her.

And the biggest thanks goes to you, awesome zombie romance readers. If the zompoc ever finds me, may I find allies as fearless as you.

About the Author

Tera Shanley writes in sub-genres that stretch from Paranormal Romance, to Historic Western Romance, to Apocalyptic (zombie) Romance. The common theme? She loves love. A self-proclaimed bookworm, she was raised in small town Texas and could often be found decorating a table at the local library. She currently lives in Dallas with her husband and two young children, and when she isn't busy running around after her family, she's writing a new story or devouring a good book. Any spare time is dedicated to chocolate licking, rifle slinging, zombie slaying, friend hugging, and the great outdoors. For more information about Tera and her work, visit:

www.terashanley.com

check out these titles from
OMNIFIC PUBLISHING

← ┄ →Contemporary Romance← ┄ →

Keeping the Peace by Linda Cunningham
Stitches and Scars by Elizabeth A. Vincent
Pieces of Us by Hannah Downing
The Way That You Play It by BJ Thornton
The Poughkeepsie Brotherhood series: *Poughkeepsie* & *Return to Poughkeepsie*
by Debra Anastasia
Recaptured Dreams and *All-American Girl* and *Until Next Time* by Justine Dell
Once Upon a Second Chance by Marian Vere
The Englishman by Nina Lewis
16 Marsden Place by Rachel Brimble
Sleepers, Awake by Eden Barber
The Runaway Year by Shani Struthers
The Hydraulic series: *Hydraulic Level Five* & *Skygods* by Sarah Latchaw
Fix You by Beck Anderson
Just Once by Julianna Keyes
The WORDS series: *The Weight of Words* & *Better Deeds Than Words* by Georgina Guthrie
The Brit Out of Water series: *Theatricks* & *Jazz Hands* by Eleanor Gwyn-Jones
The Sacrificial Lamb by Elle Fiore
The Plan by Qwen Salsbury
The Kiss Me series: *Kiss Me Goodnight* & *Kiss Me by Moonlight* by Michele Zurlo
Saint Kate of the Cupcake: The Dangers of Lust and Baking by LC Fenton
Exposure by Morgan & Jennifer Locklear
Playing All the Angles by Nicole Lane
Redemption by Kathryn Barrett

← ┄ →Young Adult Romance← ┄ →

The Ember series: *Ember* & *Iridescent* by Carol Oates
Breaking Point by Jess Bowen
Life, Liberty, and Pursuit by Susan Kaye Quinn
The Embrace series: *Embrace* & *Hold Tight* by Cherie Colyer
Destiny's Fire by Trisha Wolfe
The Reaper series: *Reaping Me Softly* & *UnReap My Heart* by Kate Evangelista
The Legendary Saga: *Legendary* by LH Nicole
The Fatal series: *Fatal* by T.A. Brock
The Prometheus Order series: *Byronic* by Sandi Beth Jones
One Smart Cookie by Kym Brunner
Variables of Love by MK Schiller

New Adult Romance

Three Daves by Nicki Elson
Streamline by Jennifer Lane
The Shades series: *Shades of Atlantis* & *Shades of Avalon* by Carol Oates
The Heart series: *Beside Your Heart, Disclosure of the Heart* & *Forever Your Heart*
by Mary Whitney
Romancing the Bookworm by Kate Evangelista
Flirting with Chaos by Kenya Wright
The Vice, Virtue & Video series: *Revealed, Captured* & *Desired* by Bianca Giovanni
Granton University series: *Loving Lies* by Linda Kage

Paranormal Romance

The Light series: *Seers of Light, Whisper of Light* & *Circle of Light* by Jennifer DeLucy
The Hanaford Park series: *Eve of Samhain* & *Pleasures Untold* by Lisa Sanchez
Immortal Awakening by KC Randall
The Seraphim series: *Crushed Seraphim* & *Bittersweet Seraphim* by Debra Anastasia
The Guardian's Wild Child by Feather Stone
Grave Refrain by Sarah M. Glover
The Divinity series: *Divinity* by Patricia Leever
The Blood Vine series: *Blood Vine, Blood Entangled* & *Blood Reunited*
by Amber Belldene
Divine Temptation by Nicki Elson
The Dead Rapture series: *Love in the Time of the Dead* & *Love at the End of Days*
by Tera Shanley

Romantic Suspense

Whirlwind by Robin DeJarnett
The CONduct series: *With Good Behavior, Bad Behavior* & *On Best Behavior*
by Jennifer Lane
Indivisible by Jessica McQuinn
Between the Lies by Alison Oburia
Blind Man's Bargain by Tracy Winegar

Erotic Romance

The Keyhole series: *Becoming sage* (book 1) by Kasi Alexander
The Keyhole series: *Saving sunni* (book 2) by Kasi & Reggie Alexander
The Winemaker's Dinner: *Appetizers* & *Entrée* by Dr. Ivan Rusilko & Everly Drummond
The Winemaker's Dinner: *Dessert* by Dr. Ivan Rusilko
Client N° 5 by Joy Fulcher

← ── →Historical Romance← ── →

Cat O' Nine Tails by Patricia Leever
Burning Embers by Hannah Fielding
Seven for a Secret by Rumer Haven

← ── →Anthologies← ── →

A Valentine Anthology including short stories by
Alice Clayton ("With a Double Oven"),
Jennifer DeLucy ("Magnus of Pfelt, Conquering Viking Lord"),
Nicki Elson ("I Don't Do Valentine's Day"),
Jessica McQuinn ("Better Than One Dead Rose and a Monkey Card"),
Victoria Michaels ("Home to Jackson"), and
Alison Oburia ("The Bridge")

Taking Liberties including an introduction by Tiffany Reisz and short stories by
Mina Vaughn ("John Hancock-Blocked"),
Linda Cunningham ("A Boston Marriage"),
Joy Fulcher ("Tea for Two"),
KC Holly ("The British Are Coming!"),
Kimberly Jensen & Scott Stark ("E. Pluribus Threesome"), and
Vivian Rider ("M'Lady's Secret Service")

← ── →Singles and Novellas← ── →

It's Only Kinky the First Time (A Keyhole series single) by Kasi Alexander
Learning the Ropes (A Keyhole series single) by Kasi & Reggie Alexander
The Winemaker's Dinner: RSVP by Dr. Ivan Rusilko
The Winemaker's Dinner: No Reservations by Everly Drummond
Big Guns by Jessica McQuinn
Concessions by Robin DeJarnett
Starstruck by Lisa Sanchez
New Flame by BJ Thornton
Shackled by Debra Anastasia
Swim Recruit by Jennifer Lane
Sway by Nicki Elson
Full Speed Ahead by Susan Kaye Quinn
The Second Sunrise by Hannah Downing
The Summer Prince by Carol Oates
Whatever it Takes by Sarah M. Glover
Clarity (A *Divinity* prequel single) by Patricia Leever
A Christmas Wish (A *Cocktails & Dreams* single) by Autumn Markus
Late Night with Andres by Debra Anastasia
Poughkeepsie (enhanced iPad app collector's edition) by Debra Anastasia

— Sets —

The Heart Series Box Set (*Beside Your Heart, Disclosure of the Heart &
Forever Your Heart*) by Mary Whitney
The CONduct Series Box Set (*With Good Behavior, Bad Behavior &
On Best Behavior*) by Jennifer Lane
The Light Series Box Set (*Seers of Light, Whisper of Light, Circle of Light &
Glimpse of Light*) by Jennifer DeLucy

coming soon from
OMNIFIC PUBLISHING

The Playboy's Princess by Joy Fulcher
The Jeweler by Beck Anderson
The Fatal series: *Brutal* (novella 1.5) by T.A. Brock
The Vice, Virtue & Video series: *Devoted* (book 4) by Bianca Giovanni
The Divinity series: *Entity* (book 2) by Patricia Leever
The WORDS series: *The Truest of Words* (book 3) by Georgina Guthrie

CPSIA information can be obtained at www.ICGtesting.com
Printed in the USA
LVOW10s0858240115

424201LV00001B/110/P